Copyright 2016 © Esther Dalseno

This edition published in 2016 by
OF TOMES PUBLISHING
UNITED KINGDOM

The right of Esther Dalseno to be identified as the author of
this work has been asserted by her in accordance with the
Copyright, Designs and Patents Act 1988.

Book design by Inkstain Interior Book Designing
www.inkstainformatting.com

All rights reserved. No part of this publication may be
reproduced, transmitted, or stored in a retrieval system,
in any form or by any means, without permission in writing
from the publisher, nor be otherwise circulated in any form
of binding or cover other than that in which it is published
and without a similar condition being imposed on the
subsequent purchaser.

All characters in this publication are fictitious and any resemblance
to real people, alive or dead, is purely coincidental.

THE VOLATILE DUOLOGY

Gabriel and the Swallows

Orlando and the Spirits

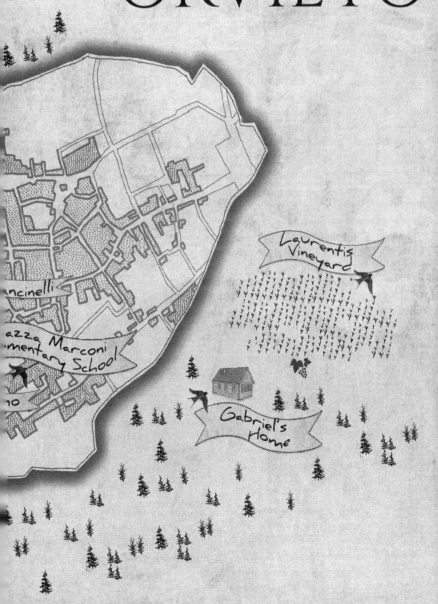

Because like Gabriel, every little boy should come of age.
For Anthony, who did so spectacular and dangerous;
And for Ethan, who was never given the chance.
In loving memory

Gabriel and the SWALLOWS

AUTHOR'S NOTE

The festivals and other events described in this novel are factual and strive to remain true to the culture of Northern Italy during the fifties to the eighties. However, *Donne Notte* was borrowed from the Carnival practices of French Guiana, and is based on a traditional Creole event, the *touloulous*.

BASILICA CISTERN
ISTANBUL, 1972

He'd gotten used to the sound of running water. For months now it had been clawing at his brain, fraying his nerves, the constant *drip drip drip* leaking from ancient walls, stirring the stagnant pools.

Darkness. Infinite underground nothingness. Him and her, awaiting the arrival of more. Preparing this place for the *others*.

"Look what you've done," he snapped, for the thousandth time. "Why am I always made to suffer for your mistakes?"

"You've no choice," she said, beaming. How could she be happy at a time like this? And as usual, whenever she was happy, he was not. Whenever she was angry, he was calm. When she was spent, too tired to lift her head, he'd be positively giddy with energy. Ebb and flow. Opposites attract.

"Reckless," he muttered, tracing the sharp blue veins over his arms and they prickled under his touch. "All for that boy."

"Hypocrite," spat the girl, her wings standing on end like a startled cat's.

He regarded the massive stone Medusa's head impassively, upside down and lying lichen-glazed in its cistern of brackish water. It had been there since the earliest days, they said. The sightless gorgon, eyes frozen open, in this underground cave with its thousand carved columns, and its *drip drip drip* all night long. And always that stale grey water that smelled of smoke and worse things. Thankfully his kind had no desire to drink.

The female had returned to sitting, and an anaemic light surrounded her, eyes shut tight in concentration. A quiet humming vibrated from her, a little like music, if such a sound could be called that. "Stop it!" he hissed.

"Be quiet. I am trying to create," she spat.

"You will get us in worse trouble. What was it they said? That the next punishment would be more severe than we could imagine?"

"I don't care," she replied. "What else could they possibly do to me?"

"To *us*, selfish ingrate," he moaned. "To *us*." He paced over to her, the damp earth nearly shuddering with every step. So much power. And for what?

He shoved his forearm under her nose. The ropey veins rose up, as if desperate to break free of his skin. They formed lines, cursive paths of foreign writing. "It keeps changing," he stated softly, shaking his lion's mane of black tangles. "I don't know what they want from us anymore."

She smirked, but suddenly a sound echoed all around, scuffling footsteps in the dark. The female jumped to her feet, a swift, glorious movement, blue-grey wings unfurled. "It's him," she breathed, her voice thick and hungry.

But the male was still as a corpse, his only movement the slight trembling of his nostrils as he sucked in the air slowly, deliberately. "No," he whispered, catching the scent. "It's the *other boy*." A strange light entered his eyes, and with the sudden snap of oil-spill wings, he vanished.

But the female hugged herself in the dark, gently swaying. "Gabriel," she groaned, and her eyes rolled back into her head. "Gabriel, Gabriel."

His name was like a prayer.

WAKING LIFE

PART I

UNO

I don't dream the same dreams anymore.

It hurts but the pain is the same one feels when starting to run again after a winter sitting by the fire. Heaviness in the lungs. Tightness of tired joints. And my heart burns when I wake. I have to remind myself that this is what's best for me, that I have trained myself back to life, and I can't return. Every morning when I wake, I feel I am conducting a sort of Alcoholics Anonymous meeting with myself. "Hi, my name is Gabriel and I am a…"

A what? A dream-aholic? Well, doesn't that sound romantic?

I'm sure it would look that way to someone on the outside. But it was all I lived for, for a time. Those dreams. I threw myself into them so deeply, I was nearly lost. I almost drowned. And I owe it to myself not to give up now, to keep swimming.

"Don't go back to the dreams, Gabriel," warns my wife, and I listen.

I am constantly anxious, weaning myself off dreams and memories, too. *She* still exists, if only in my head these days. Her face still scorches me. I clutch the pillow to my chest like a child, a grown man approaching senior years. I stare at the mattress and pretend to ignore her ghost hovering over me. The ghost whispers from the corner of the room, *Go to sleep*.

"Don't go back to the dreams, Gabriel," repeats my wife as she takes the pillow from me. "Don't go back to her."

Her.

I don't know if I am still in love with her because you can't be in love with two people at once. Can you?

Is it love if I, for instance, see the ghost's shadow accompany every living creature? Sometimes, when strolling down the cobbled stones of Corso Cavour, I detect someone else's shadow billowing out from my wife's ankles. A dark sheath, transparent like women's stockings, hovers over her head like an umbrella. Its arms bounce haphazardly while my wife's remain rigid and just slightly tapered at the elbows. The shadow's head bobs about in that funny, familiar nod while my wife's stature, as her mamma strictly decreed, remains perfectly straight, like a new knife. Wherever she steps, glides too the ghost of someone I once knew. And not only my wife. My father and olive-skinned Orlando are followed by this shadow. Sweet Vittoria and the memory of Alfio Gallo still stomping about my head, who is now also a ghost and probably very angry about it.

But is not death merely a migration? That's what Volatile used to say, once upon a time, in the vineyard I used to dream about.

GABRIEL AND THE SWALLOWS

I have lived in the vineyard nearly all of my life. In those days, it was not important enough to have a name, and all anyone cared about was that it yielded enough grapes to meet the yearly quota of *Orvieto Dolce Fantasia*, that sweet dessert wine that leaves sugar crust in the corners of your mouth. That's all I care about too these days.

The vineyard lies in a hooded valley in the province of Umbria, barely more than a hundred kilometers from Rome, in a little patch of land where, from the kitchen window, the view of the volcanic slopes of Orvieto can be seen with a slight craning of the neck. Once protected from medieval invaders by the fortress wall carved from volcanic tuff that encloses the perimeter of town, Orvieto once kept secret a Pope with a death warrant. Historically the center of art, wine and culture in a land not yet called Italy, it was a haven of wealth preceded over by the master of corruption himself, Cesare Borgia.

But now, these walls snare tourists from Germany and Sweden and troves of *Americanos*, dining on overpriced wild boar, buying postcards printed in China and pottery replicating our town's Etruscan history. They speak of their politics and compare their countries to ours, clicking their tongues over Italy's inevitable bankruptcy, while stuffing their faces with *porchini ravioli*. They wave around pamphlets of the underground labyrinths of Orvieto and gush over the old symbols engraved in the cave walls. They wonder if they can order jewelry made with those pretty designs -- not realizing they were carved by parched skeletons of heretics during the siege of Rome -- because they didn't read their brochures, they just looked at the pictures. And away they go, bustling about with their lumpy, middle aged thighs, wearing sweatshirts embroidered with the symbols of their Alma Maters, under our vine-wrapped canopies and cobbled tunnels of road, visiting the chocolatier and buying pound after pound of hand-dipped caramels at a whopping three Euro a piece.

And for the past fifteen years, my neighbors, the owners of vineyards much like my own, have opened their cellars to tourists, taking their Wall Street dollars, permitting them to fill their homes with French perfume and the powdery stench of underarm deodorant. They dirty glasses with lipstick stains and slurp down our wines without a thought of the bouquet, the carefully cultivated aftertaste of almonds. They don't know to swirl the wine, to let it breathe, to inhale and let layers of aroma tickle the nostrils and fill the lungs. Instead, they glug it down in a gulp, and when my neighbors' backs are turned, refill the glass and swallow it whole. They do it all afternoon, until they begin to sway into each other and attempt making love in the vineyards, but are too drunk to remember how to unbuckle their belts. Oh, how we love to complain about them in the squares and on market day. We are grumpy old-timers, after all. Our bloom of youth has gone.

When I was young, I used to wish myself away from Orvieto, to the bustling glory of Florence and Milano, the large wine region of Tuscany. Although I had no aspirations to return to Rome, where they tease us for our provincial accents, I wanted to run away and become anything but a wine maker – a carpet seller, a tobacconist, a pigeon trainer.

I used to run though the paths of the vineyard when I was a child, both hands skimming the peaks of the infant vines as my arms stretched out in flight. I made aeroplane noises that caused saliva to bubble and pop upon my lips. It was springtime, and the swallows were returning to Italy from somewhere far hotter – Morocco, I imagined. Madagascar.

I remember every detail of that day. The setting sun on my face, encouraging the freckles Mamma complained of. The cheap fibers of the hand-me-down cardigan scratching at my neck. The smell of liquid sugar in the air and my head fuzzy because I wanted to sleep. I always wanted to sleep, even in those days. Somewhere in the distance, my mother calling out, "Gabriel, five minutes until dinner time," because unlike the vineyard, I was important enough to name.

I suddenly stopped cold as I heard it. A blood-curdling shriek, animal-like, horrifying in its urgency. It was long and wounded, filled with desperation. It seemed to be coming from the monotone woods that lay in the back of our house. Another shriek followed and with it, Mamma calling me, so that the two sounds bonded and I have never heard my name since without the accompaniment of that desperate scream.

I fled toward the house, long white-gold curls of despised hair in my eyes, anything to silence that sound. I felt relief as the warm lights of home engulfed me, the smell of dinner. But as I reached the threshold, my heart twisted inside me, and through my own terror I was struck by the torture within the scream. I swallowed and built up my little-boy courage brick by brick, clenched my fists and charged toward the uproar.

Pushing back the inevitable guilt of disobeying Mamma, I ran. It was difficult to follow, that screaming. It sometimes drowned out and became a barrage of whimpers, varying in speed and volume, and I became disoriented. Then the creature would renew its strength and howl and I would race toward it, only to be lost again in the shadows of the woods, bare branches striking my face and arms.

The heavy pounding of steel-capped boots suddenly echoed all around, sending fresh waves of horror through me until they dissolved into nothingness. I could hear the boots breaking dry branches that had fallen to the earth with unnatural violence and purpose.

I shuddered, remembering that night had fallen. I was so far away from the farmhouse that I could no longer hear my mother's calls. There was no light; all the stars and the moon had gone out. And suddenly, silence. I prayed not to hear those footsteps, muffled noises only but somehow ravenous and horrible, again.

I felt relief at the sound of water gushing over flat river stones, consoled that I could navigate my way home from there. In my immediate pleasure, I almost forgot the entire reason I was alone in the night, when I abruptly sensed a presence close by. Too close. It was wheezing intentionally softly, its hot breath brushing against my ankle. It was so silent by the water that I could hear its small heart thundering in its chest. I crouched down onto my haunches, and cautiously extended my hand, for it might have teeth. I'm not sure why I spoke then, but I am certain now that it was to reassure myself rather than it, "It's okay.

I won't hurt you." And my fingers brushed something soft like down. I pulled my hand back, a sticky liquid coating it. Blood.

I leaned over and blindly felt around the form of the creature. I detected two large wings, big enough for a crane or even a nighthawk, its body concealed and convulsing beneath a feathery expanse. Something long and sweaty slid over my arm and I shuddered. It felt too human for comfort. It was far heavier than I imagined, but I managed to pick it up with both arms, hooking my chin over it for extra security. I detected blood and goo oozing onto my chest from somewhere beneath its right wing. All the way back, on that moonless homebound trail, I whispered words of comfort to the bird and to myself.

"About time!" Mamma remarked, as I pushed the door open with my foot. Her wiry black hair was caught up in an unraveling chignon scarfed atop her head and her face was flushed with annoyance. "Where have you been? You shall have no supper tonight!"

Her complexion paled when she saw the bundle in my arms, the growing bloodstain on my chest and shoulder. She let out a cry and dashed over to me, and in the tangle of her hands and demands for information, the bird slipped out under me and landed on the floorboards with a dull thud.

And then I began to curse myself. I should have known this would set Mamma off.

I had always been aware of how the Orvietani pitied my father and I. They whispered about my Mamma's condition behind cupped hands and over steaming cups of espresso. I saw that dreaded word *retard* mouthed at me from other children, and

I felt ashamed. "Mamma can't help it", my father would say. "Something happened when she was young, a terrible shock." But I always saw what others did: the way she could be so perfectly normal, like all the other women in town, and suddenly she would snap. Something would alarm her - a loud noise, a strange idea, a visual assault. And she would focus on the last noise she heard – a sentence, a song, a loud smash, and begin to stutter, imitating the noise over and over, louder and louder. She would fix her gaze on an unsuspecting person and stare at them while her head jerked slowly side to side, like an ill-fated bumper car. As she grew more agitated, her body and shoulders would start to quiver and all the while, the noises from her mouth rumbled on and on. The very worst and most frequent was when a near-accident would occur and someone would swear. Mamma would become fixated and Orvietani mouths would drop, children staring in awe as Mamma repeated *merdamerdamerdamerdamerdamerda*. Their mothers and fathers would cover their ears and lead them home, shaking their heads at Mamma, as if the filth was voluntary. And Mamma's eyes would fill with tears and horror while all that flowed from her mouth was *merdamerdamerdamerdamerda*.

But now Papa, his back bent from thirty years of hard labor, emerged from the washroom, drying his leathery hands with a rag and surveyed the sight before him, the creature on the floor.

"Oh, my darling boy, thank God you are all right." Mamma had tears in her eyes now, and had taken to rubbing her palms over the bloodstain in my cardigan, in a vain attempt to erase it. Then the fifth finger of her right hand began to convulse, like it wanted nothing more than to leap away from the others, who might bully it because it was the smallest.

"Ah, but what is this?" came my father's languid voice. And he discarded the rag on the table and stooped down to collect the bird. He held it to eye level and gazed at it quizzically. He lightly yet firmly extracted the wings, just a little, to see its face. "Oh," he whispered, withdrawing suddenly. "God in heaven."

"What is it, Celso?" asked Mamma, going to stand beside Papa. She stared at the thing for a moment. My heart went dead in my chest as I waited for her scream. I knew what the night had in store: her excitement, the yelling, the convulsing, the words. So instead of rushing to behold the creature like any ordinary child, I planted myself next to my mother and squeezed her hand tight. Please Zeus, I prayed, don't let her start again.

But Papa brought the creature, still secreted inside its wings, to his chest and held it there, like it was a baby. "It's...a little girl." His voice was high and strange.

Mamma's arms started twitching as her head rocked back and forth on her neck, all unnatural angles as she stared at the creature. The scarf that was wound around her head began to unknot itself. She was bouncing up and down, up and down on the balls of her feet. *Demon possession*, the kids at school once hissed at me.

"Mamma?" I whispered, clutching her hand with all my strength.

"*It's a little girl,*" echoed Mamma. I was horrified to hear her imitate the precise pitch and cadence of my father's voice. "*It's a little girl. It's a little girl.*"

"Go to your room, Blanca," said my father, a serene order.

"Show me," whispered Mamma, and her hands shook as she reached out for the expanse of the wings. "Show me the little girl." And my father opened the wings and we all held our breaths.

The hue of Mamma's face transformed from grey to golden. "*It's you,*" she purred, raising all the hairs on my body.

And like an obedient, radiant child, Mamma disengaged my hand and wandered away, her head still bobbing from side to side, her shoulders jerking. I was afraid that one day her neck would snap and her head would tumble to the floor, and would I have to put it on a platter, like John the Baptist? She shut the bedroom door, but I could still hear her muttering, "*It's you, it's you, it's finally you.*"

My father laid the creature face-up on the kitchen table, next to a bowl of radicchio soaked in oil and vinegar. Instinctively, it rearranged its wings to cover its entire face and body, as if it were somehow ashamed. There was blood on the table.

"Gabriel, hot water," instructed my father. "The pliers. Bandages and the whiskey."

I rushed around our tiny abode easily collecting these materials, as my mother, who required consistency above all else, had meticulously categorized everything in the house. As I ran past the linen closet, I snatched up two clean rags in afterthought. I placed them gingerly on the table, a little way from the body.

Papa immediately set to work. The wound was located on the outside of its wing, just beneath the shoulder blades. He doused it in whiskey and I blocked my ears to the screams of the creature as Papa deftly dipped his pliers into the wound, removing a small steel ball. During his administrations, I could not help but admire the creature for its strength of will – for even though it flinched amidst cries of pain, it would not retract its wings. From the bedroom, we could hear Mamma imitating the bird's squalls.

My father quartered the softest rag and soaked it in whiskey, binding it to the wound by wrapping the bandage around the creature's shoulder and neck. But the bird's head retreated even further into itself, making it impossible for Papa to continue. "Gabriel," said Papa, "Come stand by me. Talk to her."

Obediently, I trotted over to my father's side, pleased to be essential in this task of bird-restoration. But once I opened my mouth, I felt foolish. What does one say to a wounded animal? What does one say to a creature that made one's Mamma scream? Would it make any difference at all?

"Hello," I stammered, and my voice wavered with self-consciousness. "My name is Gabriel Laurentis. You are in our home, on the kitchen table, to be precise. We make wine here and I help too, but I'm not allowed any until I'm fourteen." I looked up at my father for guidance, and he flashed a wide smile that made his horn-rimmed spectacles soar up to his eyebrows.

Encouraged, I continued. "The person holding you is called Celso. He is my father. And the lady before is called

Blanca. She is my Mamma. But she is in her room now and you won't see her anymore tonight. And Papa needs to bandage you up. So remove your wings, if you please."

The creature twitched a little and through its long, slightly bent flight feathers, which I noticed were blue and grey in the lamplight, I saw an eye blinking at me.

It was not a bird's eye at all. It was much larger, almond-shaped, rimmed with thick black lashes. And it was bleached green, like the underbellies of pond frogs in summer.

"Go on," murmured my father.

"You must be very scared. But you should know that it was me who saved you. You don't have to thank me, because you probably can't speak Italian. I want you to know that you can trust me." But the bird's eye disappeared again beneath her expanse of feathers. I decided to change tactics.

"My name is Gabriel," I repeated, "in case you have forgotten. I am eleven years old. And I am a boy, although sometimes people mistake me for a girl on account of my hair." And I blew that infernal puff of curls out of my eyes to demonstrate my point. "I want to cut it off, but Mamma won't let me. I think the longer it is, the happier she is, because the fortune-teller told her I would be a girl, and she was sad when I was not. And I promise she will like you in the morning," I whispered, so that Mamma could not overhear, "because *you* are a girl."

And the creature spread her feathers apart even more widely, exposing a pink cheek and ear. "I won't tease you," I pressed on, "I swear. I've never teased anyone. But I know what it's like, I am always teased by the other boys because I am smaller than them and can't play games well."

My father fixed his eyes on me now and frowned, but I pretended not to notice.

"But you needn't worry about them. I won't let them see you."

I don't know if it was the tone of my voice or the length of my soliloquy, for I was sure the creature could not understand me, but she slowly unfurled her left wing and let it flop onto the table.

I gasped.

For inside the blanket of feathers was indeed a little girl. She could not have been more than nine years old, I judged, but she was small and wiry, yet not malnourished. She had a normal sized head, nose, and teeth, and from my limited knowledge of small females, perfectly unremarkable excepting those wings.

Papa seized his chance then, and resumed wrapping and pinning the bandage firmly over the wound. All the while, the bird did not take her eyes off me. She cocked her head to the side, like magpies do, and studied me with unblinking eyes. I imagined she was peering into my soul and understood my secrets. For a split second, it occurred to me that we had met before.

My smile froze when suddenly there was a pounding at the door. Papa immediately swept the girl up in his arms. His eyes darted around for a place of concealment. New fear rushed over me, and I wondered why I felt so panicked, so guilty. Like we were doing something horribly wrong.

"Over here, Papa!" I hissed, throwing the quilt back to expose the old cradle that was once mine that my parents never threw away.

There was an impatient, gravelly scuffing of feet outside and the urgent, authoritative hammering again. Papa silently laid the creature down and with the blanket, covered her up again. Then he removed his spectacles, placed them in his shirt pocket and strode to the front door. He already knew who our guest was. Only one person would have the indecency to knock like that.

Alfio Gallo was the kind of man who could fill a whole room with his presence. And when he left, it was as if a man had not just occupied it, but a large body of smoke, acrid and dark, that lingered long after the person had disappeared. I stood very still then, and took in his large, middle-aged frame, the woolly cap with the sheepskin earflaps that Signora Gallo undoubtedly knit, the steel-capped boots. It was then that I noticed the Winchester shotgun that swung from his fingers, in that careless way only true gun handlers dared treat their weapons.

"*Buonasera*, Signore Gallo," greeted my father, but the former simply pushed past him and entered our house, glaring at its fixtures and the shadows of each corner with beady eyes.

La Casa di Gallo was the largest farmland in the Umbrian countryside, not a simple vineyard like ours, and boasted a large array of *Grechetto* and *Trebbiano* wines. It was no secret that Gallo's farm had a profit margin far greater than our own, and even our most faithful buyers were becoming persuaded by his "specials": buying up coarse wines made from leftover grapes because tourists never knew the difference when ordering house wine at a *trattoria* in town. However, Gallo could never recreate the original *Dolce Fantasia*, and it was this obscure amber brew that the European wine connoisseurs came from all over the continent to sample. My father could not afford to lower prices on his wine, for our farm was already heavily mortgaged, and one hundred or so enthusiasts per annum purchasing a case of wine each was not enough to pay the rent.

Gallo made a yearly offer to buy the property for a small sum, much less than what it was worth. He had grand plans of *advertising*, whatever that meant, our wine to restaurants in Rome and beyond. During *Carnivale*, and when he was drunk and in good cheer, he would bully and humiliate my Papa, calling him a failure, more suited to life as a schoolteacher than a landowner. And in these moments when Papa grew quiet, Gallo would guffaw and slap him heartily on the back, and offer to pay off all his debts if he finally gave up the farm. Papa never did. I wonder if he worked the land, all those steadfast years, just to spite Alfio Gallo. In my heart of hearts, I hope so.

"Evening, Laurentis," grunted Gallo, poking around the kitchen, and making a good show of perusing the contents of the sink and garbage can.

"May I help you?" asked my father serenely, although he could not hide his disdain from me.

Alfio Gallo stopped short when he saw me, and instantly, I blushed all over and stared at the floor. "Who's this, then?" he growled, circling me.

"That is my son, Gabriel," stated Papa.

"Son, is it?" demanded Gallo, glancing skeptically at my hair. "Huh."

"As a matter of fact, you've met Gabriel on several occasions—"

"Enough of the pleasantries!" barked Gallo, and rounded on my father like a voracious hairy spider before strangling its prey. "I am here on serious business. Tell me, Laurentis, what do you know of the falcon?"

"The falcon?"

"The falcon," repeated Gallo, and he raised the Winchester 12 so that its barrel gleamed in the dim kitchen light.

"I've seen no falcons in these parts," replied Papa calmly.

"Then you are not a very good hunter," stated Gallo, and wiped the gun on Papa's nightshirt, as if it were only fit for a cleaning rag. I bristled to see my father intimidated in this way. But Papa did not seem bothered.

"That's right," agreed Papa amiably, "I'm a winemaker."

Gallo guffawed. "And neither a very good one, eh, Laurentis? You'd better sell this wasteland to me and put your son through university. I very much doubt, by the looks of *him*, that he'd do a much better job himself. Looks more like a....bookish type." Gallo looked as if he felt a "bookish type" of person was equal to a dirt-eater, and he made a very loud belly laugh, and didn't care that he was the only one to do so.

"There is a falcon," reminded Gallo, serious now, "that I have been stalking for a very long time. Magnificent creature. Blue and grey wings."

"If it's so magnificent, why don't you leave it alone?" I was horrified by my own outburst and the sudden protective surge that swelled through my chest.

And then Gallo was upon me and I could smell the stale cigarettes on his coat, the rank wine breath. "Because, little boy," he proclaimed, "I am very fond of taxidermy."

"We have seen no falcons, sir," repeated Papa firmly. "And it is getting late."

"Something disrupt your dinner?" inquired Gallo with faux-politeness, regarding our stone-cold supper and neatly laid out tableware. "Tsk, tsk," he clucked, regarding our meager fare with delight, "no *antipasti*, no *primi piatti*? I suppose the Laurentis family eats like heathens, not Italians." A cold light entered his eyes when he saw the bloodstain the bird-girl had left. His stare sought me out, her dried blood all over my cardigan.

"I was helping Mamma chop the meat. I was sitting right there," I stammered, motioning to the pot of rabbit ragout.

"He's a clumsy boy," added my father helpfully.

Our visitor was silent for a moment, his brow creased in thought. "I see," he conceded. "And clumsy boys should not be permitted to play with knives. I hope you will see to this, Celso. And where is Blanca this evening?"

"She is resting," replied Papa.

"Ah," said Gallo. "Perhaps she has had, how can I put this, another *episode*?" And he chuckled cruelly, approaching the front door.

"Good night, Signore Gallo," said Papa tautly.

"Back to your books then, Laurentis," he tormented, and placed the barrel of his gun over my father's spectacles, hidden inside his pocket. "*Bang,*" he silently mouthed, sneering.

"I hope the safety's on!" I snapped from where I stood near the bloodstained table.

"It is for tonight," replied Gallo smoothly, "and until I see that falcon again. Good luck with the knives, little man."

"Good luck with the hunt!" I added willfully.

"A smart-mouthed boy you've got," he murmured to Papa, "you must be so proud. And I trust, if you see that falcon, that you'll do the right thing."

"I assure you," stated Papa, "I will always do the right thing."

"Good man," sneered Gallo, "my love to Blanca."

When he had disappeared into the fields, Papa turned off all the lamps but one. He shut all the windows, and with them, the curtains. I returned to the cradle and peeked under the blanket. There she was, asleep on her left side, her right wing curled around her. I looked down upon her very ordinary face and wondered where she came from.

"She looks nothing like a falcon," I commented to no one in particular.

""You shouldn't have spoken to Signore Gallo like that," chided my father gently.

"But he held his gun to you!"

"As a means of intimidation. He never would have used it."

"He's a mean man."

"He is all bark, no bite," assured Papa, but I did not believe him. "The Gallos have owned that land for generations. And when this farm is yours, you will have to deal with them. And the less bad blood between us, the better."

"I hate that whole family!" I spat.

"Come and have supper," said Papa, sitting down and spooning out the stew with gusto.

"Why did you have to call me clumsy in front of him?"

"One potato or two?" continued my father.

"Can I sleep here on the floor tonight?"

"I think your mother's asleep, so we'll save this for her breakfast," said Papa, and portioned out a perfect serving with all Mamma's favorite pieces.

"Do you really think I'm clumsy?"

But Papa didn't respond, and I watched him chew thoughtfully as I pushed food around on my plate.

"Go to bed, son," he said when he was done eating.

"Are you coming too?"

"In a minute," he replied, and as I was closing my bedroom door, I saw him sit next to the cradle, pull out his spectacles and examine them, as if he didn't know what they were for anymore.

DUE

I was a child that reveled in sleep. Unlike other children, who are up and brimming with anticipation as soon as a new sun hits their windowpanes, I would screw my eyes shut and will myself back to slumber. It became an achievement to sleep solidly for long periods of time, and I hoped to beat my personal best of thirteen hours thirty-five minutes. In that way, I was similar to my mother, who always retired early and rose late. My father didn't seem to mind, if it wasn't harvest season.

I would be lying if I said it was the rest, the unconsciousness of sleep that I loved. It wasn't.

It was the dreams.

But the next morning, I was up at the crack of dawn. My mind was fuzzy with faded memories of a new arrival, and Signore Gallo was there too, and a 1912 shotgun. Something told me it was no dream, and I wanted to confirm my suspicions by whatever sight lay in that cradle. When I opened my bedroom door, I realized that I was not the only person in the house with ideas.

Mamma and Papa, both in their night robes and nursing steaming cups of espresso, were peering over the cradle. The bird-girl was awake, both her wings stretched around herself. Only the top of her head and her eyes were visible. She stared at them like a rabbit caught in headlights.

"I suppose," said my father with resignation, "that calling the authorities is out of the question."

"If you want to hand her over to Alfio," said Mamma with a rare hint of authority, "that's the way to do it. You know Gallo has lined police pockets for years."

"I worry," muttered my father, "for Gabriel."

Silence. Then, "She will be good for him. Like she was for me."

"Blanca—" warned my father.

"Where do you suppose she came from?" whispered my Mamma.

"The sky, my dear," responded Papa.

"But what is she for?" asked Mamma.

"For?"

"What did God make her for?"

"What do you mean?"

"You know, Celso. Cows are made for milk and meat. Bees are made for honey, *for honey*. That sort of thing."

"Then what are humans made for?"

Silence. Then, "I don't know. Something."

"Then that something," stated my father like the good Catholic he once was, "is something only God knows."

"Do you suppose," began my mother, her voice wavering, "that God didn't make her at all?"

"Maybe she is God," I said from behind them. "Maybe she is the daughter of Zeus or Apollo." I was learning about Greek gods at school and lived part-time in an imaginary world where I fought alongside them in their great red battles.

"Don't be blasphemous, *bambino*," said Mamma, coming to her senses. Papa merely chuckled.

We were silent for a moment, just gazing at the creature in the cradle. For once she had heard my voice, her eyes had swiveled over to me, and she seemed to regard me like she knew all my secrets (correction: secret. At that age, I had but one. It was so large and so heavy and so important that I never imagined it were possible to have more than one).

"But what if she is an abomination?" my mother insisted. "What about her parentage? One is human and the other – a bird? Is it even possible?"

"But Mamma," I interjected, "don't you already know her?"

"I doubt that is the case, Blanca," said my father, giving me a hard glance that I could not mistake the meaning of: *don't ask*.

"Or what if there is no God, just hundreds of little ones, and she is a goddess?" I insisted, changing tactics. This was my preferred belief system at the time. "Maybe she is the goddess of the sky. Or wine! Or healing," I added slyly, glancing sidelong at Mamma, in hopes of her approval. I already wanted it as a pet, despite what Sweet Vittoria might say.

"Maybe she is a devil," murmured my mother, and her speculation sent chills up my spine. "Maybe she has been a devil all of this time." A strange light entered Mamma's eyes, and she appeared as in a trance. "I let the devil inside me," she whispered.

"Do you know what I see?" interrupted Papa. We all looked up at him then, for his next statement was to be vital: it was to seal our fate and the way we regarded the creature forever. "I see just a little girl. A little girl who happens to have swallow's wings."

I nodded slowly, and much to our relief, Mamma did too. Soon we all felt hungry and chattered about food.

"If I cooked us all omelets, would she eat one?"

"She probably came from an egg, Mamma, she's not a cannibal!"

"What do swallows eat?"

"She's not a swallow. But seeds perhaps?"

"Swallows eat the insects before the insects eat our grain," interjected Papa wisely.

Mamma: "I could empty out the bug catcher."

Me: "We could make her a bug sandwich."

"Why not try people food?" reasoned Papa.

Mamma: "Look! She's moving!

Me: "She's turning over!"

Silent and in-awe speculation. Finally...

Mamma: "Is that a *tail*?"

Me: "I think it is! I think it is!

Mamma: "My God! This is just like those two-headed babies one reads about in the paper. Or that fifteen-toed Indian child!"

Me: (beginning an enthusiastic jig) "Yeah! A freak!"

Mamma: "I do not like this, Celso. I don't like it at all." And her eyes became round and wary, and as her heavy head swiveled slowly on her shoulders, fear descended over the three of us that it was going to happen all over again.

But Papa leaned over the cradle to observe the creature. The blue forked swallow's tail, with its white underside, did not protrude from her bottom. Instead, just inches below where the scapular wing feathers met in the middle of her shoulder blades, glided the graceful tail, centered in the small of her back. The overall effect was not remotely gruesome or freakish, to my disappointment.

"Of course she has a tail," remarked my father like it was the most natural thing in the world. "How else do you suppose she could fly?"

At that, Mamma seemed to disregard any previous doubts and launched straight into motherhood. "She's *naked*!" she shrieked, realizing for the first time. "Oh, you useless *men*!" And Papa and I exchanged bashful glances, high color spreading over both our faces. "Where's your decency?" she demanded, and began rummaging through my chest of drawers, pulling out a t-shirt far too small for me, which I had saved because it had frogs on it, and I dearly loved frogs.

"Not that one, Mamma, not that one," I begged.

"Too bad!" sang my mother, and with a pair of scissors, sliced a large square in the back to accommodate the roots of the bird-girl's three feathery appendages.

And she returned to the chest of drawers and found my rocket ship underpants, also too small yet saved for love of the print, sniffed them, and convinced of their cleanliness, brought them over to the girl. "Come here, Celso," she commanded, "hold her up."

My eyes widened at the spectacle of dressing this strange creature in *my* human clothes. "Close your eyes!" demanded my mother. "And go to your room!"

I sat on the bed and sulked, and came out again when I heard the sizzle of the frying pan. To my great surprise, the bird-girl was sitting upright, my frog shirt hanging down to her thighs, the healthy wing protruding easily from my mother's hole, the wounded one hanging pitifully at her side. I could even make out the forked tail that curled around where she sat. She looked so perfectly normal, like a baby sister even, that I couldn't help but stare. What made it stranger was that she munched heartily on buttered toast.

My mother deposited pastrami and fresh bread rolls on the table, as well as a chunk of ewe's cheese, *pecorino*. "I wonder if Lulu is a carnivore," muttered Mamma.

"*Lulu?*" I bellowed.

A few hours passed and I found myself again sulking on the bed, listening to Mamma bathing the creature and speaking to it in hushed tones. Papa had gone out to the vineyard, even though it was Sunday. Stupid Mamma, I thought, with her stupid ideas. And stupid Papa too, for leaving us here alone. I'm the one that saved her. She's *my* pet.

I felt a stab of guilt for assigning such an insult to my parents, especially my father. Then I felt foolish for feeling any ounce of guilt over my own private thoughts that I made up new ones to prove my grown-up independence of opinion to myself. Damn Mamma, was one ferocious consideration. And damn Papa too!

Suddenly I was so overcome with shame for using such a terrible curse word against them that I made up an elaborate prayer full of mournful adjectives to send to Zeus, including a vow to wash the dishes for a month in penance, and a promise never to swear about my parents again.

"Repeat after me, Lulu," my mother was whispering, "the water is warm, it is lovely."

Splashing but otherwise silence.

"The water is warm," directed my mother again. "Repeat. The water is warm, it is lovely. Repeat. Repeat!"

Nothing.

Mamma sighed, and I was sorry for her.

Since she was a teenager, Mamma went to town monthly to visit Signora Silvana, the ancient fortune-teller. Since it became determined that her illness was not a phase, as supposed, but a neurological discrepancy that would last her entire life, Mamma sought the Signora for advice on all matters. There were no photographs to prove that Mamma was ever young, and I had a difficult time believing it. To me, she was always middle-aged, with a slightly stooped back and a head that hardly ever remained still – jerking from side to side – sometimes rapidly, sometimes violently with jitters, and sometimes slowly with precision, like a piano teacher's metronome.

"Your doctors are wrong," was the first statement Signora Silvana ever made to her, hunched over an apple crate in a dirty orange tent in an alleyway off Piazza del Popolo. Paintings of Cleopatra and Houdini hung from the tent beams, as well as a faded holographic picture of a UFO. A silk embroidered scarf covered the apple crate, and a crystal ball had been laid ceremoniously in the center of it.

"I have been in and out of specialists since I was eight," said sixteen-year-old Mamma.

"And they are all…" Signora's kohl-lined eyes widened for dramatic effect, "*misinformed*".

"Misinformed?"

"Tell me the details of your condition, if you please."

"Isn't that your job?" queried my mother skeptically. It was her first visit after all, and she was not addicted yet. She glanced behind her to the slight figure of another teenage girl waiting beneath the awnings of the stationer's store, wringing her hands and watching. The girl was wearing a somber black veil that covered everything but her face, and she nodded to Mamma hesitantly. *Go on*, the nod said. *Just get it over and done with.*

"My dear, a fortune teller whose predictions are as accurate as mine does not associate with a wide array of spirits, oh no. I commune with one or two very close, very established beings that speak through me and only me. Unlike other two-bit circus performers, I *specialize*. And unfortunately for you," she sniffed, "the spirit of health is simply not one I am acquainted with." And she flipped the edges of her headscarf haughtily off her shoulder and glared at Mamma, daring her to disagree.

Mamma looked down at her knotted hands and began. "It's uncontrollable, most of the time. I get...uncomfortable, in a way, and I start twitching. It's unnoticeable, at first, but as my anxiety grows, so does the twitching. And sometimes, when it gets really bad, I begin...saying things."

"What sort of things?" demanded Signora. "Do you prophesy? Speak to the dead?"

"Nothing like that," assured Mamma. "I repeat things."

"Oh," said Signora Silvana, relieved she did not have a rival.

"Say my mother is angry with me and says 'Don't leave your clothes on the floor'. If I get an attack then, I might run around twitching and repeating 'Don't leave your clothes on the floor, don't leave your clothes on the floor' for hours sometimes. I try to stop, but I can't – because those words repeat in my head over and over."

"Well, this is very obvious," stated the fortune-teller grandly. "There's no illness inside you. There is a parrot."

Mamma blanched. "A parrot?"

"*Si, si*," affirmed Signora. "Wait." And she closed her eyes and held a finger to Mamma's lips and began nodding as if receiving a very important message. "A parrot. A very wise parrot, very exotic too, from Central America or somewhere like that. Let's see." She closed her eyes and consulted the spirits again. "She will repeat the most important statements in your life, through you, for the rest of your life."

"'Don't leave your clothes on the floor' is a most important statement?"

"Never disregard the gravity of tidiness," advised the fortuneteller gravely.

"Anything else?" asked Mamma wearily.

"Yes," said Signora. "The parrot's name is Lulu."

For the years that followed, 'Lulu' became a code word of sorts for Mamma's disease. "How is Lulu this week?" Signora Silvana would query.

"A little on the quiet side," my mother would reply.

"Has Lulu said anything interesting lately?"

"Only, 'Catch that thief!'"

"Catching thieves is most important," Signora would confer.

"Indeed," Mamma would agree.

And now here was Mamma, believing her Lulu had come to life, but this Lulu was failing the repetition test. Yet my mother would not be discouraged. She dictated phrase after phrase, in hope that a parroty voice would echo it back to her. But this Lulu merely covered her head (and subsequently, her ears) with her wings and fell asleep.

It was only when Papa came home for a late supper, when I was supposed to be in bed but really spying through the crack in my door, that she stopped. She looked up at him with tears in her eyes.

"It isn't her," she confessed. "I thought it was Lulu at last."

"But isn't Lulu a parrot?" said Papa, crouching down beside her.

"Yes."

"And isn't this one a swallow?"

"Yes."

And Mamma began to cry, and Papa was stroking her head and cradling her like she was a child. He murmured all sorts of embarrassing endearments that shall not be mentioned here.

"I don't think," he said at last, "that you should believe in Lulu anymore."

"I know, but if Lulu doesn't live inside me, what does?"

"You know its name," pushed my father gently, "the doctors told you."

"I forget."

"You know."

"I don't."

"The disease is named…"

"It is not a disease; it is a parrot. And its name is Lulu."

"The doctors said…"

"The doctors," said my mother's new voice, icy and impenetrable, "have been *misinformed*."

TRE

The swallow-girl was still asleep in the cradle when I woke the next morning. She looked too big for it, lodged in between the headboard and the base, her wings wrapped around her and her face burrowed beneath them. I noticed the bandage around her wounded wing no longer leaked blood, but instead boasted a distinctive stain the color of rust.

"Your father's making a cot for her," said Mamma, indicating toward the barn outdoors, where all manner of hammering and sawing could be heard. She handed me a lunch pail, filled with a hard roll, two boiled eggs and an orange. "Have a good day at school."

I sighed; for I had hoped to be excused from the event, wanting to stay with my pet and watch her, train her. I was secretly begrudging the fact that the creature would be in Mamma's care all day, most days, and would bond with her over me, like a dog whose loyalty lies with the one in closest proximity.

"And Gabriel," added my mother as I opened the front door, "not a word of this to your friends."

I nodded solemnly and sighed. Even had I wished to, I had no friends of which to recount the weekend's wild adventure.

Closing the rickety wooden door with one foot, I shuffled on the front step, balancing my book bag and lunch pail in readiness for the long walk ahead. The front step was ancient, just like the farmhouse, and made of dirty tiles forming an earth-colored mosaic. Two concrete steps slippery with moss and I was on the ground. I walked past the chicken coop, the makeshift vegetable patch, and cut through the vineyard to make my way toward Orvieto town. I weaved through the grapevines and ducked under olive trees with earl-grey leaves, the ones with parasitic lichen clinging to their trunks like children to their favorite grandfather.

It was here that I turned for a last look at the farmhouse, atop the valley of grapes, woods surrounding it. It looked tiny from where I stood, and I could barely make out its old roof consisting of a plethora of misshapen curved tiles, like fingernails. A tiny sheath of smoke exhaled from the chimney. My refuge. I sighed and continued on my way as the sun ascended its ladder.

The cobblestone road was a stiff, steep climb. On my right, fir trees soared elegantly into the clouds, their thick, angular branches fragmenting the light that fell on my face. To the left was the volcanic wall of Orvieto, and as I craned my neck, I could see where the wall turned into houses at the very top, with arches and windows and laundry flapping in the wind. I sensed faces full of *biscotti* and *cappuccino* looking down on me. I tarried, hoping to delay the eventual moment in which I arrived at the dreary jailhouse of school.

I saw Sweet Vittoria trotting down the road, in the proud swagger of one who's had a successful night out on the town. I waved at her and wished her to stop, but she merely looked at me from the corner of her eye haughtily, and continued on her way.

The ground began to shudder ominously, and I lunged off the road into the brush as a shiny black Chrysler sailed past. The road was barely wide enough for a pair of donkeys, and I found myself gripping the brick railings as the tires crashed past my toes, mere inches away. Just for a moment, I could see the haughty profile of my arch-nemesis in the window and I recoiled in fear of the teasing the day would bring. As the vehicle soared past, I toyed with the notion of waving my fist in vindication, and resolved to do so once Zeus and his mighty armies deigned to fight beside me.

But in a moment, the Chrysler was long gone. It was once more quiet and lonely, save for the caws of the early ravens, and I mourned that I was the only child too poor to be driven to school. My papa did not have a car, and would not own one in his lifetime. Sometimes, he would go to town on the back of the old donkey Tomasso, and I had taken lately to staying at home because I was ashamed. Last year, when Papa went to market, I would ride behind him because I was so slight (boys at school taunted that I would fall over if they sneezed on me, which they often did). I used to be able to ignore the children talking behind their hands, laughing at my Papa's mismatched clothes and poor Tomasso, who was cross-eyed. I would hold my head high and scan the crowds for a glimpse of Mariko.

I entertained these gloomy thoughts as I passed through the summit, the monstrous cylindrical Fortress Albornoz with its narrow slits for windows. But when I had taken that last step through the crumbling golden canopy, there I was. In Orvieto.

The tall, ancient stone buildings, with walls so high one could only see a sliver of sky between them. A jigsaw puzzle of misshapen apartment on top of apartment, with stained glass windows and doorways in the wrong places. The streets seemed like tunnels with crossing bridges and irregular archways that soared above the head, a kind of reverse labyrinth across the city. Walled-in gardens draped in moss and roses sat fifteen feet above ground. Wooden window-shutters flung open, potted berry bushes and chrysanthemums unfurling. Someone was always practicing the piano.

As I dragged my feet along, the Baroque lanterns that lined the narrow streets began to go out, thanks to electricity, one by one. I barely registered the street signs carved into marble at every twist in the alley. Instead I watched as grocers opened glass doors to reveal purple artichokes, oranges, and crisp yellow apples. Potters were already deep inside their vine-covered caverns, whirring away at the wheel. I stopped for a moment and peered inside a ceramics store through red and blue glass. I drooled over glazed pastries in the baker's window, promising to burst open with custard at first bite. And already, at this time of morning, the amateur theatre group, Signore Belivacqua and Co., were downing coffee from thermoses and shouting King Lear's threats at passer-bys. They were waiting for S. Belivacqua to unlock the doors of the magnificent Teatro Mancinelli to begin rehearsing this season's production, and I tried not to stare at Signora Marino, the mime artist, wiping tiredness away from her strangely shaped eyes.

Convinced I must certainly be running late, I hastened my pace past the Duomo, the grand Byzantine basilica that hovered over Orvieto like a great striped gargoyle. We learned at school that Luca Signorelli, the famed artisan, had crafted the façade of the Il Duomo – lifelike frescos of devils and angels and people engaged in agony, warfare or debauchery – that served as inspiration for the Sistine Chapel itself. I crossed myself as I hurried past it and said a prayer. "Please Zeus, let us move to town," I whispered. It was cooler up in Orvieto than our farmhouse in the valley. And if we lived in town, I wouldn't see the black Chrysler sail past every morning.

I reluctantly turned my back on the Duomo and wandered away. And as I stood on that circular plateau of the town, all around and beneath me lay the green farmlands and woods, where people who were not Orvietani belonged.

Alas, despite my tarrying I arrived at Piazza Marconi Elementary School five minutes before first bell. It was a fairly modern, formidable white building, two small sunken courtyards under the shade of mammoth Jerusalem trees to either side. To the left, a schoolyard existed, simple concrete with shabby fencing. The sight in the schoolyard was typical; clusters of children forming tightly knit cliques that would last their whole lives. There were the academics, serious boys and girls with complexions wan from too many nights pouring over books in puddles of lamplight. Close by were the strong boys, athletic and too tall for their ages, who considered taunting and goading as much a sport as football. Pretending not to look at them were the pretty girls, apples of their papa's eyes, in their store-bought dresses and a different hair ribbon for every day. I prayed for the moment that just one of them would gaze adoringly at me, particularly Mariko, but today she was fiddling with the strap of her book bag, and would probably not notice me all day. And scattered around these groups, like dandruff on a jacket shoulder, were those weird, solitary persons who could not boast a fair face, sharp tongue, mindless boldness, or bookish mind. They were the ones with buckteeth, a limb shorter than the other, a speech impediment, one green eye and one brown. Poor farming folk, or charity orphans taken in as work boys. They had an instinctive, unearthly pull toward others of their kind, attracted like magnets, and clung to each other like drowning rats. And even they did not deign to speak to me.

Unwilling to draw attention to my ever-apparent exclusion, I thrust out my chest in faux nonchalance and marched up the marble stairs to the school doorframe. Hoping to dissuade any opportunity of teasing, my step was hurried in the attempt to reach the sanctuary of the classroom.

"What's the rush, lady boy?" came the dreaded purr behind me. I froze momentarily, and turned slowly to behold my arch-nemesis. Darlo Gallo stood, her legs spread apart and planted in the soil like unearthed roots, arms crossed boldly over her chest. Behind her was her band of strong boys, their fathers all workers at *La Casa di Gallo*, snickering and appraising me with mocking eyes. She was like her father in no way but her presence, that sickly-sweet phantom presence that could fill a room like the remnants of body odor. Darlo tossed her head and licked her lips. "What's the matter, lady boy? Do you like my dress? Jealous, perhaps?" And she twirled around, the full skirt of her rich garment swirling around her, the boys snickering.

"No," I mumbled.

"Do you know what I think?" she hissed, pushing her face within inches of mine, "I think that you *are* jealous. Not of the dress, but of my hair." And she ran her fingers through her auburn waist-length hair, grabbed a fistful of it to fashion a whip, and smacked me across the face with it.

The boys began to laugh as I staggered back. They circled me, and one reached out his calloused hand to stroke my face. "Pretty boy," he murmured, "so beautiful I might take you for my wife one day." I recoiled at his breath and stumbled. "What's the matter, pretty boy? Embarrassed of the rags your Mamma dressed you in? Don't worry, it's not your fault she's retarded." There were roars of laughter all around, and my eyes began to smart with tears. The boy locked both his fists in my hair and began to drag me even closer.

And as his nose grazed mine and I could see every black patch between his teeth, Darlo Gallo pushed him back. "That's enough, Christopher!" she barked, elbowing him out of the way. "He's mine." And her hands flittered over my face gently, but the look in her eyes was feral. "Don't be frightened, lady boy. I know you want to be just like me. But you must be content, for now, to be my slave." And she sank her teeth into my bottom lip.

I fought the urge to scream and in those few moments, my mind found refuge as I thought about the swallow-girl, and how she would turn her head toward me and stare when I spoke to her.

"What on earth is happening here?" shrieked Signorina Greco, the teacher. Darlo released me and whirled around, flustered. She appeared shocked, as she should be, for it was a well known fact that Signorina Greco always sat behind her great oak desk and did not move from the period of seven-thirty to eight-fifteen, after every pupil was seated before her. I had never seen her in the corridors before this day. "I beg your pardon, Signorina, I was just—"

"That's enough, Miss Gallo! Kissing your boyfriend in front of the classroom like a common girl, and you so well brought up! Wait until your father hears about this!"

Darlo gazed up at our teacher with a well-practiced expression of wretchedness. "I'm ever so sorry, Signorina, if you could only punish me instead of disturbing my poor papa. He has been so overworked lately and..." The lies slipped from her tongue as easily as grease.

"Enough," commanded Signorina Greco. "Go inside, we will talk about this later."

Darlo lowered her head in false humility and obeyed, followed by her group of boys. But when the teacher's back was turned, she glared at me and mouthed, "Later".

"And as for you," began the Signorina, but I had already reached for her hand and grasped it.

"*Grazi*," I whispered, "*grazi tanto*".

"Why, Gabriel—" stammered Signorina Greco, astonished.

"And I am not," I murmured, rearranging my tousled shirt and picking up my book bag where it had fallen, "her boyfriend." I noticed that out of the two eggs that had rolled from my lunch pail, one had been trampled on.

"I suppose then that I am glad I was alerted in time," stated the Signorina, and sailed past me back into the classroom.

"Alerted?" I called after her.

It was only then that I saw olive-skinned Orlando slinking in the shadows. He winked at me and held open the classroom door. "After you," he said. His rich accent curled around me like a cat's tail.

Orlando Khan was an entity unto himself. Tall and as thin as a cigarette, the smell of mothballs and tobacco followed him like a shadow. Nobody at school bothered to associate with him, for he was a foreigner. That alone would have targeted him as a potential candidate for bullying, but it was well known throughout Orvieto that Orlando Khan did not stand alone. In fact, the Turni province was dominated by the Khan clan who boasted an army of fifty or sixty dark-skinned, rough-talking men that would as soon knock you down for looking at them than say hello.

The Khans had emigrated from Turkey generations ago, and with their old money established a number of trades in and around Umbria. Some member of the Khan family owned every tobacconist and sandwich bar in Orvieto. Lamp sellers and curtain outfitters were Khan territory too, importing exotic and impossible materials from their connections in the Eastern regions. Every lottery ticket was purchased from the hand of a Khan. Orlando lived with his parents and two sisters on top of a grocery that did not sell brooms, canned dog food and gardening tools but rather Moroccan spices, Cuban cigars, Darjeeling tea and thick yellow curry powder. And as these faraway ingredients were all the rage, the Khans profited enormously.

They were a handsome bunch, straight-backed and elegant, with noble foreheads and that trademark curved nose. They were schooled, mostly, reading Italian newspapers and large religious texts marked with coiled Arabic script. Their conversation turned often to politics and economics, mostly peppered with complicated and strange tales serving as metaphors to their thesis. Occasionally, one would marry an Italian girl and sire a troupe of children with skin the color of honeycomb, but the Khan women stuck to their own kind, much to the disappointment of many a young man.

I had often noticed Orlando at school, sitting in the back corner of the classroom, a book held open to his face either to shield his view of Signorina Greco, or the other way around. He would disappear at lunch times, but once I thought I saw him under the canopy of a Jerusalem tree not far from the schoolyard, smoking a pipe. He never looked at or acknowledged me, and most students flatly bore witness to my harassment, like it was as common as a birthday. I wondered why he chose today to intervene.

I was resolved to overcome my shyness and ask him this very thing after school, and entertained hopes that we could walk home together; or rather that I could walk him home as a token of my gratitude. At lunchtime, when the stench of my boiled egg excited the other children's ridicule (the Orvietani only use eggs as an ingredient to a meal, and eating one by itself was equivalent to consuming a bag of flour), I was too enraptured to care.

But when the final bell rang, Orlando Khan had vanished. Only then did I remember my savior worked in the grocery at three and left early each day to do so.

"Mamma, can we go to the Khan Emporium in town?" were the first words that gushed from my mouth as I flew in the front door. The swallow-girl looked up brightly from where she was sitting upright on a low stool. Her wings were folded around her back, and she looked so perfectly normal, her hair brushed and braided and her face scrubbed clean. I noticed traces of seedcake down the front of my frog T-shirt.

"Whatever for?" said my mother from her pots and pans.

"I don't know, to look around?"

"It's seven miles to Orvieto and I'm too tired to walk."

"Please?"

"And what does the grocery have that we don't have here?"

"Tea?"

Mamma eyed me with disapproval. "I'll never understand all that longing for foreign tea. It's just so bitter. No thank you, Gabriel, our own tea is quite good enough."

"Maybe I could bring back something for you tomorrow after school?"

"There is nothing of interest to us there. Tobacco and turmeric are of no use in this house. And it's best to stay away from those dreadful Khans." She was beginning to grow agitated, and repeated herself. "*Dreadful Khans, dreadful Khans.*"

"Why do people say they are dreadful, Mamma?"

A pause while she screwed her eyes tight, willing her head and shoulders to stillness. "Because they are different, Gabriel."

"Why are they different?"

"They don't go to church."

"Neither do we."

"They act strange and talk even stranger." Mamma's head jerked and she began to rub her nose with ferocity, as if it had become the center of her concentration. "*They talk even stranger. They act strange and talk even stranger, stranger.*"

"But so do we sometimes."

Mamma looked at me steadily. My heart began to pound as I realized what I'd said, and I was frightened. But this time, my mother sighed and stared at her feet. "Why don't you show Lulu your room?" she asked, too brightly, and turned her back on me.

I gently took the swallow-girl's hand and led her to my room. I noticed the way she walked, hunch-backed and unsteady, like she was unused to her legs, as if the wings were far too heavy for her frame. I decided I should like to cut them off, and she could be my sister, and accompany me to school. But then I realized that would take away all her wonder, and she would be ordinary, like me.

My room was small with a window looking out toward the vineyard. The walls were brick with tiny nooks where I stuffed schoolbooks and old socks and the occasional pinecone. There was a narrow bed and a chest of drawers that contained my meager wardrobe. A wicker basket in the corner held my short life's collection of oddities: some dried carcasses of enormous elephant-beetles, a sucked-out stalk of sugar cane Papa bought me at a travelling fair, a bag of marbles, a top from Signora Silvana, a handmade wooden train. The creature made a strange sort of cry when she beheld the contents of the basket. She grabbed the train and began spinning its wheels, and promptly swallowed the elephant-beetles.

I sat on the bed and watched her.

"I met a real-life hero today," I said softly. The girl looked up at me, cocking her head to one side, like a puppy that doesn't yet comprehend commands. "He saved me. Maybe even saved my life. I believe he was sent by Zeus."

She disengaged her stare and resumed her exploration of my treasures.

"His name is Orlando Khan and he lives in town. Did you know he has thirteen uncles? I could never imagine so many relations. I have only Mamma and Papa. I should have liked an uncle."

The girl would look up at me from time to time, her expression fathomless, as I continued my babbling:

Orlando Khan is a mathematics expert, says Signorina Greco.

Orlando Khan carved a peacock on the topside of his desk and he never got in trouble.

Orlando Khan's sister is supposed to be the most beautiful lady in Umbria but I have never seen her.

Orlando Khan sometimes wears slippers with curved toes to school for no good reason.

After I had exhausted myself with every good thing I had catalogued on the subject of my olive-skinned savior, I looked over at my companion. But she was fast asleep on the wooden floor, her fist curled tightly around the train. I was frustrated. She hadn't understood a word I said.

Later that week, I happened upon Orlando Khan as we arrived at the school's gates. "Hello," I stammered eagerly.

"Ah, hello, Laurentis," he replied softly. He strode through the gates with purpose and I trotted behind him.

"You can call me Gabriel," I said breathlessly, jogging to keep up with his long strides.

"Is that your name?" said Orlando, not looking at me.

"Yes," I replied, "and can I call you Orlando?"

"Well, that is my name," Orlando said, distracted.

I summoned all my courage and blurted out, "Will you have lunch with me today? Under the Jerusalem tree?"

But Orlando suddenly froze, and stared at the sky with a quizzical expression. He was silent for so long that I began to deeply regret my enthusiasm.

"You don't have to," I mumbled. "I didn't really mean it anyway."

"Shhhhh!" Orlando hissed, his gaze still fixed on the heavens. His eyes darted over the clouds and the treetops like a madman.

"What is it?" I inquired, deliciously petrified.

"It is the damndest thing," began Orlando, finally lowering his gaze to mine. "I could swear I'm being followed."

My imagination soared by this confession, and I was deeply touched by being brought into the realm of such close confidence. "For how long?" I whispered.

"Every morning and afternoon this week. They follow me to and from school, they wait for me outside, like an escort. Like a guard."

"They?"

"The swallows."

QUATTRO

Time passed; as this is time's sole responsibility. The swallow-girl remained with us, and I grew to rely on her silent company, and would tell her all my musings. She never revealed a sign that she understood or commiserated with me, but occasionally her head would nod about empathetically in a funny little bob, and I would laugh at her.

Mamma stopped calling her Lulu, and although she didn't treat her quite like a daughter or even a human child, garnered her with more attention and affection than I had expected. Papa and I began to call her *Volatile*, the fleeting bird, and it suited her. All day she would accompany Mamma in the house if it rained, her legs growing stronger and her wings folded archly across her back, her tail flitting up at a mathematical angle. Mamma had sewn dresses for her, simple things made from old pillowcases, with slits in the back to accommodate her bird-like appendages. She grew steady on her feet, and it wasn't long before she could run through the vineyard with Papa and I when it was dusk and no one could see her. I had a fit of giggles the first time I witnessed this – her wings beginning to unfurl and assisting the wind in lifting her upwards with every leap, tripping over her tail which was proving tiresome in this activity. Papa had looked at me very sternly then but I couldn't stop. Volatile merely ignored me.

Volatile grew more accustomed to human food, although she cared a great deal more for sandwiches than our homemade pasta, *umbrichelli*, and turned meat away. Once when Mamma presented us with stuffed pigeon at the table, Volatile had stared at the dish and begun to quiver. Papa immediately removed the pot, and lectured my mother a little too severely. Mamma had had a fit then, and threw the pot on the floor, and I picked up the pigeon legs and wings and middle bits and placed them quietly back on the table. And when Mamma was in her room, crying and rocking, and Volatile had hidden under my bed, Papa and I washed the dirt off the sad, deflated pigeon and we ate it in the barn, because we couldn't waste food.

Sometimes Volatile dug holes in the dirt and slurped the worms below like they were spaghetti. And as it turned to autumn, she watched the birds of the air migrate in magnetic V formations overhead, and she would make strange, strangled cries from the base of her throat and I would be sad for her.

I liked to talk to Volatile, for there were few people I could really confide in. In those days, my favorite topic was Orlando Khan.

Oh, how I loved Orlando Khan. The son of Zeus himself, so strong and tall and two whole years older than me, my only friend. My comradeship with Orlando Khan did not so much as cause a ripple in the schoolyard society – everyone ignored me as they previously did, and never looked our way. The strong boys did not bully me quite as often as before, for when they did, Orlando Khan would stretch out his arms and make his brown fingers into claws, and his long, curving nails scared the boys, as well as his guttural tiger growls. He would mock them, hiss at them, and thrust his claws at them like a caged animal. The bullies would call him *figlio di puttana* -- whatever that meant -- and something about his kind taking over Europe, and something else about his religion -- whatever that was -- but Orlando would promise his cousins would be waiting for them outside the school gates the very next day, and the bullies would pretend they didn't care. But Orlando would laugh his loud, musical laugh as we watched them run to the lavatory, because they were about to piss their pants.

Orlando taught me many things. How to swear -- colorful, wonderful words that were much worse than 'stupid' and 'damn'. He called everyone "God-damn *bastardo* salami-eaters, except for you Gabriel," and I learned that the pretty girls would not always look the way they did, that one day they would possess this thing called "bosoms" that my mother had, and I was terrified thereafter to ever look at my mother's chest region.

Once, he bought a pipe to school and presented it to me. I took one puff, inhaling deeply as he instructed, but I coughed and spluttered because it was the most God-damn awful thing I had ever tasted. My head swam and my eyes watered and Orlando laughed. When I tried to explain to him that my mother was probably retarded, he shrugged and said, "Everyone's mother is a little retarded", and that made me feel better. But I never told him about the swallow-girl, and I never told him my secret. But he would watch me watch Mariko in the schoolyard and sigh, and his eyes lit up like mother's fortune teller, like he could read the cards that lay in the future between her and I.

And when Volatile's eyes glazed over from boredom, I would whisper to her with a surprising lack of shame of my dealings with Darlo Gallo.

It had all started, as far as I knew, at *La Casa di Gallo*. I remember that place, a stone palace in the valley, with its manicured lawns and a hundred pruned fir trees, the fountain spouting crystal water from the urn of a marble maiden. I was in a chamber somewhere deep in the house, on a thick sheepskin rug, and I was six years old. My parents had left me there while they drank coffee, possibly in futile business negotiations, with Alfio Gallo. There were toys all round, ceramic harlequins and stuffed bears, wooden alphabet puzzles, and a bleached Pinocchio puppet with hinges in its limbs. But my eyes were drawn to a naked doll stuffed inside a toy truck. I pulled it out, ran my fingers over its hard plastic body, the high arched breasts, the big inane head, the painted blue eyes. I was entranced by its hair, long and white gold and curly, just like my own. I was kneeling on the rug, stroking this hair, when I saw Darlo Gallo for the very first time.

She screamed. She ran over to me, snatched the doll from my hands, and cuffed me over the head with it. I fell back, not with pain, but with shock.

And as I staggered to my feet to behold this little girl, trussed up in a dress that looked like it had been assembled from five miles of lace, her long auburn hair and her wet open mouth, I was astonished by the blankness within her eyes. Even at that young age, I sensed her soullessness. *Enemy,* my little mind predicted. But something strange happened in that three-minute encounter. As she stared at me, all the rage disappeared from her face, and something seeped over the nothingness in her eyes, something foreign and disconcerting, that made ghost pimples sprout on my flesh. She dropped the doll, in a trance, and her hand slowly stretched out toward me. I recoiled, resisting another slap. But Darlo's hand remained in mid-air, and she did not break her gaze from mine, until she suddenly became aware of herself and sharply withdrew her hand, running from the room with a loud door slam. I sat back down on the rug, slowly this time, and cradled my knees to my chest, and did not touch another toy until Mamma returned to take me home.

From that day on, Darlo Gallo teased and humiliated me every chance she got. That trance-like look never appeared in her eyes again, only pure hatred. In the first years of school, whenever I bent down to retrieve a missing pencil or paper, she or one of her posse would kick my behind until I fell over, often grazing my chin on the concrete floors. In sports games, which I excused myself from soon after, she and her strong boys would tackle and secretly wound me, a knee to the ribs, a strong kick to the ankle or head. And then when we were older and learned the power of words and wit to degrade and belittle, Darlo and her gang would begin their tauntings of subjects it was too easy to designate to me: my appearance, my mother, my lack of friends, my poverty.

Because of Volatile's gentleness, her awareness whenever I spoke, although her comprehension was doubtable, I trusted her. So much so that I decided to tell Volatile my only secret. It was something that I held to me like a beggar his one scrap of food, tucked into his underpants and never consuming it, saving it for a special day that never comes. It was something I wouldn't dream of mentioning to a single soul, not even my conquering hero, olive-skinned Orlando.

"I'm going to tell you a secret," I said one night to Volatile. We were sitting in the vineyard after dinner, a distasteful meal of unflavored garden roots seasoned with oil and vinegar that we ate so courteously and without complaint that Mamma let us play outside in the dark as a special treat. Volatile looked away from me and I felt safe to continue. "It's something you can't tell a soul," I said, "but I know there's no way you could anyway." And Volatile stumbled to her feet and walked a few meters away to investigate the trees.

"My dreams are not the same as other people's," I spluttered, all at once, a huge messy sloshing of alphabet soup. "I know this because I told Mamma about them a long time ago. She shrieked and covered her ears. She told me I wasn't normal. And she told me to never, ever repeat it, because then people would be afraid of me, and I would end up like her, poor and friendless and living at the bottom of the world."

Volatile continued to ignore me as I went on. The moon was high in the sky. And it was full.

"I don't remember when they first started. The dreams. I used to have dreams like everyone else. About cars and races and cakes and Sweet Vittoria, and also things that didn't make sense. But then one night, they changed." I clutched my head with my hands and shook it, hard. I inhaled deeply.

"And now, every night, I have the same dream. Not over and over, but one long continuing one. I dream about what happened during the day, but it's different…and it's more real, *more real than real life*. I can't really explain it. But I always remember my dreams when I wake up. I think about them all day. Whatever happened in the dream before continues the next time I go to sleep. And the worst part is, I mean, the reason why it is a secret is that…"

Volatile turned to me violently and fixed her pond-green eyes onto mine. "…is that I am not always sure which is the dream. What happens after I fall asleep, or what I'm living right now."

Did Volatile's eyes just light up or was I imagining things?

For in my dreams, I lived in the same Orvieto I always had, surrounded by the same people and places. But the colors were more vibrant, and I never felt hot nor cold. The dreams were so intricate and real, and almost impossible to distinguish from waking life. The dreams were addictive because in them, everything was a better version of itself.

For example, I had the same Mamma and Papa but they behaved differently. Papa was still a winemaker, but he was rich and Mamma wasn't sick, no, she was beautiful and smart and cooked delicious dinners and had banquets for all her friends. We had a shiny black Chrysler that Papa drove me to school in every day. Signorina Greco adored me because of my cleverness, and the boys always played football with me, and visited me on the farm on weekends. Every lunchtime, I sat under the Jerusalem tree with Mariko and she held my hand. And every day, I was allowed to do something mean to Darlo Gallo. I pulled her hair and called her names because she was so ugly, not beautiful as she is in real life, and she cried mostly and I danced around her and all the boys joined me, and Signorina Greco clapped her hands in time to our music. In my dreams, I was so happy I could cry and when I woke, I felt so sad I could cry because my life when I was sleeping was so superior to my life when I woke up.

Volatile was really listening now, or so I thought, and she sat down beside me as I continued. "But there is one thing that I am happy about when I wake up. You see, when Orlando Khan first saved me, my dreams began to include him too. But there, I hate him. His skin is dark like oil and he smells strange and the curved slippers he wears makes him look a fool. And he stares at me from behind his school books with his eyes narrowed like a tiger and he doesn't have hands, just black claws. So I am happy that when I wake, he is still my friend, and none of the things he is in my dreams."

"But something else confuses me, Volatile. I dream about everyone I know, each person in Orvieto. If it is Sunday, in my dreams it is Sunday too. If I have a geometry test on Monday, I will have the same test in my dreams that night too. If Mamma has a fit one day, then that night, she will do something extra special, like dance in the ballroom our house has in the other world. If Sweet Vittoria snubs me, then she will be nice and listen to me and lie on my bed. When I met Orlando Khan, that night I dreamed that I found him under the Jerusalem tree and he disgusted me so that I fought him and won. But since I found you, you have never appeared in my dreams. It's like in that world, you don't exist, and I don't know why."

Volatile shifted away from me, and averted her eyes, probably because she had lost interest in my long soliloquy. I sighed. And then I said, in a very small voice, "I wish they were real. And sometimes I get confused. I never remember that it's only a dream when I am in it, only when I wake and recall everything. But I know this; this moment now has to be reality, because I am unhappy here. And I know more than anything that I was never meant to be happy."

Volatile stood up and brushed the twigs and dead leaves from her knees, and wandered inside. I sighed, and got up too, and I felt instantly better wondering what would happen in tonight's dream. If I would ride around the vineyards on the back of the old donkey, which had Alfio Gallo's face and Alfio Gallo's voice, and I would whip him while he complained of his nothingness.

Yet this was what happened in my dream:

Mamma was wearing a red evening dress and she laughed as she brought the *osso bucco* to the table, because she had burned the red wine sauce. Papa grabbed her about the waist and whirled her around the kitchen and I rolled my eyes. She told me to go outside to play and when I ran out, I beheld the acres of vineyards we owned, the last of our multitude of workers going home for their suppers. I felt around in my tailored jacket pocket and found a note that Mariko had concealed there. "Handsome Gabriel," it read, "meet me at St Patrizio's well tonight, I have something to show you." She had drawn hearts and kisses all around the border. The smell of wine – white wine, red wine, pinot noir, chardonnay and bubbling frothy champagne stung my nose. Yet there was something more. The overpowering smell of moss, dried leaves, dampness, mold, the inside of eggs, of unwashed flesh and the entrails of insects – whatever those scents combined was, it eluded me. It took me many, many years to discover what that smell was, that aroma that engulfed every dream I ever had, from my birth until my death. And when I finally did, it explained everything.

The stars glistened and the wind ruffled my white gold hair that all the girls loved. The moon was full.

And I left our vineyard and climbed the fortress wall into Orvieto town, but it did not seem dreary and exhausting, it seemed magical, because in my dreams I was stronger and the distance was lesser. Every upward step felt like I was descending and the tree branches parted the moon's milk and bathed me in fractured luminescence. The town was deserted, but the lights in the ancient stone houses and apartments that lined the streets were turned on, and cast Orvieto in a pool of golden calm. Cats curved around shop signs and on the ledges of windows, and the coins that lay on the bottom of a plaza fountain glimmered as they granted each wish. As I passed the Piazza Cahen, I noticed S. Belivacqua singing in a rich tenor to a lady who looked very much like Signora Marino, but I couldn't tell because her eyes were shrouded in shadow. I wondered if she was waiting for Mariko too.

When I reached the well, Mariko wasn't there. I leaned over the edge of it and smelled the dankness inside that was the aroma of the hundred-year-old bodies that had lived and died there, still remembered fondly by the well that stored their scent in its walls. Completed five hundred years earlier, St Patrizio's well was a colossal structure of paths leading to Orvieto's underground city, a city that had existed longer than the earth could probably recall. The Etruscans had built the passageway for masses of people and livestock in exodus, journeying deep into the darkness on an incredible descending double helix.

I sat there and hummed to myself, fingering the note Mariko had given me, my heart swelling with love. An hour passed, maybe two, and still Mariko did not come. I began to feel worried when –

"She's not coming," said a voice behind me. Something emerged from the shadows of the trees and moved closer to me. "You shouldn't wait anymore tonight."

My heart began to pound. "Signora Marino?" I whispered, and wondered how much trouble Mariko would be in when her mother got home.

And she stepped out into the light, and I saw it was not S. Marino at all, but a tall woman with swallow's wings, some sort of *Carnevale* costume. She had long brown hair to the middle of her waist and piercing green eyes. And she was lovely.

"Who are you?" I said, jumping to my feet.

"I am Volatile," she replied. And her voice was like that of a little girl, but I calculated her age – twenty-five perhaps. She wore a white dress that made her look like an angel, on account of the costume wings.

"Do I know you? Have we met before?"

"Yes," said the creature, "and you will remember me when you wake."

"What do you want?"

"To be in your dream."

"But I'm not dreaming, I am awake now, this is real life."

"Is it?"

I furrowed my brow. "And I'm not exactly friends with old people anyway."

"Old? I thought you thought I was twenty-five?"

"Are you?"

"Not really, but I look older tonight."

"You're confusing me. Go away."

"All right," said the swallow-woman, and turned to leave.

"Wait!" I said. "Are those real?"

"My wings? Yes."

"Can you fly?"

"Of course."

"So what are you? Some sort of half human, half bird? You're a foreigner anyway, I can tell. We have a foreigner at school and his name is Orlando Khan and I hate him."

"But you don't hate Orlando Khan. You love him because he saved your life."

I laughed. "You're strange."

"Perhaps. But I'm not half human and half bird."

"Then what are you?"

"I am a human with bird tendencies when I am with you. And I am a bird with human tendencies when I am with them."

"You're weird. What did you do with Mariko?"

"I prevented her from coming."

Rage began to boil within my chest. "Why did you do that? Who do you think you are?"

The woman frowned darkly and suddenly, the moon was leached of its light. "I am someone, who in this world, has power over it," she said cryptically. "I know all about your dreams. And before tonight, I never wished to enter them." And she spread her wings and flew away.

The next morning, I awoke, filled with fear and wonder. It was early and Mamma was still in bed. I marched into the kitchen and Volatile's head surged up at my entrance from her cot near the open window. Something inside of me jumped when I recalled her face from the night before – lovely. But old. Not like her at all, and it was uncanny how I was filled with a creeping dread, like my childish heart already recognized the undoing of me. And I hated it. I sensed my own destruction and I hated it.

"Why did you do it?" I hissed, and grabbed her forearm too tightly. "I know you did something last night. Who are you?"

But Volatile wrenched her arm away and dropped her gaze. I felt foolish then because how could she be responsible for anything? She was just a little girl with birds' wings, not a magical being. "If you did do something," I whispered, as a precaution, "don't do it again. Stay out of my dreams. I'm warning you."

Volatile's wings shuddered a little and she began to desperately gaze out the window at the sky. I began to feel guilty for scaring her, and remembered how distorted the Volatile I met last night was, and doubted myself. "I guess I'm the idiot here," I confessed mournfully. "I'm standing here talking to a struck-dumb bird-girl who doesn't even know her own name."

Volatile looked at me out of the corner of her eye. She took a sharp intake of breath, and stood up poised for flight, her wings spread out like a speckled cape. *"You're an enormous idiot,"* snapped Volatile in a clear, clipped voice I recalled from the night before, "and I don't know why I bother with you! I won't meddle with your dreams again."

And she soared out the window, completely ignoring my open mouth that was undoubtedly hanging to the floor, and I wondered how I was going to explain this to Mamma.

CINQUE

Like a child whose guilt grows like a monster in the dark and eventually paralyzes him, so the incentives of Volatile's departure consumed me. I decided not to say a word about it, knowing my parents would immediately interrogate me, and I was the world's most transparent liar. How on earth was I going to explain this to them? *"Sorry Mamma and Papa, but I told Volatile all about my secret dream life where you two are better versions of yourselves, and she appeared in it. So I got angry and she flew away. By the way, she can speak Italian. But on the plus side, it looks like her wing is fully healed."* Unlikely. I squeezed my eyes shut and prayed to Zeus that Volatile would return and all would be forgotten.

"Where is she?" queried Mamma, who got out of bed shortly after Volatile had flew away. She scanned the fields from the open window. "She knows not to go outside during the day."

"I don't know!" I squeaked, pouring myself an extra-large glass of milk, which I glugged down whole.

Mamma began to search the closets and the bedrooms. When she returned to the kitchen, her brow was creased into three horizontal lines. "You haven't seen her, Gabriel? Was she not in her cot when you got up?"

"No," I stammered, and threw a huge chunk of cheese in my mouth, and began busying myself with rearranging the jars of spice and herbs on the counter top.

"Gabriel…"

"I said I haven't seen her," I spluttered.

"Gabriel…" Mamma's eyes were wide and she stared into mine, pulling the truth out of me.

"I haven't seen her!" I cried. "Leave me alone."

"*Leave me alone, leave me alone,*" repeated Mamma.

"That's what I said!" I screamed, slamming the milk glass back on the table with more force than required. It splintered and shards of glass fell on the floor. I ran into my bedroom.

"*Leave me alone!*" repeated Mamma, and then shook her head hard, like a dog emerging from a river, trying to regain control of herself. "Well, I would leave you alone, Gabriel, but I think you know something that you should tell me! *Tell me, tell me!*"

"I don't!" I wailed from my bedroom. I grabbed my book bag and starting stuffing my homework into it.

"*Leave me alone, leave me alone!*" said Mamma, and entered my room. She stopped still for a second, pressing her forehead with her shaking hands, willing herself to concentrate. But she was angry and her disease was betraying her. "You had better spit it out now, young man, what did you do to her?"

"Nothing!" I yelled, planting my feet solidly on the floor. "Nothing! Nothing!"

And Mamma blinked her eyes rapidly and held up her hands with fingers splayed like a mime, and her little fingers began to twitch demonically. "*Nothing!*" she shouted. "*Leave me alone! Nothing! Leave me alone!*"

I ran to the door, my book bag flopping over the floor, and pulled on my boots. Mamma had not been up in time to make my lunch, so today I would go hungry, but I didn't care. "You get back here this instant young m—*leave me alone!*" shouted Mamma, and suddenly a violent tremor coursed through her body and she sank to her knees.

I swung around and glared at her – my own mother, clad in a threadbare nightgown, breasts exposed from the upheaval, lined with stretch marks like rings on a tree trunk. Her wild hair, all black and grey, tumbling from her head like a mad woman, as it jerked on her neck. Her hands had landed on the shards of the glass and began to bleed. Here she was, pathetic and textbook ridiculous: the reason why no one spoke to me and teased me so unmercifully, while I tiptoed around on eggshells for her sickness, fraying my nerves, and now she was blaming me for a stupid damn bird-girl who had tricked us into thinking she couldn't understand a thing.

"Get back here, Gabriel!" she cried.

So I did. I took two steps toward the house and said, "I hate you, you know that? You've ruined my life!"

"*I hate you!*" echoed my mother, and began to cry. "*I hate you, I hate you!*" She covered her eyes with her bloody hands, and her fingers convulsed savagely. "Why do you hate me, Gabriel?"

And seeing my own Mamma crying on the floor made tears well up in my own eyes too, even though I hated her. But I would be strong, or else she would start about Volatile again, and I would be undone.

"I hate you because you've ruined me! Everyone hates me and it's because you're a retard!"

A strong hand on my shoulder and suddenly, someone was shaking me so forcefully I could feel my teeth rattling and I bit down on my own tongue – hard. "What did you just say to your mother?" bellowed Papa, his spit flying on my face. His spectacles fell to the ground and in my clumsy haste to get away, I stepped on them and they shattered. I squeezed my eyes shut, but the tears coursed down my cheeks regardless. "You will answer me immediately!" he shouted.

"*Leave me alone!*" shrieked Mamma. "*I hate you! Retard, retard, retard!*"

"No!" I screamed at Papa, and wrenched my shoulders free. "You God-damn *bastardo* salami-eater!" And I grasped the strap of my book bag and ran like the wind. I sprinted toward Orvieto, and didn't look back.

But if I had, I would have seen Papa pick Mamma from the floor and examine her hands. He would wipe them down and try to extract the splinters, but do a bad job, because his glasses were broken.

GABRIEL AND THE SWALLOWS

Instead of taking the direct route to school, I deviated. It was early and I didn't want to be present for extra teasing, so I needed a place to hide out. Without thinking, I flew past St Patrizio's well and its spider web of ancient aqueducts, up the slight inclination of Via Roma until I saw it blazed on a wooden sign:

The Khan Emporium.

The shop was still closed, as it was very early, and I peered through the windows. I had never been inside the Emporium before, and I gasped as I beheld its contents. Curved jars of loose-leaf teas lined the shelves behind the cash register. Just above it, beeswax candles in impossible shades and shapes, so slick and shiny they looked like marble. Lanterns of glass and papyrus, and paper umbrellas of the Orient with hand-painted cherry blossoms. There were plates and bowls not made of fine white china, but of cracked and glazed clay, shimmering like fish scales. Rugs hung where curtains should be, with patterns so curved and deliberate they made me dizzy if I stared too long. A glass case boasted cigarettes and cigars from all over the world, and another spiced, musky perfumes that Signora Khan mixed herself. There were embroidered robes so deliciously ornamented that nobody in town could possibly wear them, except perhaps for *Carnevale*, and Indian saris in saffron and teal that probably served as costuming for S. Belivacqua's theatre troupe. I noticed a strange wooden box containing

Asian cosmetics: a pot of black henna for the eyes, a tub of red henna stain for lips. And suddenly, a face in the window.

I gasped and pulled back at the strange white monster: no hair, no neck, just a white face hovering; bodiless. As I hastily gathered myself and turned on my heel to escape, the door opened. The doorbell chimed so merrily that I couldn't be afraid. There was Signora Khan, dressed head to toe in black, a scarf covering her hair and neck like a nun. "What do you want?" she demanded, but her voice was gentle and infused with glorious, curled vowels. "We do not open for another half an hour."

"Nothing," I said. "Sorry." But I stood there, staring at my feet while she waited for me to turn away.

"Oh I see," said S. Khan and smiled. I noticed then how beautiful she was, and her emerald eyes. "Are you looking for Orlando?"

"Yes," I stammered, surprised.

"You're Gabriel, aren't you?" she said, smiling so wide I could see her perfectly white teeth, and the gap between the front two. "I should have known. Come in."

I followed her into the Emporium, inhaling the scents that descended upon me like a crowd of insects. My head began to grow fuzzy but I enjoyed it. She turned on the lights as she passed, and I felt like I was inside a rainbow. "Sit down," she said, leading me into what had to be the kitchen, and placed a pink and gold glass of thick coffee in front of me. I was about to mention that I wasn't allowed coffee until I was fourteen, but to hell with it, I'd already upset Mamma and Papa so terribly that one little coffee couldn't hurt. It tasted vile and bitter but it made my heart race and clarity exploded through my thoughts like a thunderbolt. "Orlando will be down soon. He's saying his prayers."

"I say my prayers too," I said, the energy from the coffee pushing me past customary shyness, "only not to Jesus."

"Oh," said S. Khan, "the same as Orlando."

"I pray to Zeus though," I informed her seriously.

"That's a very good idea," said Signora Khan kindly, seeming amused, and poured me another cup. "You're a very handsome boy," she stated.

I set my cup down and looked at her straight in the eyes. "I'm not. You don't have to say that."

"I'm not just saying it, Gabriel."

"Well, you're an adult. And adults always have to say silly things like that. My Mamma says that all the time."

"You don't think it's true?"

"Of course not. But all Mammas say that little boys are handsome, especially their own. I bet you say that to Orlando all the time."

"You're very observant and quite right," said S. Khan, and looked impressed, although I could tell she was trying not to smile. "But all Mammas happen to believe their sons are the most handsome boys in the world."

And at the mention of my mother, I began to feel sorry for how I had behaved. I remembered that I loved her and I wanted to go home and tell her so, but then recalled I was angry too, and scared for Volatile.

"Your mother is Blanca Laurentis, no?" queried Signora Khan.

"That's right," I sighed. "Sorry."

"Sorry? Sorry for what?"

My shoulders drooped and I shook my head. "Just sorry. You know. Everyone knows she's a…"

"She isn't," stated Signora Khan in a voice so loud it startled me. "She has a medical condition, that is all. It's quite common, you know."

"But she's the only one who has it!"

"Yes, in this small town whose citizens believe is the center of the universe. But in the whole world, she is one of many. Don't be too hard on her."

"Do you know my mother?"

"I went to school with her," said Orlando's mother, and cleared her throat.

"Was she always…you know…like *that* at school?"

"Not always."

"Papa said something happened to her to make her like that."

Signora Khan looked distinctly uncomfortable and shuffled in her chair, choosing her words carefully. "Then your father must be right. Are you an only child?"

And without thinking, I gushed, "I have a sister but she flew away!"

"Don't you mean ran away?"

"Yes, sorry. She ran away."

"Well, that is very serious. I am sure she will be back. Your parents must be beside themselves with worry. I didn't realize you had a sister."

I must have looked monstrously horrified, because Signora Khan stopped cold. My face turned white, and beads of sweat began to drip from my forehead, and I remembered why Volatile must be concealed; because there was a man with a shotgun who was looking for her, and there were people out there who would not understand and would scream, "Lock her up! Take her away!" And I had betrayed her, again. Just like my parents.

"Please, Signora Khan, please."

"What is it, Gabriel?"

I was paralyzed with the realization of what I had done. "Don't…just don't…"

And S. Khan leaned over the table and I smelled ginger and fat yellow lemons. She looked me in the eye and saw deep inside me, to all my secrets sliding over each other in the pit of my stomach, like bloated worms. "I won't tell a soul," she breathed, "so you just rest easy."

She smiled at me, and the thought inanely crossed my mind what it would be like to slide a pencil between her two front teeth. She reached out a hand and smoothed back my hair. "At least you comb your hair," she said, but her voice was different now: jovial, too loud. "I hope you can teach my son."

Orlando approached the table and kissed his mother on both cheeks. He nodded at me, and for the first time, appeared awkward as he shuffled his feet. I noticed the long, curved slippers he wore, and how he was slightly duck-footed. He was wearing a silk robe embellished with peacocks and roses. He blushed and said, "It's Imelda's," and slid it off his shoulders, where it shimmered in a gleaming puddle on the floor. "Let's go, Laurentis," he said, grabbing my glass of coffee and swallowing it down like a shot of vodka.

"*Ciao!*" I called behind my shoulder to S. Khan, and before I knew it, I was being led up a flight of shining spiral stairs, and all around me hung the Khan's laundry, shiny and satin and bold, that it seemed I was walking upward in a tunnel of leftover circus tents. There could have been rooms to the right and to the left, had to be rooms, where the legendary Imelda beheld her beautiful face in a mirror, where a cupboard held all her silk gowns and pajamas, a closet of thread roses and peacocks. Word had it that she could have been a model in Rome, but her father wouldn't allow it. And there must have been Signora Khan's room and the chamber of Signore Kahn himself, and the other sister too, whatever her name was.

But Orlando led me to the very top of the staircase, and I judged we had gone up four levels. When we stepped out, it was into a decaying old loft, with original ancient wood flooring and a solitary window. I rushed to the window and looked out: there was Orvieto town down below, people lining Via Roma to buy tomatoes and lantern oil. There was the Duomo in the distance, and I could see its medieval piazza, where one day I would drink wine on the stone steps, underneath the canopy of the *bibliothequa*, where the four flags flew. Yes, that's what Orlando and I would do when we were big, every night. And we would call out to girls and they would come and share our wine, and someone would produce a guitar and everyone would sing, and occasionally Mariko's eyes would meet mine. I would wear my hair long at the front, and style a lock to fall directly over my left eye. I'd find money somewhere for new clothes and I'd smoke American cigarettes.

I turned from the window and looked around. Orlando's bed was nothing but a thin mattress on the floor, covered with an array of quilts and sheets and scarves with golden tassels. His clothes were thrown into an open wooden chest, like one that used to contain pirate's booty. A melee of rugs covered the entire floor, and I realized they were imperfect shop goods: soiled, burned by a stray candle, or sold to a customer who deliberately damaged it and returned it the next day, because her husband thought it godless. I noticed that the walls had been painted a chartreuse green, and Orlando himself had drawn haphazard snatches of himself on the walls: a street scene, a sphinx, a depiction of what could have been the Eiffel Tower, an elephant with a decorative trunk.

"Sit," Orlando commanded, and kicked a large pillow shaped like a sausage toward me. As I sunk into the floor, I felt like I was sinking into clouds. He rummaged through the pirate chest and found a pair of black satin pants that he slid over his narrow hips, covering his pajama shorts. Then he lay down, stretching his long brown body over the rugs and yawned. He lay with his eyes closed for a minute or two, and I began to contemplate leaving, when his eyes snapped open. He leapt to his feet and from the pile of fabric that was his bed, he pulled out a red something. It looked like an ornate vase or candelabra with a hose attached. Silently, Orlando felt around in his black satin pockets until he located a little pink disc, wrapped in cellophane. I watched in awe as he lit existing coals on the instrument with a match, and the water inside it bubbled.

Finally, he placed the little disk on the clay bowl on the very top, and the most delicious scent filled the air.

"What's that?" I asked.

"It's breakfast," replied Orlando, and placed the hose in his mouth. He sucked on it deeply and exhaled a smoke cloud that was pink and purple, awash with lights.

"Aren't we supposed to go to school?"

"You are my guest Gabriel, and it is customary for us to receive our guests until they wish to leave."

"So you can't go until I go?"

"It would be considered bad manners."

"And if I don't go?"

"Then I would be obliged to entertain you under my roof until you do. And you want to stay all day, don't you?"

"Yes."

"Then it's settled. No school today." He took his third mouthful of the concoction and passed the hose to me.

I took it and inhaled, expecting it to be horrible like the coffee. Instead, my mouth was full of strawberries and my head became blissfully light and cloudy. "Wow," I managed, passing back the hose and sinking deeper into my sausage-shaped pillow.

"It's called a *huqqua*," informed Orlando, "a water pipe. It was invented many years ago by our ancestors in Rajasthan and was smoked throughout the Persian Empire. Do you like it?"

"I love it," I said truthfully, for I had never felt happier in my life. I had almost forgotten about my parents, about Volatile. "Does your mamma know you have this?"

"Of course! My father gave it to me for my birthday two years ago."

"You've been allowed to smoke since you were my age?"

"Well, it's not really smoking. Father says there's only a tiny bit of tobacco in mine, he fills it up himself. It's mostly fruit oils and spice."

"It's really very good," I said.

"Why are you here?" Orlando replied.

"I don't know," I said, and took a big puff of the pipe.

"You've never come here before."

"I've never been allowed to."

"Most kids aren't," Orlando conceded. And his long dark curls fell over his forehead and he smiled his perfect smile.

"I think you look just like Zeus!" I exclaimed, for the coffee and the tobacco had truly gone to my head now.

"How do you know what Zeus looks like?" Orlando laughed.

"Picture books that Signorina Greco has," I mumbled.

"Isn't he that old man with a big beard?"

"No, that's God."

"Aren't they the same thing?"

"No!" I giggled.

"Well, let's see," Orlando stroked his chin and squinted his eyes at me, "who do you look like?"

I threw my head back and posed like a fashion model on all the Lambretta billboards I'd seen on my one trip to Rome. Orlando and I descended into a fit of giggles, and I felt tears rolling down my face. After we had finished laughing, and

Orlando was wiping his cheeks with long brown fingers, he said, "I know. Those painted cherubs inside the Duomo."

"Those fat babies?"

"Yeah."

I threw a pillow at him in my defense. "Just in the face!" Orlando cried.

After we had smoked all that the little pink disc provided, which was now a pile of grey ash in the bowl, we lay on our backs and listened to the rain. I thought about my father, who would have picked grapes with our neighbor all morning, and they would have had to quickly haul their sacks into the shed when the rain began. And then I remembered that there was no way he could have done that.

"I broke my Papa's glasses this morning," I said.

"Why did you do that?" drawled Orlando lazily.

"I stepped on them. It was an accident."

"Just take one of my father's pairs before you go," he offered.

"I couldn't do that!"

"Of course you could. He has about fifty and he'd never miss them."

"Okay. Thanks."

"You can have them if you tell me one thing."

"What?"

"Why'd you really break them?"

I was silent. I thought about my mother with the remains of my milk glass in her hands and I was ashamed. I couldn't go home and look them in the eye. Not after that. I could never go home again. I wondered if Orlando would permit me to live in the loft until I was old enough to work.

"Was it because of your sister?" he pressed.

"You heard that?" I moaned.

"I kind of did. I can unhear it though, if you want."

"I do want."

"You never told me you had a sister."

"She's a secret. I don't tell anyone."

"Is she like your mother?"

"Kind of."

"I see," Orlando nodded seriously. "It's okay. I won't tell anyone about her." A slight pause. "Is she pretty?"

"No!"

"Can I meet her if she ever comes back?"

"No!"

"Okay," Orlando shrugged.

"Okay," I said, and we were silent for a long time, and then I realized we were both asleep.

I stayed until sundown. Signora Khan came upstairs at one point and lay down a tray of tea, and hot flat bread with no yeast. Orlando taught me how to dip it in an array of pastes contained in long, flat rectangle dishes, some made of peppers and sweet chili, some of ground chickpeas and sesame. It was delicious. We talked, and slept, and smoked more *huqqua*, and as the sun came creeping down, I knew it was time to leave and I dreaded it.

S. Khan made a big show of calling me a taxicab, but I refused, saying I had no money. She offered to pay for it, but she and I both knew it was impossible for me to accept such kindness, no matter how she insisted. So I left quietly, and a little sadly too, and stood on the doorstep of the Khan Emporium waving much longer than I should, looking very foolish. I turned to go, and was grateful for the bulge in my pocket – a brand new pair of glasses from the store that Signora Khan insisted on presenting to me, if I wasn't to take the offer of a cab. "For your mother, with the compliments of Ayisha Khan," she said formally. But I knew there would be no such compliments, and that Mamma should never know where I spent that day.

When I arrived home, it was as if nothing had happened. Volatile was gone, and Mamma and Papa were quiet and contemplative. They showed no surprise at me showing up late, and if they detected the hints of tobacco and strawberry concealed in my clothing, they made no comment. I could not manage to say a word, I was far too ashamed. I ate all of my dinner gratefully, and hoped my downcast eyes and hanging head would convey all the apology that words could ever say. When I had finished, I pulled the little eyeglass case out of my pocket and placed it quietly beside my father's plate. He opened it, and with great surprise, beheld his brand new, shining pair of horn-rimmed spectacles. He put them on, and Mamma laughed, for they were a strange shape on his head, and made his face look funny. I laughed too and Papa blinked many times. "Perfect," he said, and did not ask where they had come from. I ducked my head and went to my room, where I lay in bed in the darkness and tried to cry because I was so happy to be forgiven.

The next day, everything returned to normal. Papa continued to wear the spectacles, and indeed wore them for many years of his life, until the frames were tarnished and the glass too scratched to see clearly.

"Mother says thank you," Orlando said at school days later.

"Thanks for what?"

"She received five bottles of *Dolce Fantasia* yesterday. She said she couldn't drink them herself, but will keep them until we have guests that will."

"Oh," I said, not wishing to show my surprise. "You're welcome."

I looked up at the sky and there they were again, the flight of swallows that followed Orlando wherever he went. There was a very large one amongst them. It was black and menacing and I couldn't look at it for very long. It stared at me like it knew me, and had hated me all its life.

SEI

My dreams continued as normal, a beautiful life and a beautiful lie. I excelled at all that I did, had adventures and forged relationships that I couldn't conceive of in my waking hours. At school I would daydream and relive my visions from the night, and at times would get so befuddled that I would confuse the two. Oh, how I lived for night. How I lived for sleep.

However, upon waking, I would often recall a kind of bewilderment that existed in my dreams. I would recollect that in my dreams I was looking for someone. In fact, several times that week I found my dream self journeying to St Patrizio's Well for no reason but to sit there. I would sit and be very still, holding my head in my hands and willing myself to remember, remember. And once, a breakthrough: I stood up and cried out, "Come back to me," and had an image of a lovely woman with swallow's wings. But no one would come. In the morning, I knew I was summoning Volatile, that in reality I missed her terribly and was consumed with guilt, and that was so strong it permeated my perfect dream life.

Winter came and went, and in the spring Papa attended to the vineyard and the olive grove, detracting old brittle branches. In April, when spring was promising to fully bloom, the swallows returned to Orvieto. "They spent their winter in the Sahara and Arabia," Papa said, consulting his *Oxford Guide to Birds*. "I'm sure happy they're back."

"Why, Papa?" I said.

"Because they eat all the insects that want to eat our grapes," my father responded. One strict regulation the DOC – the Italian wine board – had in making the *Dolce Fantasia* wine was that very limited pesticides were permitted in the vineyards, and our farm relied mainly on nature to keep us afloat.

"Oh," I said, and Papa laced his arm over my shoulders, and we watched a flock of swallows descend upon an olive tree. I wanted to say something about Volatile then, but I couldn't. My parents hadn't mentioned her to me since the morning she disappeared, nine months ago.

Orlando was a brilliant student and even though he acted otherwise, I knew he secretly liked school. He excelled at mathematics and languages, and Signorina Greco once mentioned that he could go all the way to Cambridge, his English was so fluent. He also spoke another language at home, something grating yet earthy, like fine cigar ash ground out in a glass bowl. So when Orlando stayed bedridden for a week with influenza, I was forlorn: lonely and fearful that one of the strong boys would notice his absence and it would begin again.

They did not notice. And if they did, very little was done about it. Once, I caught Darlo Gallo glaring at me with her cat-like eyes, and she whispered something to Christopher Esposito who shared her desk, and he turned around and looked at me in a way that made my stomach crawl. All during the lesson he would look at me this way, and often when he was sure I wouldn't notice.

It was during cursive writing class – the stupidest and most pointless of all classes, and to this I hold to this day – that I excused myself to go to the bathroom, more out of tedium than necessity. There were no mirrors in the small, whitewashed lavatory, and as I stood at the cistern, with my pants around my ankles and my undershorts supported by my left hand, I heard the door close quietly behind me. A chill ran up my spine as I heard soft, labored breathing. I willed my urine to stop its flow, told myself there was hardly any left, but it trickled out of me in what seemed to be a slow, never ending stream. Footsteps closer. My right hand began to shake and the flow began to deviate onto the wall. There was a sigh, and Christopher Esposito's clammy hand cupping my buttock.

I did not scream. I could not look at him in the eye. In a flash, I had whipped up my pants and buttoned them, ducked under his arm, and ran out of the lavatory as fast as my feet could carry me. Aware that there was a growing stain on my trousers – Goddammit, was I *still pissing*? I fled past the classroom door and down the hall, through the front doors and down the steps onto the street of Piazza Marconi and the two Jerusalem trees. What if he comes back for more? I hesitated, and ran. I thought I heard Darlo Gallo's voice calling my name.

I don't know why I didn't run toward home or to my only friend, perhaps a fear of discovery and a terrible shame that began to overcome me, a notion that I had become dirty. Christopher Esposito's face kept returning to my mind's eye, and even though I checked that I wasn't being followed, I could not trust my own eyes. All along the city wall I ran, on the path that had no name, the enormous volcanic tuff barrier rising and falling, the valley and vineyards far below.

I noticed a little cavern in the yellow umber wall, the entrance mostly concealed by white-tipped vines. I thought it would be enough to hide me for a moment. No, I didn't want concealment; I just wanted to be in a small, dark, cramped space for a moment, for a lifetime, just to think. I crawled in and to my surprise, the hole opened marginally, and I saw a little path of descending steps carved out of the tuff. Cautiously, with one hand upon the wall to keep my balance, I walked down. There the steps turned right as they fell into darkness. I inhaled sharply the scent of birds' nests, old eggs and feces before I found myself in an enormous cavern, perhaps fifteen feet below the ground.

Awe brushed every thought of the lavatory incident from my mind. I had heard of these places. Ancient Etruscan caves that riddled the bowels of Orvieto, huge enclosures that once housed cattle and goats, olive oil mills, entire wine cellars, fugitive popes and their wayward cardinals. I was beneath Orvieto.

The air was dusty and it was cold, and I noticed several precise squares carved into the back wall, as my eyes adjusted, perhaps fifty or so. Pigeon holes, of course. Where the birds once flew with the sun through the one window and returned in the eve to roost in these notches before they were slain for supper. The three layered water troughs, the first designed to spill over into the second and third, which the pigeons were trained to drink from. All empty now, save for dry mint-green lichen that sprouted like clouds. And a mass of something. A mass of a quivering, dusky, shadowy something, covered with a substance dark and dense, like hair.

I couldn't help it. I screamed.

The mass jolted and became alive, a heavy blur of blackness. It happened so fast, but I can still see it in my memory to this day: the shadow took form, white skin caught the sunlight and glimmered, wings unfurled, and a face I recalled with glittering green eyes and waving light brown hair.

"Volatile?" I whispered.

The swallow-girl jumped out of the water trough, hovered in the air for a moment, her wings stretched to their full capacity, reminding me of one of the frescos in Signorelli's Duomo. When she landed on her feet, the wings immediately folded around her body, to protect it from my sight. She was taller, and her back was straighter. Her face had become sharper, more angular.

"Hello, Gabriel," she said softly.

I felt shy all of a sudden. "What are you doing in here?" I demanded, my voice sterner than it should have been.

"Sleeping," she said, and did I imagine it, or was there a bite of sarcasm to her words? Did bird-girls even know of sarcasm?

"Underground?" I looked around distastefully. "But it's all wet and smelly…"

"It smells fine to me."

"But it's so dark."

"It keeps me hidden from predators and hunters."

"How long have you been here?"

"We've been here for three weeks now."

"*We?*"

It was then that *it* emerged from the shadows.

This is how he appeared to me then, when I was a child and knew no better. A tall, monstrous being. I remember his arms, muscular and powerful, skin as pale as marble and riddled with veins like blue cheese. I recall his wings: oil-spill black and so enormous they seemed like a cape that engulfed him. His eye fixed on me: I believed they were blue at the time. But one thing I recall, and I dare anyone who has met him to defy me: that his pupils were shaped like crucifixes. And it dawned on my childish mind that he was the shadow of death, the Grim Reaper, Hades – and I would meet him again one day, when he came to collect for the underworld. Suddenly, there was a sound like a hurricane, and then he was gone.

When I returned to my senses, I saw a single black feather, still quivering from the speed of the creature's movement. I deftly rescued it and pocketed it. "Who was that?" I demanded.

But Volatile would not answer. Instead, she watched the window, as if she could see him fly away.

It was getting dark. I was hungry and increasingly aware of the smell of drying urine from my pants. I could hear the birds in the valley, crying out to each other, preparing to come home. Soon swallows would invade the chamber, and I did not want to be present when they arrived.

"Mamma misses you," I said. "Won't you come and see her?"

"I will stay with my own kind."

"You were happy with us, remember?"

"I have tasted the human life, but it did not like me," Volatile replied.

"Just for tonight," I said in my most reassuring tone, and suddenly it was a year ago, when Papa asked me to speak to a swallow-girl as he attended her wound.

In response, Volatile unfurled her wings, forgetting about her nakedness, and flew away.

Defeat engulfed me as I trudged home wearily. Stars hung in the sky as I cut through the olive groves, and all I could think about was Volatile and with a shudder, the enormous winged man. I kept my hands in my pockets, and fingered the spine of the black feather gently. It shivered. As I shuffled up the steps, reality hit me, and I wondered how to explain my lack of book bag and lunch pail to my mother.

But as the door swung open, my worries dissolved. There was Volatile, apparently freshly bathed with hair neatly combed and a new dress made from some sort of bedding, and Mamma fussing with more energy than I had seen the past months. With her wings folded against her back, I noticed how they had either shrunken, or she had grown to accommodate their size.

Papa was heaping potatoes grilled with sage and Roman artichoke onto her plate, and they both looked up with joy as I entered. Volatile would not meet my eyes, and her cheeks were scarlet.

"Look who it is!" gushed Mamma, as if I didn't know.

"She's come back!" added my father helpfully, looking more happy than I ever saw in my life.

"She's come back to stay," said my mother hopefully, and I saw tears shining in her eyes and realized she had loved the girl all along.

We ate dinner in sheer joy that night, no one saying much. I didn't want anyone to notice how much I was staring at Volatile, but I couldn't help it. She used a fork like a native, and she was different somehow. I felt a stab of jealousy when I contemplated the possibility of her joining another family all those months. I was so engrossed in her return that only later I was struck by my parents' seeming nonchalance to her speech.

"So, she can speak," I said after a while, hoping to startle my parents a little with my knowledge.

Mamma screwed up her face. "Well, of course she can speak," she exclaimed.

"Where have you been all this time, Gabriel?" queried my father, as he cleaned the horn-rimmed spectacles.

"Not listening properly, I guess," I muttered, narrowing my eyes indignantly at Volatile, who ignored me.

"I was in India," she said at length, "for the winter."

"Do you…travel alone?" asked Mamma carefully.

"With my flock. The same birds I was born with."

"I see," said Mamma, and I could tell she had a wealth of controversial questions stored within her. I did too, frightful and scandalous questions, many of which included: do you sleep in a nest sometimes? Do the others notice that you're much bigger than all the other birds? Do you speak swallow? How did you learn Italian? Are you a secret everywhere you go? Did a witch cast a spell on you? When was the first time Signore Gallo saw you? Do the other swallows pick on you because you are different? Who is that man who is just like you? "And your parents?" Mamma queried cautiously, trying to appear nonchalant, and I was disappointed at such a dull question.

"I don't know," said Volatile. "Maybe they are in my flock, maybe not. I have no way of knowing, you see."

My parents clearly did not see, but did not know how to go about asking more questions of the nature.

"Do you like the name we gave you?" asked Papa.

"Of course," said Volatile. "It is my name."

"Well, of course it's your name!" I interjected inanely.

"You misunderstand," replied Volatile. "It has always been my name, long before you called me that."

My parents exchanged a confused look.

"It is all our names," continued Volatile. "Every swallow calls me Volatile. And I call every swallow Volatile. It is our name."

"Oh," said Mamma.
"Huh?" said I.

Spring passed and summer came. The harvest was strong and the house was pervaded by the scent of fermented, frozen white grapes, which I had grown used to. Flies filled our rooms and our barn, but it was worth it. I watched Papa bottle the wine by candlelight, when summer was nearly over and the days became shorter. The liquid looked like thick caramel as it was filtered into clear bottles with necks as long as swans'. My mother would apply the labels with a sponge and her fingers and gaze proudly at each bottle before she stacked them in the cellar. *Laurentis Dolce Fantasia, Orvieto, 1958.*

Volatile became an intrinsic part of our lives once more, and it was almost forgotten that she had ever left. I grew accustomed to seeing her face over the breakfast table, and playing in the fields at night. She was strange, though, so strange that summer that we gave up all hopes of ever assimilating her, of making her human. It was clear that Volatile was an in-between child, a mixed-breed like one can be mixed-race, neither belonging here nor there, yet belonging to both. I recalled what she said to me the first and only time she appeared in my dreams: *"I am a human with bird tendencies when I am with you. And I am a bird with human tendencies when I am with them."* And I understood exactly what it was like to never belong.

Volatile was a creature of few words, in those early years. She hardly spoke of her own accord, and often chose not to respond to questions. Her Italian was good, but her accent strange, clipped and stark, like it came from a beak. "Have you always been able to speak?" I asked her once, when we were folding the linen.

Volatile spat out two wooden clothes pegs from her mouth and answered promptly, "Haven't you?"

"It's just that you don't seem to say much, that's all."

"I only speak when there is something worth saying."

"Were there many things worth saying to my parents and not to me?"

Volatile shrugged, if you could call it that: a nonchalant expression crossed her face and her wings bobbed up and down behind her in a way that indicated sarcasm. "Only a fool wouldn't thank the hands that fed her."

"And you speak to the others, don't you?"

"I'm not sure what you mean."

"Who was that man that was with you that day?"

She shrugged.

"Is he your brother?"

Silence.

"Are there more out there, creatures like you?"

But no matter how I pressed, she would not answer personal questions or queries regarding her life with the swallows, partly out of concealment, and partly because she did not know the answers. "I don't tell the swallows of my human life," she would say whenever I pushed her too hard, "so why should I tell you about them?"

I never witnessed her conversing with swallows. Sometimes, she would make strange noises at the base of her throat, a weird gargling. Sometimes, when surprised, she would let out a very erratic squawk and her feathers would ruffle and stand on end, usually when Sweet Vittoria visited. Often, her head would bob about in a funny little nod, like a chicken. Like my mother when she was having an episode, which were rare that year, and every year after when Volatile visited. And when Mamma witnessed this strange head bobble, her eyes would mist over and she would gaze at Volatile like she was indeed the long-lost parrot of Signora Silvana's advice.

"I'm sorry about what I said that morning," I said to her once in our olive grove, which wasn't quite an olive grove, as it only consisted of five trees with dying roots.

"It's about time," said Volatile, smiling a little.

"I wanted you to come back, really I did. I asked you to come back in my dreams but you never came."

"I told you I wouldn't meddle in your dreams again."

I was stumped then, and something fell deep into the soil of my heart, a seed. "But…I think I want you to."

Volatile merely said, "Then one day you will have to ask me again, only very politely."

And of course, Volatile remained a secret. She did not leave the house during the day, and no one spoke of her to outsiders. We had so few visitors and lived so remotely that it became almost easy. Orlando never asked me about my missing sister again, so I did not feel guilty lying to him. Although, sometimes Volatile would vanish, for days on end, only to reappear to the relief of all. "I had to go," was all the explanation she would offer.

But at the beginning of autumn, when the pigeons and the sparrows and the ravens left Italy behind, Volatile said, "It is time." And in the sky directly above our house, the swallows cried out for her.

Mamma began to weep. Papa put his arms around her and I grew nervous, having become spoilt and used to a normal mother. I detested the thought of a long winter ridden with screams and spasms. "I will return," assured Volatile, "I will come back early."

"How early?" sniffed Mamma.

"I will be back for *Carnevale*," she said.

"*Carnevale*?" squeaked Mamma.

"For the masquerade parade. I want to join in. With all the other girls."

"But they will see you, it is impossible –"

"Goodbye," said Volatile, and flew away.

"Well!" exclaimed Mamma, for the shock of Volatile's desire had shed away any sign of hysterics, "I suppose I have all winter to make a costume!"

SETTE

True to her word, when the ice coating the streets of Orvieto cracked and turned to grey slush, and the barren trees bent over and picked up their cloaks leaf by leaf, Volatile returned to the farm. We found her sleeping on the rug under the kitchen table, for the cot had become far too small for her. She had grown, and her face had changed again, and for the first time I recognized the woman in my dream. I could see her wings in the morning light, the deep oily patterns of midnight blue that whorled along each feather. They had grown even smaller this year. It was February and I was fourteen years old.

Carnevale, the grand masked European tradition, was the most celebrated event of the year. In great cities like Florence and Venice, people came from all around the world to gasp at the spectacle of the Italian *Carnevale*. The children's parade day, where the streets were lined with floats of such epic proportions and detail they seemed both monstrous and celestial. The blasting music and heavy rhythms. The dancing, drowning in confetti made from dyed newspaper and sold by the bag, the water balloon bombs and the administration of silly string on the persons of anyone who crossed your path. And elsewhere in Europe, the balls in the street, where everyone dressed as historic characters, every man Don Juan and every woman Marie Antoinette. And later, the private balls for the rich, held in ornate palaces where women ordered diamonds for their dresses and their masks. Orlando told me about the university festival too, but I didn't believe him. "Sometimes during *Carnevale*", he whispered, "and only in Rome, there is what's called *Donne Notte*, Ladies Night."

"That sounds boring," I counteracted.

"You would think so," continued Orlando, "only it's anything but boring. It's where every man wants to be."

"Why?"

"Because the ladies choose any man they want, and take them away to do things to them."

"What kind of things?"

"Sex things."

"Wow," I said, "like kissing and stuff?"

Orlando frowned at me. "There's a lot more to sex than kissing, Laurentis. How have you not learned this?"

"Will you tell me?" I asked urgently, wondering which university Mariko would end up at.

"Not today," said Orlando, screwing up his nose in distaste.

"But what if you don't like the lady that wants to do sex things to you?" I pushed.

"You have no choice. It is said that once you enter that place, there is no escape. You must do exactly as the lady commands. Besides, what does it matter anyway? Everyone's in masks, so you'll never know who the lady is."

"Even the men are masked?"

"Of course."

"Would you go?"

Orlando sighed and sunk back into his pillows. "I doubt it," he replied. "I'm not even allowed to go to the tedious kids' parade here."

"Your father again?" I asked, by now used to the list of restrictions that caged Orlando. It was strange how in the beginning I thought him completely free, smoking a pipe at eleven years old. I was mistaken. We all have our prisons.

"Yeah," he said. "And my uncles, too. Even Mother. It's not a fitting code of conduct for us, *et cetera* and thank you very much. But it's okay. I can watch from the window anyway."

"Aren't you tired of never being able to go to parties?"

"Come on, Laurentis. As if we ever get invited."

"I have to go to one this weekend," I said quietly, because I was unsure how I felt about it yet.

"At *La Casa di Gallo*. Lucky you," sneered Orlando and rolled his eyes. "Be careful of little pig Darlo. She's sure to squeal."

Over the winter, my parents had decided in favor of Volatile joining the *Carnevale* celebrations. Mamma had prepared a costume for her, a pale blue dress made of satin, with plenty of padding at the back to disguise her wings underneath. The plan was to visit Orvieto town as a family, and pretend Volatile was a distant cousin come to stay, should anyone care to enquire. Papa could not see anything going wrong, especially during a day of outrageous noise, costume and crowds. No one was sure to even notice her. And at the Gallo's party, Volatile was to stay at home, out of sight, the whole incident forgotten. But an icy pair of fingers sunk into my heart, and I could not eat that day.

"Here," said Mamma over breakfast the morning of the parade, and placed a neatly folded something in front of my plate. She stood back and watched me with anticipation.

I swallowed my mouthful of porridge and hastily unfurled the bundle. A shiny red cloak, a pair of tight green satin leggings, a white billowy shirt with puffed sleeves, and a brown vest that seemed the only wearable garment in this group of travesties. "What the hell is this?" I cried.

Volatile was choking on her breakfast with the effort of trying not to laugh.

"Gabriel, language!" chided my father. "Your mother worked very hard on this."

And I looked over at Mamma, who was gazing at her creation with pride.

"But Papa, I can't…" I began under my breath. "Do you want me to be a laughing stock?"

"It's to match Volatile's costume," sang Mamma. "You're a prince for today! Isn't that wonderful?"

I held up the pair of shiny leggings gingerly with two fingers, as if bad taste were contagious. "Papa, do I have to?"

My father glared at me and I sighed deeply. And I don't think, to this day, with all the misery I have had to endure this lifetime, that I have sighed more deeply than at this moment.

I have to confess I was very poorly behaved that morning, and I refused to dress myself in that hideous monstrosity. I stood there like a wooden boy, while Mamma pulled and fretted over every inch of the glimmering costume that was sure to concrete my reputation as a lady boy for the rest of my days. Volatile sailed by my open bedroom door and giggled at the sight of me in my underpants, but I was too devastated to be embarrassed. And when Mamma finished dressing me, I stood there like a statue, face deadpan, my arms hanging by my sides like a puppet. "Oh, you look so handsome!" gushed Mamma, and pushed my unyielding body over to the mirror. I looked like a more ridiculous version of a court jester.

"It's perfect," breathed Mamma, "and matches Volatile's — Volatile! What on earth are you doing?"

And my reverie of self-pity was broken at the sight of Volatile kneeling on the floor with a pair of scissors, slicing up her dress. Mamma snatched the shears away and held up the dress, wailing. "This took me three months," she cried, "three months!" Her head began to jerk steadily on her neck.

"I couldn't breathe," said Volatile.

"What do you mean, you couldn't breathe? Was it suddenly too tight? It fit perfectly last night!"

"No, I mean my wings. I couldn't breathe." And Mamma unfurled the garment and saw two slices along the deep padding of the back.

"But my dear child, you can't go out like this," my mother said, "everyone will see. *Everyone will see, everyone will see. You can't go out like this for everyone will see.*"

"But if you cover my wings, I'll suffocate."

"Let her have them," advised my Papa, "people will think they are part of the costume."

"Celso, they look far too realistic!"

"Not after a few glasses of grappa," came Papa's response.

And so Tomasso was hitched to the cart and off we went to Orvieto – Volatile overjoyed and soaking up the sights that she had never seen from this angle before, and me, sulky and humiliated in my yards of shining satin. Papa and Mamma seemed happy enough, although I could sense tension, as Mamma was wary of making a spectacle of herself at public outings.

There was a farmer's market and craft fair at the Piazza del Popolo, where Papa tied the donkey and the cart, gave us 5000 lire each and told us to run along. There was a restrained raucousness in the air as I took Volatile's hand. Shopkeepers had closed their stores and parents were pushing their children to the traditional meeting place at Repubblica square, where they were assembled into lines to begin the parade down Corso Cavour. I shuddered when I saw my classmates, the boys dressed in their non-shimmery, masculine costumes. There were cowboys, matadors, policemen, and some dressed as a new hero called "Zorro", who had his own TV show and everything, although I had never seen it.

All the children from my school seemed to be clustered in a circle, as if orbiting around a particularly shining star. A few turned to regard me.

"Nice costumes, ladies," sneered a cowboy as we brushed by.

"Was that thing made from your mamma's old panties?" laughed a football player, raking Volatile over with his eyes.

"It would take more than those threadbare old rags to make a prince out of you," commented Zorro drily.

And then, as the lively music started to pump out of loudspeakers, the orbiting crowd broke apart to reveal its star. My blood ran cold when I saw Darlo Gallo, regal in a sapphire-colored silk gown and a pointy, dangerous-looking tiara. And there, curling over her spine, was a pair of costume wings so realistic, they may have been constructed from her father's hunting successes.

Sweat broke out on my brow as Darlo spotted me. Her expression changed from that of a fat, pedigreed cat languishing in attention to narrow-eyed suspicion. Then, a red fury seemed to descend over her like a visible cloud, and everything became slow motion. I cringed like a baby when she stalked over to me and I recoiled in anticipation, but to my great surprise, her outstretched claws did not graze me. Instead, they grabbed Volatile by the collar of her dress.

"Who are you?" screeched Darlo Gallo, and suddenly, we were surrounded by her band of strong boys, who served to conceal us from the world of adults. "Answer me!"

But Volatile was speechless, and I could hear her heartbeat hammering like it was my own.

"Leave her alone! That's my cousin!" I spat, but Darlo ignored me.

"Answer me!" demanded Darlo, and she shook Volatile. "I want to know! I want to know why…you…are…wearing…my…costume!" Every word was punctuated by a violent push, and then two boys had Volatile by each arm and whirled her around. I was tall enough to see into the crowd of people, but none of the adults seemed to be paying attention over the deafening music. I tried to call for help, but my mouth was as dry as week-old bread. Darlo Gallo had worked herself into a white-hot rage. "How dare you?" she shrieked. "Don't you know who I am? *I own this place!*"

And with all of her strength, hands clutching Volatile's wings at the base, Darlo tore with all her might. Volatile screamed – not the scream of a human being, but the cry of a bird shot down in flight. And through the crowd, I saw Alfio Gallo snap to attention.

At that moment and right on cue, the children assembled in the square began to dance in time with the music, moving in a line down Corso Cavour. The *Carnevale* parade had begun. The confetti and streamers began to fly, and the boys around us had no choice but to disband and join in their allotted places. Darlo shot Volatile a hateful glare and looked almost depressed that she couldn't finish the job. But instead, she sniffed, put her nose in the air, and marched away. I sighed with relief, and placed an arm over a shaking Volatile to disguise the blood stains that had already began to seep through the back of her gown. I jostled through the children and the crowd of admiring parents, my arm tightly around Volatile's shoulders. I felt the eyes of Alfio Gallo on the back of my head, so I hurried further, until I found a deserted lane. My eyes searched for a hiding place and immediately located one – a balcony concealed by cherry tomato vines, three flights of steps up. I half-dragged, half-carried Volatile up the steps. The garden was built around the entrance to an apartment, and stretched over like a bridge to the building opposite. It was silent, for everyone had gone to *Carnevale*.

Volatile collapsed. I was alarmed at the rate the bloodstains were growing, and shocked at Darlo's strength. "Wait here," I whispered urgently, "and do not make a sound. I'm going to get help."

"Don't leave me," whispered Volatile.

"I'll be back. Don't move!"

And with that, I bolted down the steps and into the fray of Corso Cavour. The children were dancing and shouting, throwing confetti at the onlookers, engaging in silly string fights as they moved across town. I longed to be like them, a faceless child in a faceless crowd; enjoying moments I would soon forget because they were common and worthless. Alfio Gallo, a cigarette dangling from his lips, blocked my path. "What's the rush, Laurentis?" he said in what he must have thought to be his friendliest voice, and his arm stretched out to catch me. I ducked under it and ran on.

Mamma and Papa were standing under Torre Del Moro, the monstrous brick clock tower. For a moment I hesitated, not wanting to disrupt this moment of rare pleasantry. Mamma's head was resting against Papa's shoulder, and she held a cup of chocolate gelato that Papa stole mouthfuls of. But the moment they saw my face, they knew. The gelato fell to the street and we hurried into the backstreets. When we were out of sight, we ran. Confetti poured from my hair and shoulders.

Nobody seemed to notice us as we collected a shivering Volatile from the balcony garden, rushed down alleys and lanes, jumped into the cart and whipped Tomasso into beginning the descent home. Mamma's head and hands were twitching, and her lips were turning white in an effort to bite her mouth closed. To avoid the crowds, we had to exit the back way of Orvieto – which, coincidentally, was the old entranceway of the town in Etruscan times, an uneven cobbled road with an enormous stone archway that many a warrior had marched under.

Along the dirt roads toward the farm, we were isolated enough for Mamma to release herself. "*Oh God, oh God, oh God!*" she yelled, followed by a stream of gibberish so ferocious and loud even the birds were startled from their trees. The cart shook from the violent shudders of her body, and I grabbed one of her hands and squeezed it shut as Papa called her name. Volatile squirmed but remained silent. Finally, Mamma gained control of herself, and trembling slightly, crossed her arms over her chest and placed her head between her knees. And so, in silence, we brought our two damaged women home.

GABRIEL AND THE SWALLOWS

La Casa Di Gallo lay in a prominent plain surrounded by vineyards and farmlands that stretched over many hills like several patchwork blankets. It could be seen from the entire western wall of Orvieto, an enormous yellow fortress surrounded by a plethora of thick, luxurious fir trees, with classical towers and turrets reminiscent of a castle in Germania. The roof was dome-shaped, like a holy church, and on top of it was a little glass room with one circular sofa, where you could sit and watch the world. It had thick stone gates, decorated with wrought-iron electric lanterns and carved stone cherubs in a variety of poses. An air of opulence would enfold you simply by gazing at it. And tonight, as Tomasso plodded down the tree-lined drive, I could already hear American jazz music in the air. There were more lamps than I remembered in the estate, hanging from trees and sitting amongst the flowerbeds. I could smell honeysuckle and basil, and I glanced down at the case of *Dolce Fantasia* that Papa had brought along as a gift – for it would be more shameful to arrive without one than to arrive hitched to a cross-eyed old beast.

A servant barely disguised his distaste as I leapt from the donkey and helped Mamma down. She looked well that night, her hair was sleek and pinned up, and she had taken great care with the black muslin dress that still smelled vaguely of mothballs. She had even dabbed a little perfume in the hollow of her throat, perfume from Sienna that Papa had given her as a wedding present. I could see its oily shadow shimmer there, like a secret. She looked a little nervous, the tiniest bit vague, like a portion of her mind was out to lunch. But Papa laced his arm fiercely over her shoulders and steered her past the enormous fountain and the monstrous wooden doorway with its wrought-iron gargoyle doorknockers.

The Gallos were standing in the foyer, a brilliantly lit, elegant room that reminded me greatly of the interior of the Teatro Mancinelli. They were proudly planted in front of two marble staircases that melded into one enormous balcony on the second floor. A glass and crystal chandelier trickled from the ceiling. Antiques and polished oak furniture were meticulously placed in all the right corners, and sumptuous red velvet curtains with gold cord tassels hung from every window. A great many Renaissance-inspired artworks hung in gilded frames, and waiters in suits served champagne and hors d'oveurs on silly little platters. Mamma and Papa greeted the Gallos with restraint, and Signora Gallo's little eyes gazed at Mamma with some curiosity.

She had the air of an aged belle of the ball; a definitive example to all the Orvietani boys of what Darlo was bound to genetically inherit. It wasn't bad. She was small and striking with smooth, young skin – but her red sequined gown and satin gloves that hugged her elbows attracted more attention than her face. Her greying hair was swept to the side, thirties-style. A jewel-encrusted piece depicting a bunch of grapes sat in that hair. She wore diamond and ruby rings on top of the gloves, which reminded me of pictures I had seen of a college of cardinals.

I only needed five minutes to assure myself that there would be no trouble tonight. All the strong boys, trotting after their mothers and fathers like well-fed dogs, were too in awe of

La Casa Di Gallo, their parent's wrath, and loyalty to Signore Gallo to bother with me. I took the liberty of staring at the boys in their finest duds, how like strutting cocks they appeared. So transparent. Suddenly, Papa's stern voice was in my ear: "Gabriel, please answer when Signore Gallo addresses you."

I jumped a little to find Alfio Gallo observing me with his shadowy eyes. "I'm sorry, sir," I managed to stutter.

Alfio Gallo cleared his throat grandly and said, "I said that I was wondering, boy, if you had any smart-mouth words this evening, but it looks as if you are rendered speechless." A loud guffaw that no one else joined in on. "Don't worry, boy," he continued, shoving a blur of hair and silk and lavender water at me, "this one gives me enough snarky remarks these days, don't you, *bella*?"

And he leaned down and kissed Darlo loudly with a large, juicy smacking of his lips, and pushed her toward me. I was terrified. "Show young Laurentis around, will you?"

Darlo looked equally as horrified as I and stood staring at me, her mouth gaping open, doubtless wondering if this was some sort of trap. "Go on!" her father boomed, and then turned his back on us. Darlo collected herself, rolling her eyes, and I reluctantly began to follow her, watching as Alfio Gallo lit a cigarette and began to bully my father into selling the vineyard.

I seized an abandoned half-empty goblet of something brown on a table and swallowed it down. It burned. I was suddenly feeling courageous.

"This is the ballroom!" Darlo was declaring, as we entered the room with the dome roof. Frescoes decorated the walls and wooden fixtures had been brazenly, pretentiously painted gold. I had grabbed another glass of thick, brown, strong stuff and had poured it down my throat as fast as lightning, not caring if Darlo saw. She looked at me in distaste and wrinkled up her nose. She opened her fat mouth to speak but I cut her off.

"You can shove this tour up your *culo*," I said. She gasped in shock as I whirled around, stuffed my fists into my pockets, and strode away as carelessly as I could.

Of course, the Gallos had an even bigger fountain at the back of the estate. This one had three sculptures inside it, spouting sparkling water: a sea-god with a conch, a mermaid with a trumpet, and a lost-looking little boy with a pail. Milling around it were people I had never seen before, and amongst the shadows of the firs their conversation ranged from their children to their spouses to their lovers to their favorite summer food. A waitress, yellow-haired like me and perhaps only a few years older, had taken to serving me brandy whenever no one was looking. I sat on a park bench; partially obscured by wild berry bushes and a waist-high stonewall, and watched.

Volatile had to have twelve stitches – seven in the right wing and five in the left. She did not cry, but Papa's spectacles were misty as he deftly worked the needle from feathers into flesh, *The Oxford Guide to Birds* open on the kitchen table, section: *Anatomy*. Mamma was confined to her room for two days after the parade,

I brought in all her meals and spoke to her in soothing tones, all of which she ignored. But today, it was as if nothing had happened, and Mamma seemed serene, her eyes cloudy and glazed, which I suspect had something to do with a little bottle of formulae that Papa had procured in town.

"Who was that?" asked Volatile, when we were alone the next day. She was lying in a bed that Papa had made her in what used to be a closet of sorts, a small room containing Mamma's bridal trunk, bottles of preserved tomatoes, and dried wild boar meat.

"That was Darlo Gallo," I hissed, "and I hate her."

"You shouldn't hate, Gabriel," responded Volatile.

"And why is that? I've always hated her and I always will!"

"Because hatred does *things* to you. I've seen it. Don't ask me anymore."

"Well, she hates me, so why shouldn't I hate her?"

Volatile gazed at me, almost through me, and I felt uncomfortable. "Darlo Gallo does not hate you."

"Yeah? And how would you know?"

Volatile narrowed her eyes. "I just know."

"*Buonasera*," came a sticky sweet voice behind me, and the devil herself appeared. She had a flute of champagne in one hand and waved it about, trying to draw my attention to her hollow rebellion. What was she hoping for – my admiration? "May I sit?" she inquired, a mocking ruse of good manners.

I didn't respond, but my whole body sighed with impatience.

"Since you ran out on my tour, I've felt like such a terrible hostess," she chattered, flinging a rope of hair from her shoulders, the silk of her dress whispering as she lowered herself onto the bench. She sat on the edge of it precariously, not wanting to dirty her bottom. Her ankles betrayed her as she buckled in high heels. Darlo took a dainty sip of her champagne and glanced around her, as if embarrassed that someone she knew would see her there.

"What do you want?" I asked, my voice hard.

"Oh, I don't know," she responded flippantly. "You were on your own and I would be a horrid hostess if I just—"

"Drop the *merda*, Gallo."

"Oh, well…I…yes….sorry…" she stammered, and fidgeted with her hair, twirling it around an index finger. There was a long pause and she drained the glass. Wait, did Darlo Gallo just *apologize*?

"What do you want?" I repeated, and noted even through the fuzziness of my head, that she was acting strangely.

"Did you know I'm off to boarding school next week? To Paris. Charm and etiquette school for young ladies. I can hardly wait!" And she let out a strange, forced giggle.

"I really couldn't care less," I counteracted truthfully, and got up to leave.

But Darlo Gallo grasped my hand, and I felt her clammy skin against my own. I instantly recoiled and violently withdrew my hand. "Why don't you care?" she said, wide-eyed, her skin ashen.

"I just…*what?*"

"All the other boys care. They care a lot. Some even cried," she continued softly. I saw my chance had come at last. I knew what I had to say.

"Because I hate you, Darlo Gallo," I said coldly, somewhat shocked at my own boldness.

"You...*what?*" And there was inexplicable, genuine horror in her expression.

Oh, how she sickened me, sitting there in those ostentatious heels, feigning oblivion to all the torture she had put me through. Anger and alcohol overpowered my cowardice and I said, "Is this a surprise to you, Gallo? You, who have tortured and humiliated me every chance you got? You, who called me a lady boy and made fun of my clothes and my mother?"

"No, it's not true, I make fun of everyone, I was just kidding around..."

"Sending Christopher Esposito after me into the bathroom?"

"What? I never did! He knows that you belong to—"

"And then you dared, *dared* to hurt Volatile!"

Darlo's face changed now from stricken to rage. "Volatile? Who is this *Volatile?*"

"Just shut up!" I shouted. "Shut your goddamn mouth!"

"Gabriel," sobbed Darlo Gallo, "I'm so sorry, I never meant to –"

I leaned in, brandy making a brave man out of me. "You're a pig, Darlo Gallo. If you ever come near her again, I will kill you. Do you understand me?"

Tears were streaming down her cheeks now. "Christopher Esposito," she stuttered, "did he touch you?"

"*Vaffanculo,*" I swore with hostile irreverence. "Go to Paris, I hope you rot and die there."

"Who is she, this Volatile? What does she mean to you?" cried Darlo through tears and snot. But I had already left, and was stomping off to find my parents. Forget this party. Orlando was right. I was filled with a strange exaltation as victory swept over me. I had defeated my arch-nemesis. I felt like I owed Zeus somehow, but was too old and wise now to say a prayer to him, even if I were drunk. Darlo Gallo was going to France for eternity, as far as I was concerned. I would no longer be bullied, hit, sworn at, fondled. I was free.

It was a long, long time before our paths crossed once more, a time when she no longer had the power to hurt me. But I never saw Christopher Esposito again. Not long after the party, the Gallo estate fired his father without explanation. In search of new work, the family left Orvieto.

OTTO

I had been in love with Mariko Marino since the moment I first laid eyes on her. It was during a fall farmer's market, when I was too young to care how unfashionable Tomasso was, and used to accompany my father to town as often as I could. I would always take any opportunity to visit Orvieto in those days; to be lost in a city with walls so high, a sliver of sky would only present itself after the most painful elongation of the neck. The winding, breathing tunnels containing everything from nook-and-cranny apartments to concealed grand ballrooms and monasteries, wrapped in volcanic stone. Every door so monstrous and grand, like an empirical entry to a medieval dungeon. Surprises around every corner – roses growing horizontally five floors up for no reason at all. Little gargoyles and stone lions appearing around every corner to glare at you with critical expressions, and gossip about you once the town had gone to sleep.

Papa had brought several bottles of *Laurentis Dolce Fantasia* to the market in Piazza del Popolo, in hopes of trading them for a weekly supply of grain and cheese. I jumped off the donkey, clutching the few thousand lire in my grimy hand, the very last of my birthday money. I don't remember how old I was, perhaps six or seven, but my primary obstacle was to get to the *panetteria* and stuff my face with *torrone* – those sickly sweet slabs of nougat stuffed with almonds – as fast as possible.

And it was there, as I stood at the counter of Montanucci's bakery on Corso Cavour, my hands and face all sticky from the candy, that the strangest creature walked in.

She was tall and stick-thin, with no bumps and lumps along the way that a woman should normally possess. Apart from her odd yard-stick shape, she had a face so weird that I couldn't help but stare: impossibly white skin, a flat nose that almost disappeared in profile, slanted eyes with puffy, fat lids that would effortlessly slide over them. She had no eyelashes, and her brows were scattered and scarce. An unusual hairstyle did not help to assimilate her: the black, straight stuff fell in an asymmetrical angle over her forehead and ended just under her ears.

Suddenly, all the women in the *panetteria* were atwitter, glaring and staring, all the while pretending not to. The woman was not alone, her arm was looped through the elderly Signore Marino's, the retired schoolteacher.

Word had it that Signore Marino, an educated man, had bad luck in love with the Orvietani women. Two broken engagements, one of which the fiancée called off the morning of the marriage, left S. Marino so frustrated that he fled to

Japan, wherever that was. There he lived for a decade or so, teaching English in the schools of Kyoto, until he fell in love with a high school student, Matsuyo.

His elderly parents, opposed to the match, refused their son's offer of an all-expenses-paid journey to Japan for the wedding. Declaring a war with the elder Marinos, who wouldn't even budge on their decision once their son wrote that his wife was pregnant, Signore Marino did not return to Orvieto until the elder Marinos had both died, leaving him the apartment along the eastern wall he had grown up in.

Orvieto was rife with gossip when it finally beheld the notorious Signora Marino. It had expected a tiny, childish bride who spoke in a strange, foreign tongue, wearing silk kimonos and wooden shoes. "She will surely have the body of a seven-year-old girl," sneered the first ex-fiancée, the wife of Orvieto's post-master. "She will hardly be able to see from her slitty little eyes!" declared the second ex-fiancée with so much glee that the two women promptly mended their rift.

But she was neither of those things: she was so tall she towered over the women of Orvieto with so regal a bearing the women were secretly afraid. Her Italian was fluent and sculpted so beautifully from her soft Japanese accent that the Orvietani felt mesmerized as they watched her order daily fresh flowers in the Piazza Duomo. She wore the flowing black clothes of a deadly samurai, and in winter, expensive furs and leather high-heeled boots. Those that knew her intimately said she could create beautiful little paper animals and birds with a few clean movements from her fingers. They said she owned a small projector and would turn out the lights after a dinner party and perform the most amazing shadow puppets. They said she was a mime artist.

I was too busy staring at this creature that it took me some moments to discover the little girl clutching her mother's hand. Mariko Marino. Large hazel eyes, creamy skin, jet black hair. And she stared at me too, or stared at my girlish blond curls, and I felt at that moment some kind of destiny between us.

Alas, destiny would have to wait, because during my childhood and adolescence, I could never summon the courage to even speak to Mariko. I would watch her at lunch times, as she played with Darlo Gallo under the Jerusalem tree, her movements ethereal and mysterious to me. I would stare so hard that Orlando would elbow me in the ribs, and Mariko would notice and look a little frightened. She would avoid my gaze and the thick perimeter of air around me at all times. I never caught her watching me out of the corner of her eye. I never overheard my name passing her lips. Still, I would hopelessly dream about her all night long, and in my dreams she loved me.

After Darlo left, the strong boys seemed to disappear too, as if they had had enough of education, and joined their fathers picking grapes in the Gallo vineyards. I stayed at school until I earned my high school diploma, but did not make many friends, even though my arch-nemesis was no more. Olive-skinned Orlando filled all of my friendship requirements, and together, we sailed through the years of school until it was all over, and we left the white building in Piazza Marconi behind forever. Orlando finished a year before me, and I visited him behind the serving counter of the Khan Emporium for espresso most afternoons. Mariko stayed too, because her father was a stickler for education, and I had heard it rumored that she was to study economics in Rome.

My heart sunk at the news, for I could not imagine a day where I wouldn't wake in anticipation for seeing Mariko, or a weekend spent dreaming about Monday. On the last day of school, I tried to summon all my courage to just walk up to her and say something light and hearty like, "So what's next for you?" or "Are you glad it's all over or is that just me?" but I stood there on the steps like an idiot, and watched as she sailed past me, down the front stairs with her friends, a cloud of perfume and giggles. I felt my ribs separate from each other with a sigh, and my spine bend forward from disappointment.

As I trudged home, on that last day of school, I felt like a child and not an eighteen year old man. I had never hated myself more. Twelve years of school with the same girl and I still couldn't speak to her, apart from that one glorious, incandescent occasion that I relived in my head at least once daily. It alone had given me hope.

It had happened two years ago.

La Teatro Mancinelli, the heart and soul of Orvieto's artistic community, was a grand little feat of classical architectural sturdiness and general good taste. It hosted a variety of events and productions that took place on a weekly basis: a Tuesday and Thursday night engagement, for example, with a Saturday gala performance and a Sunday afternoon matinee. Religious passion plays too gruesome for the Duomo,

Latin-American tango troupes, lesser operas from Rome or Florence, and sometimes a saucy new American play with no music and no dancing whatsoever. No matter the event, all of Orvieto, including the wealthier of the farming folk, would put on their best clothes and could be seen sipping aperitifs in the theatre caffé as the first bells rang announcing the commencement of the performance. The men would stub out their cigarettes and usher their women in, and there would be an air of electricity and anticipation so thick, you could scrape it with your fingernails.

No matter the performance, from *La Boheme* to Tennessee Williams, nothing drew the crowds like the local amateur theatre group, Signore Belivacqua and Company. Whenever a travelling act could not be booked, Signore Belivacqua and his troupe of talented misfits could be counted on to hold the Orvietani in its thrall with their astonishing array of daring productions. Shakespeare, popular musicals, love poetry, folk music: nothing was safe once S. Belivacqua had one of his epiphanies, translating any material whatsoever into a grand, sometimes questionable, production. I had never attended any of them before, and when I saw the posters for the new show, I made up my mind.

S. BELIVACQUA *&* CO. THEATRE COMPANY
Proudly presents:
The Nightingale
by Hans C. Andersen
"a sweet song, an Emperor and the Grim Reaper unite in imperial

China to create music, poetry and eternal life..."
Starring:
S. Vitale Belivacqua as The Emperor &
S. Matsuyo Marino as The Nightingale

**LIMITED ENGAGEMENT!
14-18 JULY**

I requested a ticket to the opening night for my birthday. Mamma gave me a funny look but Papa pulled his billfold out of his front pocket and withdrew the exact cost of a ground floor ticket and placed it in my hand. In afterthought, he withdrew another stack of lire, the price of a Campari spritz.

On the 14th of July (my birthday was ten days prior to this, on some Americano holiday, I have since been informed) I arrived at the Teatro in my best suit, which wasn't really a suit, but slacks and a vest reserved for weddings. Strange Oriental music poured out of the theatre as I alighted the stairs, clutching my ticket that I meticulously acquired days earlier, choosing the seat carefully and to the best of my advantage.

Classmates at my school worked part-time as ushers, in little suits of red. One youngster checked my ticket and pointed up the stairs. As I followed the crowd through the powder-blue hall, I suddenly felt foolish that I hadn't asked Orlando to accompany me. I overcame my shame and found myself at a second-floor box, opened the creaky little door and pulled back the red velvet curtain. I sat and gazed down at the ground floor, the plush seats aligned in two columns, the Orvietani people hastening to theirs seats as the bell sounded. I gazed up at the famous chandelier, powered by electricity these days, and the fresco of brightly colored maidens that danced around it. As the lights dimmed, the Oriental music grew louder, and a stage decorated with minimalistic origami-inspired trees emerged, I finally saw what I had come here for: Mariko Marino, in the front row.

I can't remember the performance at all, as I stared at Mariko most of the time. Sometimes she gazed with pride at her mamma, sometimes cringed with embarrassment, but I could tell she was fond of her papa, whose hand she regularly patted.

During intermission, I fled down to the café and ordered a glistening red glass of Campari and soda, stuffed with ice and garnished with a floating orange slice, before the crowd of ravenous people arrived. As I sat at the bar sipping it, my heart did a backflip as Mariko materialized beside me.

"What do you want, my dear?" asked her elderly papa.

"A Bellini," replied Mariko in her beautiful voice, and as she brushed her straight black hair from her shoulder, her eyes caught mine and I blushed. She swallowed and stared straight forward.

"I don't like you drinking, Mariko," said her father, but it didn't sound like an admonishment, but a prayer. I sensed correctly that she was the apple of his eye, and could have consumed a dozen Bellinis in his presence, for all he cared.

"Oh please, Papa. All my friends' daddies let them have a drink on a special occasion!"

"I suppose, just this once," said her father. "Isn't your mother wonderful tonight?"

"Yes," replied Mariko, her eyes lighting up on the jewel toned cocktail set before her. "*Salute*," she said, and tapped her glass to his.

As she took a sip from her champagne and peach juice, her eyes caught mine again, and I was about to wish her a good evening when three girls flew by and surrounded the Marinos in a fortress of giggling and dangerously waving arms and perfume too suffocating for the season. I downed the remainder of my aperitif and placed my empty glass on the bar. One of the girls eyed me strangely as I turned to leave. The bells began to chime in warning, the intermission was coming to an end.

When the performance was over, there was polite applause, confused expressions, and a great deal of loud chatter as to what the Orvietani liked and did not like about *The Nightingale*. (Liked: the Emperor, some of the trees, the costumes from the Khan Emporium. Did not like: the Nightingale, the makeup, some of the trees, the paper palace, the music, the Nightingale's solo, the length of the play, how the Nightingale did not die at the end.)

As the crowd poured out of the Teatro Mancinelli to discuss the production in detail over cigars and red wine, and perhaps a late supper of rabbit stew or a plate of antipasto, I remained in my box, waiting. I watched the Marinos, Signore Marino's hand shaken by many a patron, Mariko looking bored. I dug my hand in a pocket to pull out the remains of my lire, for I had chosen a cheaper box ticket in order to save for two cups of coffee. My hands shook.

One or two cleaners began to file into the theatre, and as I looked down upon the ground floor, I knew my moment had arrived. Mariko sat in the front row alone, her father undoubtedly gone backstage to congratulate and collect his wife.

"*Buonasera,*" I said meekly behind her, and her head whipped around to see me standing in the aisle, hands thrust deeply in the pockets to conceal the shaking.

She looked around her, searching for a way out, or perhaps for somebody who would see her, I didn't know. I was filled with dismay.

"Your Mamma was great tonight," I said, and I meant it, because everything associated with Mariko was grand, wonderful, just magic. I kind of just stood there, waiting for her to speak. An old lady cleaner sailed past me with her broom and rolled her eyes, as if she knew exactly what I was up to and did not approve.

"Uh…thanks. Thanks, Gabriel," said Mariko, and my heart soared. She knew my name. *She knew my name!*

"Did you…uh…did you help her with her lines?"

"Not really."

"Well, someone had to, because she was great."

"I think the rest of the cast would have done that, during rehearsal."

"Oh," I finished lamely. "Can I sit down?"

Mariko looked flustered. "Um…I don't know, well, maybe for a minute…"

I understood immediately. "Your father?"

But Mariko frowned. "No." Her voice trailed off. "I'm not supposed to talk to you," she said flatly, and turned away.

One by one, the house lights began to go out until we were sitting there in near darkness. Mariko squirmed uncomfortably.

I felt terribly foolish, and the distant dream of the two of us, laughingly perched over cups of steaming cappuccino, seemed ridiculous indeed.

But instead of apologizing and slinking away, I grew indignant. I had dealt with rejection for too long, you see, and in my back knuckle-like bones began to click together like beads on a bracelet: the beginnings of a spine. And suddenly, I was weary of her, of her beauty, her unattainability. Sick to death of unrequited love from such a terrible distance, I realized the haunting truth: I was tired of Orvieto.

"I can guess why," I replied peevishly. "I'm poor. My clothes don't match and I never eat anything the way it's meant to be eaten, because we never have the kind of food that you Orvieto folk do." My hat quivered as I held it in my lap. Suddenly, the hat felt far too adult for me, and I must surely look laughable in it, a fifteen-year-old acting like Humphrey Bogart. *Shut up, idiot!* my brain said, but I continued on anyway. "And I know you all think I'm a reject of society or something. The boy who has no friends, except for that foreigner nobody else likes, and a mother that's considered retarded."

"Gabriel!"

"Oh, and not to mention, ugly as sin. '*Look at that lady boy! Is it a boy or is it a girl? What a mystery!*'" And I stood up, feeling like my whole body was shaking now, and I felt miserable, foolish and righteously angry all at once. All I wanted was to run along home, and hurl myself into Volatile's bed, and keep her up all night moaning about it.

"Thanks for letting me sit here, Mariko Marino. What an honor it was to sit next to you for just a moment, considering how you're not *supposed* to talk to me. What a privilege," I scoffed, turned my back, and exited the theatre.

I hurled the hat away from me in disgust as I fled down the steps. Damn Humphrey Bogart, I mused viciously as I resolved to never think about Mariko Marino for the rest of my days.

But suddenly, I heard my name being called, and footsteps echoed behind me on the cobblestone street, and a cold hand clasped the bare skin of my forearm.

"So what if you don't eat the way the rest of them do?" said Mariko, letting go of my arm and thrusting my discarded hat into my chest. "We eat uncooked fish sometimes. And sticky rice. And raw baby octopus when we can find it. And *edemame*, my favorite – that's steamed green beans that Haha cooks for me."

"Haha?"

"It's Japanese for 'mother'."

"That's funny," I said, and grinned. We were alone on Corso Cavour, with only the Gothic wrought-iron street lamps and rooftop gargoyles to see us.

"And if Orlando Khan is a foreigner, then I am a foreigner too."

"But why is it you have so many friends? Why is it no one seems to care?"

"Oh, they care," said Mariko, somewhat moodily. "They used to laugh when Haha would paint my face white and dress me as a geisha for *Carnevale* and her dinner parties. They used to turn up their noses when they visited the house because of our furniture and tableware. They used to complain that I smelled…like *seaweed*!

But after they would tease me, *she* would kiss me and say that it was all right, that I was her little China doll."

"She? Your mother?"

Mariko frowned. "No, silly. Darlo Gallo."

The name struck me with dread, that name I hadn't heard for an age now. "What does she have to do with anything?" I scoffed, rather naively.

"Oh, come on, Gabriel. How have you not realized this? *She owns this place.*"

Goosebumps broke out all over my skin at these words. "But she's in France!" I spluttered.

"Maybe so," said Mariko, "but she is still here." And she glanced over her shoulder, as if the villainous creature were standing right behind us. "Darlo Gallo is my cousin," she said finally, and the admission seemed like a heavy burden she was finally free from, "only that's not well-known. It's not really something the Gallos wish to...*advertise*." That word again. Only this time, I knew what it meant.

A voice came to us on the evening breeze, calling Mariko's name. "That's my papa," she said, "I have to go."

"Do you want to go to a caffé?" I blurted out.

Mariko looked flabbergasted. "Now?"

"Well, yeah," I replied, and I could see her blush in the lamplight.

"Maybe someday," she said, "outside this place." And she looked around us as if the walls of Orvieto were a prison.

"Well, goodnight," I said.

"Bye," said Mariko and smiled at me, a heart-rendering smile full of promise. "Oh, and one more thing."

I drew one step closer to her. "What?"

"You're not ugly. You're actually, well…anything but ugly. But I'm sure you hear that all the time." She was really blushing now, and so was I, because I had no idea what she was talking about.

"Well…thank you, I guess?"

She laughed and headed back inside the theatre.

"So that was a yes to coffee?" I shouted after her, encouraged.

"Someplace else!" she called back.

"I would take you all the way to Rome!"

"Well, come and pick me up sometime! You got a car?"

"For you, I'd get one!"

"Who are you shouting at, Mariko?" came her father's voice from the shadows.

"Ladies should not shout in public, they should be demure," came Haha's strange little voice.

"Oh stop it, both of you," said Mariko, and she laughed.

I disappeared down Corso Cavour, the grin on my face threatening to split it in half. It was the happiest day of my life.

But this day, the final day of school, was surely the worst day of my life, I thought, as I hurled my school bag into the kitchen corner for the last time, and dumped my body into a chair, consuming in one gulp the steaming espresso that Mamma set before me.

"Gabriel?" said Mamma softly, and I could see her through my fingers, because both my hands were covering my face in despair. Her head was bobbing gently on her shoulders, and she had a wild look in her eyes. I could tell immediately, after all these years, that she was excited. Papa appeared beside her and then there was Volatile, her long brown hair hanging to her waist, nearly concealing the speckled wings that curled against her shoulders like a shawl. One of mother's old dresses hung past the knees of her long legs, and she was bouncing the handle of a mop between her hands like it was a football. She smirked at me. She was always smirking in those days.

"We're so proud of how well you've done in school," began Mamma, and she began to speak, nervously and haltingly and feverishly.

They knew I enjoyed academics. They wished they had enough money to send me to university. They had been saving for it since they were married, but *Dolce Fantasia* is not as popular as they wished. They wanted a better future for me than a peasant wine-maker. I could be a writer, a teacher. If they had enough money, I could be anything I wanted.

But they never stopped saving, and last night, they figured they had enough for one year's university, my choice, board and food and a little spending money besides. It wasn't enough for a full degree, but it was better than nothing, right? But of course, if I didn't want it, I could take the money as a gift and save it, or buy something: a car, perhaps? A nice watch?

But they needn't have given me that choice. I chose university. And I chose Rome.

NOVE

Volatile had been such a successfully-kept secret that I could have strangled Orlando Khan when he just happened to "drop" past the house one summer's day for a "surprise" visit, to put it in his terms.

I had never given him license to visit the house. I had never invited him, never hinted that he ever come of his own volition. If anything, I painted the farm in a greyish, dreary, unflattering light. It was unremarkable and dull, and nobody ever visited, and we wanted it to stay that way. But somehow, Orlando Khan, probably bored in the scarce months since he finished school, decided to venture into the valleys of Orvieto, march through the olive groves, enquire of a few farmers the location of the Laurentis vineyard, shuffle up the lichen-covered front steps, and rap presumptuously on the front door one hot Sunday morning.

I was in my room at the time, but I should have known it was he, because through the open window, I could hear the infernal chatter of that whole circus troupe of swallows that followed Orlando wherever he went. I sat up straight; my body all stiff angles with readiness, and listened as Mamma opened the door.

"*Sì?*"

Mamma and Orlando Khan beheld each other for a moment, Mamma in her apron, a smear of flour on her face, a fistful of dough in one hand. "Good morning, Signora," said Orlando pleasantly, "is Gabriel at home?"

I jumped off the bed and threw my book on the floor. I hastily searched my own mind. *Where is Volatile?* It was almost as if I could hear the same question echoing in Mamma's thoughts. *I have no idea. She could be anywhere.*

"You're Ayisha Khan's boy," breathed Mamma and as if in a trance, stepped to one side to allow Orlando entry. I rushed out of my room.

"Hi, Orlando. What are you doing here? You know what, I was just about to go for a walk. Join me." My voice was high and strange and unusually forceful. I gave my mother a reproachful glare as I hurried over to him, and snatched up my boots from where they sat near the front door. *Where is Volatile? I don't know. She could be anywhere.* I put a hand forcefully on my friend's shoulder to push him out the door.

"Uh," responded Orlando, looking confused, "okay. Goodbye, Signora Laurentis, it was nice to finally…"

But I had already pushed him down the stairs. "Goddamn it, Laurentis. What's your problem?" he snapped as I slammed the door shut. I knew Mamma was just behind it, her ear pressed against the door. I wondered if her heart was hammering as loudly as mine.

"I was just on my way out," I muttered, and stomped forcefully up the trail into the olive grove. Orlando had no choice but to follow me.

"Fine Italian hospitality," he commented drily, and rammed his cap over his ears sulkily.

"Who asked you to come over here?"

"Well, I guess I've learned my lesson," my friend growled.

Suddenly, the air around us became disturbed, and there came the sound of rushing wind, and the crackling of broken sticks, as if a very large bird had flown by and landed. *Where is Volatile?* screamed my mind as sweat broke out all over my body.

"What was that?" whispered Orlando, trying to follow the movement with his eyes. Above him, the flight of swallows perched in the treetops and stared down at us. *She's here*, they sang. I froze. Did the swallows just speak to me? Did those birds just answer my question? Could Orlando hear them too? *She's here*, said the swallows, and that was the first time of many I questioned my sanity.

The air seemed to stand still and the world became eerily silent. A sound of crunching twigs, a footstep. Then Volatile's voice said, "It's *you*."

As she stared at Orlando, I could see what she saw. Tall, olive-skinned, exotic Orlando Khan, and written all over her face was that same expression some Orvietani girls gave him as he sauntered down Corso Cavour. Delicious, juicy, forbidden fruit, their faces seemed to say. I was terrified, launching into damage control.

Maybe it wasn't so bad. That trick Volatile had of wrapping her wings around her shoulders made them seem like an elaborate shawl. Sure, it was strange to have a shawl made of feathers, especially in the summer, but maybe Volatile was just a weird girl, who knew? She had practiced and could keep her wings lifeless, without flinching or stretching them, for hours sometimes, depending on her concentration. They ached, though. She described it as holding a calf muscle taut for an age and walking on it all the while. I had tried it out, and she had laughed at the result.

Orlando turned to me, and he had that ridiculous smile he thought was so charming on his stupid face, the one that made his dimples stand out. "Is this your sister, Laurentis?"

"My cousin," I mumbled moodily, before recalling my slip with Orlando years earlier on this subject, under the multi-colored silk skies of the Khan Emporium. "I mean sister, whatever."

"Well, hello, Sister Whatever," said Orlando, approaching Volatile sleekly, moving like he considered himself a panther or some such jungle predator.

"She's just visiting!" I yelled defensively at his retreating back.

"Orlando Khan," announced Volatile, and placed a hand on her hip sassily, "we meet at last." And her eyes scraped over his body, dragging her gaze so slowly from muscle to muscle that I could sense the tremor that ran through both of them.

"I see you are aware of my paltry existence," exclaimed Orlando, giving the poor girl the entire dazzling array of his white teeth.

"My cousin-brother has a big mouth," commented Volatile drily, and she was gazing fearlessly up into Orlando's eyes, smiling in a way I had never seen before.

I wanted to throw up.

Why wasn't she running? Why wasn't she afraid?

I desired nothing more than to jump between them but I was frozen in horror as Orlando's hand stretched out to touch her. *Why was he touching her?*

The birds in the trees began to screech in warning.

The piercing, shrill sound surely travelled through the entire wood, but Orlando seemed immune to it. Volatile looked up at the swallows sharply, but it was too late.

Orlando's fingers grazed her outstretched hand and her wings bristled, the feathers standing on end like a cat's fur when it has had a fright. Orlando immediately drew back with a cry, as if she was a flame and he had been burnt. His shout seemed to petrify her, and her wings unfurled and hung stiffly from her back, their tips pointing skywards. Orlando stared at her in horror and awe.

"*Ifrit*," he whispered, and bowed low to the ground.

And then Volatile said something strange. Her tone was off-key, and the voice was hers yet not hers, at the same time. "What do you see, boy?"

Orlando raised his eyes to hers. "I see you," he said.

I vomited.

It was strange having Orlando around the farm. In one way, it was a relief, an enormous weight lifted from my shoulders. In another, it was aggravating, having him sniffing around Volatile whenever he pleased, taking her off on private strolls, giving her those deliberate glances across the dinner table.

Mamma and Papa quickly adjusted to the continual Turkish presence on the property, and Papa took a heady interest in Orlando, like he was an exquisite, mysterious artifact from a time and land trapped in the past. Mamma secretly adored Orlando, who poured his charm all over her like sticky honey, although he wasn't nearly as charming as he thought he was and I could see right through him. He'd always bring a little gift along with his visits, and Mamma was such a hypocrite, consuming the Ceylon tea, dried, smelly Chinese mushrooms, and rose-flavored Turkish delight when she had no business to.

"I thought you said the Laurentis family didn't consume strange, foreign foods," I would whine when Orlando had gone home.

"Oh, be quiet and go back to your books," Mamma would happily respond, biting dreamily into a slice of pistachio halva.

The effect he had on Volatile, however, was nothing short of alarming.

"Tell me everything about Orlando Khan," she sighed that first night, floating into my room like a cloud and arranging herself on the bed, propping her head up with one arm as she gazed not at me, but at the memory of Orlando, his big lumbering head and all that ridiculous hair that he should probably shave off. Wouldn't his religion deem all that hair inappropriate and excessive? I thought so. It was too fashionable for a good Muslim boy. It was altogether too much.

I peered at her over my book with what I hoped was my most withering expression. "You already know everything about him," I responded, acting as bored as I could.

"Tell me again," she said, and writhed around on the bed like a worm.

When I didn't deign to encourage her by responding, she began chattering anyway, mostly nonsensical things I would never have thought I'd hear utter from her rational tongue.

Orlando Khan looks like a god.

Orlando Khan's profile is like all the sculptures of the Roman emperors.

Orlando Khan's body has muscles like Hercules.

Orlando Khan's eyes are like black coals that just burn on and on forever.

"Oh, would you just stop!" I moaned, louder and more forcefully than I had wanted.

Volatile looked at me scornfully and bounced off the bed. "Is there a problem?"

"It's just wrong. He's my friend, you know?"

"So what?"

"I don't want to hear you go on and on about him. It's disgusting."

Volatile sniffed haughtily. "Well, I've had to listen to you rave about Mariko all these years."

"That's different!" I snapped.

"Is it?" She took two steps deliberately toward me. "*I tried to write a note to Mariko today but I ripped it up and flushed it down the toilet because I was scared!*" Volatile mimicked, in a silly little voice I suppose must have sounded like mine.

"Shut up!" I hollered, and threw my book at her, but she bounced out of the way just in time, laughing gleefully.

"*I love Mariko Marino and she agreed to have coffee with me years ago and I am still waiting to take her out because I'm a big, fat baby!*" simpered Volatile, snickering, and picking up the book, hurled it back at me. It hit me on the nose.

"Children, your mother is sleeping!" barked Papa from the other room.

"Shut up, Volatile, and go to your room, or closet, or whatever you prefer to call it," I hissed, rubbing my nose.

"With pleasure," laughed Volatile. "I'm going to bed to have sweet dreams about your friend!" she jeered with a wide grin, and danced out of the room.

"Well, you can go to hell!" I whined sulkily at her.

"I'm already there living with you!" she quipped cheerfully back.

I sighed and buried myself to the chin in bed sheets. We had been fighting like this for the last year; silly, meaningless tiffs about nothing, arguments we forgot about in the morning, all battled with the passion of a zealot. Volatile seemed to enjoy them, beside herself with glee when they occurred. She often picked the fights. They had a strange effect on me, I would feel somber and lonely when Volatile slammed doors and disappeared.

"What are you doing?" I demanded soon after that fateful morning. I had kissed Signora Khan on both cheeks absentmindedly, and settled into a parlor chair in the back room of the Khan Emporium, while Orlando's mother hurried to the kitchen to prepare coffee.

"What are you talking about?" demanded Orlando testily, when his mother had disappeared once more. He lifted a steaming pink glass to his mouth.

"With Volatile."

"What do you care?"

"She's my sister," I explained.

"I'm sure she is," replied Orlando sardonically, lifting his eyes to the roof, as if praying to Allah for deliverance from his stupid young friend.

I was silent, surprised by the pit of rage that had begun to deepen within me.

"I'm not doing anything," said Orlando finally, "I just like… her, that's all."

"*Like her*? What does that mean?"

"She is fascinating."

"Not after you get used to her," I snapped with finality. "She's actually very annoying."

"And your secret is safe with me," assured Orlando unnecessarily. "It wouldn't do for so many people to hear about her."

"What would you know about it?" I grumbled.

To my surprise, instead of lightly insulting me back, as I no doubt deserved, Orlando fixed me with a dark stare and hoisted his chair closer to mine, until we were almost nose-to-nose. He glanced over at the parlor door to ensure our abandonment. "I know what she is," he breathed.

"She's a girl with swallow's wings," I said drily.

"That's what she wants you to think," he said, "but she isn't. She's an *ifrit*."

"A what?"

"Ifrit, a jinn. You know, like a genie."

"A spirit?"

"Not exactly." Orlando reached over to a heavy, leather-bound book, its title embossed in gold, curved Arabic. "*One Thousand and One Nights*," he continued, "you've heard of this, I assume? It says in here that the ifrit is a winged creature of smokeless fire."

"Well, Volatile isn't made of fire."

"It's all figurative, Laurentis," replied Orlando nonchalantly, waving his hand regally, like he was wiping away my ridiculous comment. "Does she disappear sometimes?"

"Well, once in a while, and she migrates every winter with the other swallows."

"That's what she tells you. How do you know she's not returning to the spirit world?"

"Because when she returns, she has all these stories about where she's been and what she's seen…"

"Ifrit are cunning creatures, and much of what they say are deceptions," instructed Orlando. "It says here," he continued, consulting the book, "that the ifrit prefer to live underground, in ancient ruins. What better place than Orvieto?"

My mind immediately flashed back to the afternoon Christopher Esposito touched me. Where I had encountered Volatile again, in the old caverns deep below the city's surface.

"That they have their own society, kings and queens and families and clans that live underground with them…"

I thought of the dark one, the monstrous, black-winged creature of death, crucifixes in his eyes. Who was he to her? Goosebumps broke out over my arms.

"That they are born from the blood of a murder victim…"

"You expect me to believe that Volatile just emerged from someone's blood and guts?" I laughed, aiming to look braver than I felt.

"And to invite an ifrit into your life, a human being must commit that murder."

"So someone in Orvieto killed someone just to get Volatile here?"

"Not just Volatile. A whole *tribe* of spirits."

"I don't buy it."

"That's the legend, believe it or not."

"So Volatile's evil?" I snapped.

"Ifrit can be either good or evil. Our ifrit seems a good sort to me. And one more thing: ifrit can marry humans." And Orlando winked at me rakishly and I grimaced. "Oh, Laurentis," mocked Orlando amiably, "if only you could see your face." And he laughed.

"I don't think Volatile is any of these things you say," I replied. "I've known her a long time."

But my friend was thoroughly enjoying himself. "Think about it," he whispered. "Oh! I almost forgot. Ifrit are jinn, they can grant wishes."

"Is that why you're so interested in her?" I demanded. "So she can grant your wish?"

"Of course not," replied Orlando Khan sincerely. "I'm interested in her because she's pretty."

Pretty? Our Volatile? She was many things, but pretty was not one of them. Mariko Marino – now that was pretty. Volatile was kind of plain but pleasing, like a quality, well-made sofa you sat on every day without a second thought.

"Mark my words," announced Orlando, slicing through my reverie, "I'm going to get to the bottom of this. I have a deep reverence for her, no matter what she is, and I am going to *respectfully* enquire. But you," he slid his eyes over me like I was a slab of bad meat, "you have no curiosity, no wonder. So, so blind. A pity."

"Hey!" I protested, stung.

"Such a passion for the mediocre," he stated, and shook his head sadly.

I rolled my eyes. He could be so melodramatic.

But if Orlando ever found out the truth about Volatile – whether she was a living, breathing slice of Arabic mythology or simply a girl with bird tendencies – I never knew. Not really. Where they went, what they spoke of, Orlando never told me. To this day, I have no doubt that she told him everything. There was something between them, you see, that I could never touch: not with him, not with her, and certainly not with anyone else.

Mamma, a romantic, thought what was happening between them was beautiful. Papa never mentioned it, but his interest in Orlando Khan was approval enough. They grew closer and closer with each passing day, sharing the same interest it seems, for fables and books and secrets meant for just two people. Even the small things worked in their favor. Orlando could never eat meat at the house, for it wasn't halal. Volatile was vegetarian. Yet another bond to tie them closer. I felt a bitterness, like a forgotten orange left in the cupboard until it becomes a hard crystallized ball, grow steadily within me whenever I saw them together. I was losing my best friends.

In that final year of school, I saw more of Orlando Khan than I ever wanted to. I would continue to visit him at the Khan Emporium after school, but things grew stiff between us. Something hung there, a winged shadow called resentment. We were cordial, we were friendly, and on the outside it seemed like nothing had changed. But I had.

One day after school, I was walking alone in the woods muttering to myself a table of dates and events I had to memorize for an upcoming history examination. I stopped suddenly when I heard strange sighs coming from a thicket of oak trees, sharp intakes of breath, and panting. As silently as I could, I stepped forward, not wanting the crispy fall leaves on the forest floor to announce my presence.

And then I saw the most incredible sight: a man and woman, naked from the waist up. She was backed against the enormous trunk of an oak, he had pinned her there. Her skin was so white against his dark, his black hair fell into her face, hers wrapped around his wrist like a silken bandage. His other hand was upon her breast, long, elegant fingers wrapping around and clutching it with an assured possession. His mouth was at her neck, and her face was turned toward me, the eyes closed. An entire flight of swallows looked down upon them from the thicket of trees. They were singing.

Mesmerized, I watched as the hand slipped from her breast and wound around her, shifting her so part of her back was exposed to me. He began to caress the naked column of skin where her wings sprouted and soared above their heads. The wings visibly shivered, causing one or two primary feathers to fall to the ground. I stared at the feathers as they sunk to the earth. They sailed so lazily on the breeze that I felt the whole world must be in slow motion. I stared at the scar on her back, where Darlo Gallo had torn so vengefully.

The woman's mouth opened, omitting sighs so carnal that I became conscious of the stiffening in my pants that I knew to be there all along, but did not want to acknowledge. I was wondering what to do about it when Volatile opened her eyes and stared right at me. I did not stay to catch her expression.

Once I asked her, "Are you in love with Orlando Khan?"

"Does it matter?" she responded lightly.

"I think you are," I sulked.

"What would you know about it?" she quipped.

"I'm just asking you--"

"You don't know anything about love," she answered snippily.

"Well, even if you are, what are you going to do about it? It's not like he's going to marry you. What did you think, that you'd have a big wedding celebration and invite all of Orvieto to see you?" I was being cruel, but I couldn't stop. "Maybe you think you'll take his mother's place at the Emporium after she's dead. Only he will never introduce you, and you'll never see that place."

"I fly into his bedroom all the time!" snapped Volatile. "At midnight, I visit him and I stay all night! I've seen the Emporium hundreds of times!"

"Do you have sex with him?" I demanded.

"That's none of your business!" screeched Volatile.

"It is my business! How could you go into town? It is not safe, Volatile, what if Alfio Gallo, or any other hunter were to see you?"

"Stop!"

"Oh, now you remember Signore Gallo. The one that put the bullets in you to begin with. Remember that you're a secret, Volatile. You are not a person. You have no rights. You're like…you're like a pet we keep around for our amusement. There's not much difference between you and Sweet Vittoria, really. And just like an animal, you could be snuffed out, like that," I snapped my fingers for emphasis, "and no one would bat an eyelid. You will never be anyone's wife. You are never going to matter. All you will ever be amusement for some…some *bastardo*, if he can get over what a freakish anomaly you are—"

I should have seen it coming. She punched me in the face as hard as she could and ran out of the room. I felt guilt descend on me like a cloak. I was utterly wretched. What was wrong with me? Why couldn't I be happy for her? Happy for Orlando? I knew I was jealous, but I didn't know of whom.

It took six weeks for my dislocated nose to heal.

Volatile did not speak to me again until the morning I left for Rome. I had summoned all my courage and knocked on her bedroom door the night before, in order to apologize. When she did not answer the door, I pushed it open. Empty.

At sunrise, I stood in the kitchen in my best suit, hat in one hand and a small suitcase containing my meager belongings in the other. Mamma was crying a little, and gave me a paper bag of *torrone* and crusty chocolate-filled *crostini* from Montanucci's bakery for the journey ahead. Papa was hitching Tomasso to the wagon, in readiness for our short journey to the train station.

I don't remember much of Mamma's goodbye speech, but she echoed herself more than usual, and her head bobbed sadly, like a lonely buoy in bad weather. Her rapidly greying hair smelled like fresh tomatoes and basil as I held her to me. She barely reached my chest.

Orlando was there too, and he shook my hand heartily. "Write often, would you, Laurentis?"

I said that I would, and was astonished when I felt Volatile's arms wrap tightly around my waist, her head jammed up against my neck in earnest. I wasn't sure what to do, so I lamely petted her hair until she let go. When she looked up at me, I was shocked to see that her eyes were full of tears. Once more, she was the little girl on the kitchen table, paralyzed with fear in a pool of her own blood. I was flooded with a feeling that I could not explain, and I felt a sharp pain in my sternum, the pain of a seed that dropped deep into my heart a long time ago, a seed that was growing and breaking into the empty atrium, filling it with its cloying green fronds.

"Stay away from the woods," I said to her, shaking her by the shoulders gently. "Do not let anyone see you. Promise me."

She nodded, and Orlando put an arm around her.

"Take care of her," I commanded him.

"I will," he promised.

She did not say anything else, did not ask me to write, did not say I was forgiven.

But as I climbed into the cart, and Papa lashed Tomasso once with his whip, I turned and waved to the three people who stood on the mossy front steps.

Orlando went inside first.

Mamma took turns using her red handkerchief to wave and simultaneously dab at her eyes and forehead. After a few minutes, she too went inside.

But Volatile stayed, until the cart disappeared around the bend in the wall, until she was a tiny black spec amidst the trees and dust and vines, until she vanished completely.

DIECI

Dear Mamma and Papa,

Finally, I am here and I am settled. I'm sorry my first letter was so brief, but I wanted you to be assured that I did arrive safely and I found my way around without too much difficulty. This evening, I have time to write, and more importantly, I have things to write about. You will note, on the envelope, that I have included a return address, so you can write to me and tell me all about the farm and of course, Orvieto.

I must announce, with some pride, that I have completed my first week at Università di Roma! You were right, Papa, studying literature was the best decision in the end, if only for a year. It's interesting, it's invigorating, and I understand most of the concepts my professors (and the textbooks I borrow from Everard Fane across the hall) tell me. (More on Everard Fane later.) You will be very happy to hear that you were also correct, Papa, in suggesting that economics might be far beyond my comprehension. I met quite a boring fellow during orientation week who went on and on about economic this and economic that, something about a crisis and foreign export, whatever that means, needless to say I had no idea what he was talking about. I am glad I am not taking economics and turning out a bore like him! We are currently learning English classics, and some of the books were written by women. I am unsure whether I have read a book by a woman before. (Everard says I must be crazy and that in his country, there are many famous female writers.) Who knows, I may write a book of my own one day.

I have found a modest little boarding house in an area called Trastevere, have you heard of it? It's west, over the Tiber river, and it reminds me of home. Trastevere is a very interesting area — can you believe people hang their laundry from house to house, underwear and all? That's Rome for you. But it has cobbled streets like home, only not so worn, and I get blisters if I walk them for too long in exploration. The apartments are medieval, not modern as I expected, tall and old but spacious, with long lanes between them (and that confounded laundry whenever you look up!). There's the Piazza Santa Maria, with a clock tower and fountain, just up the street from me. I live in a boarding house for students, in a little room that has one window with a view of the neighbor's window, which has curtains that are always drawn, making me wonder if I live next door to a murderer or circus freak. There are six other students, all boys thank you Mamma, and they live in their own rooms. There's a kitchen with a refrigerator — can you believe it? And one bathroom that gets awfully busy in the mornings. I don't see much of the others except for Everard, who has the same class times as me, because he studies the same course.

Everard Fane is the nephew of the British Ambassador, and when I asked him why on earth he was boarding in such a cheap place if that was the case, he responded that his father was the ambassador's least favorite brother, and it was enough that the ambassador put a good word in to the university dean about him, what with his grades. I've never met a British person before, have you? He has the strangest taste in foods. Some of the smells that come from his bedroom are alarming. But he's familiar with the area, and he showed me the markets on Viale di Trastevere where I buy pizza by the slice and fresh apples.

It's getting late and I must study more. It's growing colder and I find myself glad for Papa's overcoat — Papa, you will stay warm this winter, won't you? I hope you don't still have that awful cough? You'll be pleased to know, Mamma, that I found a bank right near my university, so I can take my checking book there at any time. You were clever to start a bank account! I was so confused the first time I went there.

Affectionately your son,

Gabriel

14 October

Trastevere

Ciao Orlando,

Thanks for the postcard. I'm guessing Mamma gave you the address? I'm sure the postman wondered what kind of freak receives a postcard of Orvieto with the words, "Tell me everything, figlio di puttana!!" written in capital letters on the back. I showed it to Everard and he said he's seen worse.

GABRIEL AND THE SWALLOWS

Rome is amazing. I mean, we all knew Orvieto was old, but Rome just seems ancient. There are reminders of the old world everywhere you look, little scatterings of past civilizations upon every corner, on top of buildings, in the old churches. But it's modern too, with new technology and straight-edged buildings and people wearing the most extraordinary clothes. It's so busy here, girls on Vespa's and guys in leather jackets drinking wine around the fountains, whistling at the girls in their enormous sunglasses and neck scarves. You have to watch it here — if you don't cross the street when the little green man made of light tells you to, you may get run over!

Everard took me on a tour of the most important sites of Rome. He has a scooter (a white Lambretta) and on weekends we go to see the important things. The Pantheon has an open roof, and it rained on me as I sat and sulked that the once-great tribute to the ancient gods was now a Catholic farce. The Trevi fountain was mind-blowing, but all Everard could talk about was the summer the glamorous Americano Ms. Hepburn was here filming Roman Holiday, oh, perhaps twenty years ago. When I saw the enormous marble figure of Oceanus, all his muscles caught permanently mid-ripple, I remembered my childhood fascination with the old gods. What a long time ago, right, my friend? We saw many others things, but I'll reserve all that for later, and when it grows warmer we have planned to visit Vatican City.

You'll never guess who lives in the same district as me. Mariko Marino. Of course you knew we attended the same university, but I underestimated the size of the student population, and I have never seen her on campus. However, when I was picking up some sausages at the butcher's on Viale di Trastevere, there she was, in a rabbit-fur coat and a hat that reminded me of a Russian Cossack. She wasn't alone either. There were two dull-looking girls on either side of her, and one gangly red-haired man. They were chattering so loudly and fiercely about the picture theatre that I turned right around and didn't greet her. Before you start, I already know what you're thinking. And I'm not a coward, I am just biding my time. Did I mention she was wearing the sexiest pairs of heels? Red. At least six inches. Shoes like that make a man think he's died and gone to heaven.

I've been noticing some peculiar reactions from the ladies lately. They seem to stare at me a lot, and not in the way the Orvietani girls did, either out of pity, or belief I was some kind of freak. I would never notice it myself, but I am most often with Everard, who elbows me in the ribs and grins every time it happens. The first time I ever met Everard, he threw his hands in the air and with an expression of genuine astonishment, he cried, "Well, would you look at that? It's James Dean!" I was quite disturbed by this, but Everard assured me I was the splitting image of the movie star, although I am sure he is the only one to think so. He can be quite idiotic at times too, stopping girls on the street to ask if his friend (me) resembles anyone they know, and they always say James Dean or a blonde Warren Beatty, just to mock me I am sure. He probably paid them beforehand.

Don't tell Mamma or Papa, but I bought some new clothes. Everard said mine were laughable and I resembled a country bumpkin, so he made me withdraw some money and took me out shopping. I never thought I'd say it, but I am wearing jeans. I have two pairs, blue and black, and they are a little tight for my taste, but that's what all the Romans are wearing. He said Papa's overcoat looked like something from the charity bin, so I splurged on a leather jacket, and now will have to eat sausages and salad for a month if I want to stick to my budget.

At nights, Everard takes me to all the Trastevere bars, where I've learned to throw back whiskey and make a habit of a daily Peroni (or five). Some bars are all male clientele, and they talk about horse racing and football, which bores me. I prefer the hipper caffes. I've come to learn that Trastevere is where two worlds meet: rich young heirs come to play with painters and sculptors who pay for their beers by the work they sold in the markets that day. There are foreigners galore too. Japanese tattoo artists, French fashion designers, musicians from Nairobi with their sleek charcoal skin and almond-shaped eyes.

When I feel reminiscent, or broke, I climb to the top of Gianicolo Hill and think about Orvieto. I look down on the sun-drenched view of the domes and bell towers, and I remember how fortunate I am to be here, at this moment, to watch this sunset. And when the sky begins to turn black I wander back to my boarding house, I desperately miss home.

With regards from the Eternal City

Your friend

Gabriel Laurentis

30 November

Trastevere

P.S. University is fine, by the way. But we both know I am not in Rome to study, so I will say no more on this topic.

Hi James Dean,

So you didn't make it home for Christmas after all, you pezzo di merda. You strung us along for long enough! Sending a telegram at the last minute saying you had had a minor traffic accident was a terrible lie. And don't even deny it. I know you. I want you to know that I spent two hours on Christmas Eve comforting your mother, feeding her spiced ale to calm her nerves, all the while saying it was tea. She shook and spasmed and by Allah, how she wept! You'd have thought beloved Gabriel had died, not 'scraped his leg' as you so mildly put it. Your Papa sat there attending to your Mamma just to feel busy and not too disappointed. He kept cleaning his spectacles with his shirttail for lack of anything else to do. We put your Mamma to bed early, for she was raving about taking the next train to

Trastevere to check on you. I did everything I could to change her mind. Imagine her broken heart to enter your room, with you perfectly fine, just drunk with your British friend, I imagine. You owe me. And don't bother writing your lies back to me. I knew all along you never wanted to come home for Christmas. I don't blame you. The Ifrit saw right through you the moment the telegram arrived (great timing too, by the way) but I reminded her you're only in Rome for a short time, and you might as well enjoy it.

Christmas day was interesting. I spent the morning with your parents, and although your mother still can't grasp the notion of halal-style meat, she cooked some vegetarian food that I could stomach. I don't know what it is about you meatball-eaters, but your flavors are all the same! We drank some wine and listened to the radio. Your Mamma gave me a scarf she had knitted herself, which I wore on the walk home. It smelled a little like you, which was nauseating, but I'll live. The Ifrit arrived in my room later that afternoon and gave me a gift too, although that is private (use your imagination!!!).

Speaking of the Ifrit, she has been acting strange lately. She told me she usually migrates for the winter and that she misses her flock and not to worry. She seems cold all the time, and I feel sure that she stayed the winter to be with me. She was sullen on Christmas Day and hardly said a word. My goodness, Christmas was a sad affair at your house! I was glad to be out of there!

I don't have to tell you my sincere feelings for the Ifrit, do I? I don't know what to do about her. A part of me wants to introduce her to my mother and sisters, but it's impossible. Don't be mad — I did tell one sister (Imelda) and she was very angry, even frightened. I've bribed her into keeping her silence, but I won't be making that mistake again. It's too dangerous. I wonder how you could have kept her a secret for so long. You must have a strange resilience to beautiful, mystical creatures one room away. It's almost as if you regard her as quite an ordinary thing, when she is in fact, extraordinary. I don't know how you could live in the same house with her all these years and not be fascinated, so in awe of what she is. She is magical. She is not like us.

Gabriel, we need to talk. There's something about her — about us -- I need to tell you, why this isn't exactly what you might think it is. But I can only tell you once I'm sure you'll understand.

Before I forget (and I can't tell you its contents so do not ask) a letter arrived from Rome a few weeks ago. Initially, I thought it was from you, but your parents' stoic response put that from my mind. I wondered if it contained bad news, and when I asked the Ifrit, she frowned and was put in such a mood, I haven't inquired further.

Mother sends regards. Write to your parents, would you, and put them out of their misery, or are you too busy 'sipping Peroni in hip caffes'? You come across as a complete idiot in your letters, by the way. Much less likeable than in real life. I realise you currently consider yourself a writer, but I really don't need to picture the abdominal muscles of a statue in that much detail. Say hi to Mariko.

Affectionately,

O. Khan
29 December
Orvieto

P.S While you're strutting around Rome in your fancy leather jacket, how about sending your Papa's overcoat back? I walked into him rearranging the wine bottles in the barn the other morning and he was wearing a blanket and your mother's dressing robe. Have a heart.

Dear Volatile,

I just wanted to say how sorry I am for what I said to you last year. I still think about it whenever I touch my nose. I don't know why I said such things. I didn't mean them.

Remember that secret I told you a long time ago? Well, I managed to get some medication here in Rome to help me sleep.

That was three months ago. I don't dream anymore.

Wish you were here,

Gabriel

17 January

Rome

UNDICI

The pills were a godsend. They worked from the very first night. It was almost as if, when I closed my eyes to sleep, I watched the vibrant colors of my dreams, the faces they contained, the voices, all the sharp, poignant images of my alternative life fade to grey, and then to nothing at all. I was sad, upon waking that initial night, to realize my beautiful, healthy mother was gone, my strong, rich father too, and my canopy bed with sheets of silk that every night contained Mariko Marino.

Long ago seemed the childhood days where I had trouble distinguishing my dreams from reality, regarding them as some sort of oscillating universe where I could retreat and live the life I was meant to. The only purpose the dreams served as I reached manhood was a reminder of my own unhappiness, of the imperfection of life and the lack of what I desired most. The dreams had themselves become unbearable since moving to

Rome, they became stretched and thin and completely wretched, like scraps of old cloth, as if they couldn't stand to be wrenched away from Orvieto, as if they didn't understand Rome and the people within it, and therefore could neither function nor formulate.

And so I confessed a little to Everard, just the bones of it covered with a skin of falsehood, saying I had bad dreams and couldn't study for trouble sleeping, and away we went on the Lambretta, to a tiny apothecary near Termini station. The pharmacist, a boyish looking Asian man, sold me a bottle of pills – a new American breakthrough medication that they were testing in Europe. The effect was miraculous. For the first time in my life, I felt like a normal person with one life and one set of desires. The confronting duality of everything was dead.

The Roman winter lasted for a much shorter time than usual, the frozen silver plains of the Tiber river melting into an unhygienic grey sludge. The pigeons returned to the squares and perched upon the domes of the churches and castles where they resumed their happy defecation, and the naked skeleton trees shivered and dropped a pound or two of snow on anyone who ventured under them.

It was February and the whole city became immersed in *Carnevale* fever. Banners were erected all over the ancient city; the cobbled lanes and the busy highways were scrubbed until they shone. Shopkeepers displayed their goods in festive motifs, and the wealthy Romans stocked their pantries with rich foods, even though they would predominantly dine out. The poor broke open their piggy banks, extracting a year's supply of lire

GABRIEL AND THE SWALLOWS

saved for this very day, and ran to the market to purchase the prosciutto, salami and spiced cured lard to make the sumptuous and heavy *lasagne di Carnevale* for their extended families. Streamers, flags, heavy scaffolding, temporary stages and arenas were erected in the popular, tourist-soaked piazzas inside the city center. All the girls wore new clothes.

I chanced upon Mariko Marino on the second day of *Carnevale*. Classes had not been cancelled at the *citta universitaria*, as they were scheduled in the early morning, and I was looking forward to the stroll home to Trastevere through the crisp, clinging air. I took a long, winding route to soak in all of *Carnevale*'s particulars on the way – children in costume, old men still drunk from the night before, leaning together as they perched on soap boxes trying to remember each other's names. Street cleaners busily sweeping up confetti and broken bottles. An enormous crowd of people had gathered in the People's Plaza, and even though I was tall, I could barely see over the mass of heads.

"It's equestrian art," came a familiar voice from over my shoulder, "fancy horse riding and such."

I was momentarily stunned to see Mariko's face peering up at me, a bright smile displayed on her mouth through scarlet lipstick. A Roman addition, I thought with approval. "Uh, hi," I spluttered, trying to recover from surprise. She was wearing a French-style beret and a luxurious-looking coat trimmed with some sort of animal hair.

"*Ciao*," she said, and leaned forward, air kissing me on both sides of the face. I tingled. "Are you interested in horses?"

"Not really, no. You?"

"Not really. Are you busy now?"

Was that a trick question? I looked over my shoulder to see if Everard were playing a joke on me and had put Mariko up to this. "I was just on my way home."

"Oh, where do you live?" she asked brightly, and I think I took two steps back just from the shock of it all. She was swinging a blue tasseled purse from her shoulder and was wearing expensive-looking knee-high leather boots. And she was grinning up at me like I wasn't Gabriel Laurentis at all, like I was James Dean or something. It had to be a trap. Or the gods finally answering my prayers.

"Trastevere," I muttered, and my stomach seized up. I knew I was being flat and boring and plain uninteresting, I wanted to be fascinating and sweep her up with my charming personality and conversational skills, and I was failing miserably. But Mariko didn't seem to notice.

"Me too!" she sang, and her eyes were all sparkly. "You know, I thought I saw you there once, in the butcher's shop. I couldn't be sure though. I mean, you dress so differently…" Her eyes swept down my body. I was merely wearing jeans, my leather jacket and a scarf, nothing special. "You just look so good here. In Rome."

"Really?" I said, and I think I grinned a little. Or a lot.

"Well, all my friends noticed you that day. You must have…well, you must have a lot of girlfriends!" And then Mariko Marino, the sole object of my affection for as long as I could remember, blushed heartily and stared at her toes. I could not believe my good fortune. It was like the world suddenly changed color, and Rome had become a shining kingdom, and all I could hear was beautiful, operatic music in the flower-scented air, music as dense as cream. I had to pinch myself to check that I hadn't forgotten to take my medication, that this wasn't a dream. As if on cue, a group of young women congregating nearby caught my attention, giggling and scraping their eyes over my body, one so boldly pursing her lips into a kiss while another glared at Mariko.

"See?" said my companion, and laughed. "I mean, you were always the handsomest boy in Orvieto, everybody knew that, but here, it's like you're a movie star or something!" And as if that wasn't surprise enough, Mariko looped her arm through mine, and glared back at the group of women. "Shall we have coffee?" she chirped, steering me away from them.

I struggled to regain my composure and confidence. "You did promise me coffee a while back."

"I did?" she responded in surprise, her arched eyebrows ascending into the cascade of long, black hair that fell from her beret, "when?"

"Outside the Teatro Mancinelli, a while back," I answered as casually as I could, brushing away the memory carelessly with my hand, as if it no longer concerned me.

"Oh! I don't remember that at all. Well, it doesn't matter, we're having it now."

I didn't know where Mariko was taking me, and I didn't care. I was in a daze of happiness. I recall the overjoyed cries of children bumping into my knees as they raced through throngs of people. They carried balloons and the candy-colored remnants of eaten treats stuck between their little teeth. I remember Mariko's happy chatter and the way the skin at the back of her neck looked as she bent down to purchase *chiacchere*, a *Carnevale* favorite of sugared fried pastry. When she swept her hair off her shoulder, I was close enough to smell her perfume. I don't know anything about flowers, so I had no idea what the scent was, other than I liked it.

I was only half-aware of the Tiber river rushing beneath our feet as we crossed over the Ponte Cavour bridge, and didn't notice the type of establishment or the color of the tablecloth as we sat down at an outdoor café. The imposing, cylindrical walls of the Castel Sant Angelo and its host of mighty angelic sculptures stared down at me with dead eyes from their imposing height, but I did not care a whit. All I was aware of was the sound of Mariko's voice that had wrapped around me like spider's silk, and I knew that I wanted her to taste the bitterness of the espresso from my own mouth.

"What *Carnevale* events are you going to?" asked Mariko, placing her cup in its saucer. She left a ring of red, gleaming lipstick on its rim.

Everard and I did not have a *Carnevale* itinerary that I knew of and I was clueless about the events and their schedule. I had assumed we would walk around the city and watch from afar, presumably with a bottle of wine or two concealed inside a paper bag.

"Tell me you are going to *Donne Notte*." The way those words hung from her lips was spine tingling.

"What's that?" I wondered, although it sounded strangely familiar.

"You know, that *special* ladies night. Oh, Gabriel, please don't tell me you're too old-fashioned for it. All the kids are doing it."

My memory kicked into high gear and I recalled the first time Orlando and I had discussed it. "You're doing *that*?" I spluttered.

"What do you take me for, some kind of puritan? Of course I am doing it," stated Mariko in commanding tones. "When will I ever get an opportunity like this again? I get to pick the man I want, and then I get to do whatever I want with him."

"Is this really a good idea?" The thought of any man, masked or unmasked, touching Mariko was enough to make my blood boil.

"All my friends are doing it," replied Mariko, somewhat peevishly. "Come on, Gabriel, live a little. It's the sixties! Surely this is just another night out for you?"

I must have looked like I was sulking, or like the clueless virgin I was, bordering on twenty years old with nobody that cared enough to give me a first kiss, because abruptly Mariko stood up to leave. "I have to go back to town to pick up some things," she announced. I scrambled to my feet. Was this it? She was leaving already? When would I see her again?

"But you should know," she continued, "that I would very much like you to attend *Donne Notte*. Friday night at midnight, at *Il Serpente Nero* on Via Dandelo. Wear a mask." On tiptoes, she brushed my cheek with her lips.

"I love your hair this long," she said, and touched the tendrils, still blonde, along the nape of my neck. "I'll be the one wearing silver wings," she breathed in my ear.

I don't know how long I stood on the sidewalk after that, watching her walk away.

I started drinking heavily from sundown on Friday night. Wracked with nerves, I knew liquid confidence was the only way I would get through the evening. I was a virgin, and extremely innocent in matters of sex. Everard had given me a nude magazine once and I had flicked through it deliberately nonchalant, because he had been watching carefully for signs of shock or awe, and my pride refused to give it to him. He even tried to explain the sex act to me, as if I were a small town boy who had never had a girlfriend, which I was, but he didn't know that. I did desperately want to spend some alone time with that magazine, but had not been able to figure out how.

Tonight, it was easy enough. We were in his room at the boarding house, drinking Peroni and listening to The Doors on the radio. I flicked through the magazine on his bed as casually as I could, studying the separate parts of the female anatomy in great detail.

"What bothers me," I said for probably the thirtieth time that evening, "is what happens with all the old perverts that turn up."

I had switched to Campari on ice, and swilled down the orange-rind bitterness with gusto. I was already extremely light-headed.

"I already told you, Laurentis, the girls have created a list that is waiting at the door. That and you have to show your university ID. *Donne Notte* has been the Rome University social club tradition going back generations." He sucked deeply on his cigarette before flinging it out of the open window.

"So the girls already have a guy in mind before *Donne Notte*?"

"Not necessarily one. They submit a long list of guys they would sleep with from the university, and if you happen to be on that list, you're allowed inside."

"But what's the point of all the masks, then?"

"So the girls don't know which guys they had their way with in the morning, and hence things aren't awkward afterwards. And it gives the ugly girls a chance too."

"But they'd be able to have a good guess who they were with."

"Yeah."

"But what if you don't want to sleep with an ugly girl?"

"Your preferences mean nothing the moment you walk in that door. You get selected, and you have to take whatever is coming to you. It's a binding, invisible contract from the moment of your entry, everyone knows that. And anyway, who cares? Just pretend she's the object of your desire and have your way with her. You're in no position to turn down sex of any kind. If not, you had better make sure your bird spots you before anyone else does."

"What if you show up and you're not on the list?"

"Then you can't go inside. And you also have the pleasure of knowing that no woman you go to university with is interested in sleeping with you, ever."

"Are you on the list?"

"With these looks and reputation, you better count on it. And I'll wager I've been requested more than once." Everard winked rakishly at me.

"Do you think that Mariko—"

"If your bird said she wanted you to come, then you can be sure she put you on that list. *Merda*, we are out of beer. I'm going to the store, back in a minute." He grabbed his coat and left me there with the magazine. I wasn't complaining.

I was well drunk and thirty minutes late by the time we arrived at Il Serpente Nero. The Black Snake was a seedy underground bar on the edge of Trastevere, known for the plethora of hallucinogenic drinks and drugs in pill form available on request. Anxious about missing Mariko, I had uncharacteristically shouted at Everard when he had returned from the store, which had taken a grand total of four hours. He seemed disturbed and even drunker than I, muttering nonsensical excuses as we ran toward Via Dandelo.

An effeminate, gel-haired boy guarded the door to the pit of iniquity, with a cocktail in one hand and a clipboard in another. He was as beautiful as a young girl and appeared interested in anything but women. Everard stuttered his own name and presented his ID, swaying a little, and after consulting the board, the guard nodded and waved him in. I muttered my name.

"Mask off, please," commanded the boy.

Surprised but obliging, I whipped the cheap black mask, a plastic thing that only covered my eyes and was attached by elastic at the back, off my face. The boy peered at me with great interest. "I see," he said, his eyebrows sky-high. He looked down at his clipboard. "I was wondering what you looked like," he explained without a sliver of shyness, "because your name had been submitted all of eighty-seven times. You can put that back on now."

I replaced the mask and stumbled down the stairs. "Have a safe time! Don't forget to strap on a blanket bopper!" cried the boy cheekily.

"Everard?" I called, as my companion was still wavering at the upstairs entrance.

"I'm sorry, man," slurred Everard.

"What?"

"I'm sorry, man, I'm not going in there."

"What the hell, Everard…"

"I'm sorry for everything," Everard melodramatically sobbed, "but I just can't do it!"

"You *pompinara*! *Porca miseria!*" I swore incredulously, watching my friend stumble away. But I was too focused on my objective to care. I ran down the stairs and flung open the bar door.

Il Serpente Nero was an unexpected sight. It was nothing but an enormous sized concrete room, like a bunker from the war, its walls and rooftop painted a matte black. All round the room, caverns had been set up, covered in cushions and rugs, probably constructed with the plastic crates that usually hold cabbages. They seemed to all contain naked people, yet in the sparse candlelight, all one could see was a golden glimpse of shoulder, or the arc of someone's back upon the cushions. A low, temperate, writhing music was playing that reminded me of the records I would sometimes I hear at the Khan Emporium. Used jars, with labels still attached, were filled with singular condoms. The floor was littered with their wrappers.

My heart sank as I noticed that there seemed to be nobody waiting for me. I had arrived too late. Mariko was in there somewhere, among the rugs that were sure to be worm-holed in the light of day, with a masked man or maybe two. Or maybe three, I thought to myself as I looked around more. They were everywhere, kissing from half-masks, stroking bodies, too many tongues, hair spread all over cushions, legs like open scissors. To my amusement, I noticed a large amount of costume wings attached to the bodies. Ever the rage that year, the wings came in a plethora of sizes and colors, worn by men and women. I sighed. Everard Fane was going to pay for ditching me.

My discomfort and awkwardness grew and I was about to leave when something touched my shoulder. I turned around and, to my great relief, there was Mariko. Her dark hair was coiled into a chignon at the base of her neck, and she wore an elaborate red plaster mask, encrusted with plastic jewels. As promised, two wings, obviously spray-painted a silver hue by an unpracticed hand, were attached to her vampire-black dress that barely covered her backside. I began to speak, but she held a finger up to her scarlet lips to silence me. She took my hand and led me toward the back of the bar, to the only unused cubbyhole that was covered with a rug in fading chartreuse paisley swirls.

Mariko pushed me onto my back. In a flash, her dress was discarded and she threw it nonchalantly into the darkness. She wore no underwear, yet kept her costume wings strapped to her back. Unwillingly, I thought of Volatile, and also of Darlo Gallo, the way she had once worn wings to another *Carnevale* party, a lifetime ago, before it became a trend. Instantly, I hated myself for thinking of them. Mariko was pushing my jacket off my shoulders and my shirt up my neck. She dived onto my chest and was suddenly unfastening my belt, sliding my jeans purposefully down my thighs.

When Mariko straddled my naked body, all I could do was reach up and unfasten the clip from her hair, and it fell like a curtain, washing over me with its familiar scent. I closed my eyes and let Mariko have her way with me. And even though I was drunk and my vision hazy, I felt the immediate connection of our souls through our thrusting bodies. I knew I would never leave this woman, and that I would have no other. I could taste the buttery wax of her crimson lipstick all over my mouth and when it was over, she breathed into my ear, "I love you, Gabriel."

I awoke by a piercing light striking my eyelids. My mask had been torn from its elastic on one side, and hung uselessly from my ear. My head swam and I sat up, not immediately noticing my nakedness. To my relief, I spied my clothes, balled up in a sweating heap close to my feet.

The light was coming from the door to the bar, wide open and abandoned, allowing any old curious pedestrian access to the shocking sight. All round me, couples and threesomes or more were coming to, and in the harsh, grey light all I could see were dirty bodies, all sagging, uneven and flaccid body parts, and mounds and mounds of pubic hair. Mariko was nowhere to be found.

Staggering to my feet, I cut my heel on the remnants of a broken beer bottle, and pain seared through my head, the beginning of my first real hangover. But I couldn't help but smile. I had had sex. If only those strong boys that worked the Orvietani vineyards could see me now. I had done it all with Mariko Marino. And she loved me. Suddenly, going home did not seem so very distasteful after all.

DODICI

I wanted to be casual about what had occurred between Mariko and I, even though it was hardly the way I had imagined our courtship. I wanted to do the traditional Italian thing, taking her out frequently with a group of friends to drink and dance, slowly exposing her to my family until it was time for me to ask the question, and she would move into the farmhouse. I had concerns, in the past, that the Laurentis winery would not be enough to support her, and that perhaps she did not want to stay in Orvieto, but after she had expressed herself to me the night of *Donne Notte*, all those fears turned to dust.

My only problem, now that I had her, was that she was nowhere to be found. I did not have her telephone number or her address, I had not seen her in the marketplaces or squares for three weeks, and neither had she returned to *Il Nero Serpente*. I had even braved the masses of administrative buildings at the

Universita, asking one assistant after the other for Mariko's address. I had finally found one willing to assist me, and as she was sorting through drawer after drawer of badly filed manila cards, the telephone began to shriek, the queue behind me began to lengthen and squabble, and a few superiors flooded her desk and began to barrage her with demands. Fed up with the chaos, and after one regretful look at the discarded student cards on her desk, I had no choice but to dig my hands deep into my pockets and walk away.

I began to feel deep remorse about my stupidity that night. Why did I have to drink so much? Why didn't I at least give her my address? Some sort of guarantee that we would see each other again? I could imagine Mariko, waking that morning in the squalor, embarrassed by the light of day, quickly gathering her things and leaving in an attempt to preserve what was left of her modesty. Had she been waiting for my call? Had she too been roaming the Piazza Santa Maria in search of me? Did she feel completely abandoned? Why hadn't I told her that I loved her back?

All these thoughts would circle around my head like a train of desperation. I wondered if Mariko thought I didn't care, that I had used her, because I hadn't been in touch. I felt like an important detail was eluding me, although I did not know what, nor want to know.

I finally tracked down her address, a mere ten-minute walk away from the boarding house, after an afternoon spent leafing through a telephone book at the Trastevere post office, summoning the courage to call her apartment in Orvieto, and stuttering through a long and awkward conversation with Haha, after explaining time and time again who I was and what I wanted with her daughter. Everard had been no help whatsoever during my search, the selfish bastard. In fact, I had seen him so rarely since the *Donne Notte* that I couldn't help but feel sorry for him; he must have felt so humiliated by his cowardice that night. He was avoiding me to be sure, and was so jealous of my success that night he would hardly let me describe it in detail. Did he feel shown up by what that effeminate boy had said about me? Eighty-seven requests. Now that was something to brag about.

Mariko's apartment appeared from the outside a better-maintained, more colorful version of my own. Large balconies adorned the brick façade, and creeping ivy covered the entire expanse of the second floor. Springtime flowers budded in pots, reminding me of home. I knew that staring up at the lacy lingerie strung over the balconies would make me seem a complete pervert, but I couldn't help it.

She looked different when she threw the door open, there was something unusual about her face, was she glowing? Even though I already knew her, shall we say intimately, my heart thundered in my chest and I was once again a little bullied boy and not a James Dean lookalike with eighty-seven girls willing to sleep with me. I felt small, not good enough for her.

"Gabriel?"

"*Ciao*, Mariko. You look wonderful."

"It's a surprise to see you."

"You're a hard one to track down."

I waited for a barrage of tales as to how she had waited for me and searched for me too, but they never came. Perhaps life really wasn't like the American movies. Her awkwardness was discouraging at first, but I was reminded of the shyness she must feel at seeing me again, remembering that night, so I made it easy for her. She was biting her lower lip and looking down at her shoes. "Do you feel like coffee?" I asked.

"Sure," she responded, as if it were a spoonful of cod liver oil I was pressing upon her and not an espresso. But as if she instantly resolved herself to the fact that cod liver oil was good for her health, she recovered and said brightly, "But not here. Our machine is busted. There's a café down the street."

She disappeared for a minute and appeared again with her purse. We walked down the lane in silence. Mariko did not grasp my arm as she did that day in the city, nor did she prattle on. I felt a heaviness between us that I could not define, but I knew time would reverse our unorthodox beginnings, and we would be as one again. I was too thankful for her presence to wish to make love again, all I wanted was to be beside her, to hold her hand, to claim some sense of ownership.

The café was a little hole in the wall, and we had to stand at the bar to drink our espressos. No other clientele were present, and as soon as the coffee was poured, the dour old woman disappeared behind the faded blue walls, leaving us alone. Operatic ballads were playing on the radio, interrupted by sudden bursts of grey static.

"How have you been?" Mariko asked sweetly.

"I've been well. Worried about you, though."

"Oh, I get along fine by myself. You are a darling though for caring."

"What have you been doing?"

"Oh, class. Going to the theatre with friends. Same as always. And you?"

"Everything you said. Plus looking for you."

"You found me."

"Yes."

"You wouldn't believe the trouble I went to! I even called your Haha," I continued.

"Did you?" responded Mariko, seeming as interested in the matter as she would a dung beetle.

It occurred to me that Mariko was too much of a lady to broach the subject of anonymous sex, so I wracked my brain for ideas of how to tactfully begin the conversation. But I had once again underestimated her.

"I'm sorry for leaving you there that night," she suddenly stated, reaching across the bar and grasping my hand. All of the cells in my body recognized her touch, and I began tingling all over.

"It's okay," I said, and raised her hand to my mouth, grateful for the contact, grateful for any of herself she wanted to give me. I wanted to tell her then, in that moment, that I loved her. The words formed in my head but they refused to escape from my lips. Instead they lodged themselves in the back of my throat, like a pebble.

"Gabriel," she said, my name one warm breath exhaled her parted red lips. I kissed her hand and her palm and she said, "Gabriel," once more, with urgency. I paid her no mind and continued to kiss her. "Gabriel!" she snapped, and her voice became ugly, her hand was wrenched away, and she slapped my face.

Instantly, the offending hand covered her mouth, and her expression was pure shock. "I'm sorry, Gabriel! *Merda*! I'm sorry."

I rubbed my cheek. I wasn't hurt. Not physically, anyway. "I'm sorry, I shouldn't have done that," I muttered.

"I didn't mean to hit you. *Merda*!"

"I shouldn't have kissed you, I wasn't a gentleman. Forgive me."

"I just…I don't want to be kissed like that."

"Why? Too public a place?"

"Yes. No. I don't know."

Something was wrong, dreadfully wrong. She was getting flustered, and I noticed a smear of lipstick on her front tooth. Her hair began to unravel out of its ponytail and fall around her face, which she brushed away violently. "What is the problem, Mariko?" I asked, willing my voice to be as gentle as possible.

"I don't want to be kissed…by you. I don't want, I can't believe I have to say it, I don't want this with you, Gabriel."

I must have just stared at her like a large, floundering, stupid fish, its slack jaw hanging open. She reached for my hand. "Gabriel, I am so sorry. *Merda*, I am so, so sorry."

"Why did you invite me in the first place?" I demanded.

"I thought I wanted it – I mean, *you*…"

"And you just changed your mind? Like that?"

"No. I mean, yes. You wouldn't understand."

"Was it something I did?"

"No, nothing! You didn't do anything wrong."

"Then why?" I was beginning to grow angry, deeply angry. I felt like a little boy with a Humphrey Bogart hat shaking in his hands, standing in the aisle of the Teatro Mancinelli despondently, the lire saved for two cups of coffee burning holes in the pockets of my hand-me-down pants. "I want to know what is going on here," I commanded, as adamantly as I could. I suddenly hated that little boy in the theatre. And I was beginning to hate the girl he was staring at, the one whose breath smelled like Bellini.

"This is a little creepy, Gabriel. I mean, you search all over for me, you even call my mother back in Orvieto?"

"*Creepy?*"

"She rang and told me you had called her! A little much, don't you think?"

"I was trying to do the right thing! I thought you would want that!"

"If I had wanted to see you, I would have found *you*. I know where you live."

"I didn't want you to think I didn't care about you. That I used you. But I guess you beat me to it. I guess you used me."

"I did not use you, Gabriel." She was staring me down with those green eyes. "You're being a little melodramatic, don't you think? I admit I made a mistake. I should never have invited you to *Donne Notte*. Happy now?"

How could she be so heartless? How could I, for all of these years, have been in love with such a careless creature? And it was all my own doing, harboring feelings for a harpy of Darlo Gallo, who was revealing herself to be as spoiled and selfish as my enemy. And why, after all these years, was *that name* coming up again? If Mariko had been right about one thing, it was this: Darlo Gallo was everywhere.

Regardless of my inner ranting, shaming Mariko as an invisible punishment for rejecting me, there was a deep pain in my chest. I wanted to storm away, throw my coffee cup at the wall, something manly, something aggressive. I wanted to keep my dignity somehow and not melt in front of her. But I couldn't.

"No, I'm not. I'm not happy. You told me you loved me, Mariko."

Her face screwed up like a dried prune, like she had swallowed a lemon whole. "No, I didn't."

"You did."

"When?"

Had she taken something that night? Was it possible she did not remember? "At *Donne Notte*. After we...after we, you know, had sex."

But Mariko scoffed. "We have never had sex," she stated drily.

"Sounds like you were too drunk to remember," I counteracted lamely.

"Sure I was drunk, but what I do remember about *Donne Notte* is that I wasn't there. I invited you, but I never turned up. So whoever you had sex with, *that's* the person you should be harassing now, and not me."

She straightened up, threw some notes on the bar, and walked out.

And that was the last time I ever had dealings with Mariko Marino.

GABRIEL AND THE SWALLOWS

I was ashamed of being rejected, and instead of pouring my heart out to Everard, I took to ignoring him, as I felt slighted by my friend in my hour of need. But Everard Fane was no fool. He must have understood from the times I passed him in the hallway, my eyes dry and bloodshot, the only courtesy extended to him a terse nod of the head. Little gifts would appear here and there – a cup of espresso gasping steam and waiting for me in the empty kitchen upon my arrival, a case of Peroni outside my bedroom door, even a couple of tickets to a movie on a Saturday afternoon. I didn't understand what was taking Everard away from me, and over some weeks, I ceased caring. We even began sitting separately during lectures – Everard always being late and preferring to sit in the back, rather than disturb rows of students to sit by me in the front of the hall.

I became solitary again, a loner, my original state. I found myself simply skimming the novels and journal articles assigned to me, the bare bones of each hardly conjoining in my mind. I began to indulge in long Monday nights languishing in the dirty tub in our shared bathroom. I'd haul buckets of water upstairs to fill it myself, hardly bothering to clean it, and sit in the tepid water, a dead spider floating beside me, and the hair of whoever used it last. I would lean back and stretch my long legs out until they were crammed up against the wall, and reach for the bottle of wine, so cheap it had no label.

It was only after the water turned stone cold that I began to long for Orlando Khan. But then I would remember what I saw in the woods that day, and promptly dismiss him from my mind.

I discovered that in Rome, it was easy to find friendship for the night. I half-heartedly believed in my own newfound attractiveness, and after returning to Il Serpente Nero soon after the rejection, I began conversing with a woman at the bar. She had enormous, dark-lashed eyes that reminded me of a mare's, and after a few cocktails, her hands began wandering all over my chest.

We went back to my room after midnight, and when I woke in the morning, I discovered the heavy, dark lashes were nothing but plastic beginning to peel from her lids, and that her skin was riddled with pock marks, deep lines in the corners of her eyes that simply were not there last night. I was revolted, and ran to the bathroom. After I had vomited, she was waiting for me, her false eyelashes intact, her hair miraculously smoothed, eager and expectant. I can't describe my disappointment. Not because she wasn't beautiful. It was me. It was what I had become.

I made her coffee and she told me a little about her life – she was a telephone operator and the wife of a philanderer who had run away to Seville with a shop girl. She lived with her mother and her two little daughters. She was trying to get a divorce so she could marry her electrician lover, but she could not locate her husband. Times were hard. I walked her to the door and agreed to call her, but we both knew I never would.

That experience did not stop me. In the cheap bars of Trastevere, it became impossible for me not to get wildly drunk, and bring home a woman. I wasn't terribly picky and my judgment was severely clouded. Cabaret performers with voices like a man's they smoked so much, the wives of Polish immigrants, starving single mothers from Germany who had run away from cruel husbands. A wealthy and curvaceous woman from the Ivory Coast with a rich, cloying accent who I went with more than once. The experience was more or less the same: I would make them an espresso and walk them out the door, or if I was at their place, they would press me to make love again, and try to tempt me to stay by feverishly cooking breakfast. And then I would leave with nothing to remember them by, save for a hazy recollection of body parts and numb sensations, which, after time, all melded into one.

In those last months, I had one rule: I never went with a woman my age, and never an Italian. Those kinds of girls were all Mariko to me. So innocent, they didn't know their power. So fresh and confident, they had the cruel and careless ability to break a man's heart. So inexperienced at life they did not need to be gentle. The women I chose were more like me: disfigured by life, bent from disappointment, willing to tread on glass in exchange for kindly treatment; they were imperfect and grateful for any attention they received.

I recall one incident with a French woman. Or was she Czech? I can barely recall. She was so thin I could run my fingers up and down her ribs like a xylophone. She was sitting on me, and her back was arched. I was drunk and hazy from her marijuana cigarette, and imagined I saw large, majestic wings sprouting from her back. I shouted and pushed the woman off me, and sat on the edge of the bed cradling my head in my hands as the women fussed and fussed. And for the first time in a long time, my mind cried out, *Volatile*!

I felt instantly ashamed. I felt Volatile's eyes on me, watching as the bag of bones attempted to curl herself around my body, the sharp angles of her frame far more geometric than seductive. I felt Volatile's eyes peering past the external and through all of the pestilence and the shame and confusion, wading through all the *merda* in my soul.

And then I proceeded to pass out.

TREDICI

It was with a sense of urgency that I whirled through my final examinations, although the outcome did not matter to me. The same wild compulsion was present as I haphazardly packed my suitcase, relieved to abandon my stained bed sheets and the carnal secrets they had witnessed, into the hands of the landlady. I had scribbled a note to my parents, instructing them to expect me back at some point that week. I knew Everard was asleep in his bedroom, but I didn't bother awakening him to say farewell.

The woman from the Ivory Coast picked me up in her Fiat and drove me to Termini station, but not before she had clasped my head between her ample bosoms and covered me with kisses. I promised her I'd write, but we both knew I never would.

I felt clean again as I stepped off the train and onto the platform of Orvieto Scalo, two hours later. I breathed in a lungful of country air, the scent of ripe green grapes and sumptuous red wine barely concealed in the breeze. My suitcase was light and I decided to walk home in the sunset, carrying my leather jacket strung across my shoulder. I had no money left from my parents' gift, and most had gone into the hands of bartenders throughout the city in the last few months. My very last fistful of lire was spent purchasing a tomato sandwich and a bottle of *chinotto* from the seller on the train.

Nothing had changed in the year I had been gone. The olive groves were the same, the woods were green and beckoning, the vineyards were orderly as farmhands worked away, harvesting the grapes. Some recognized me and waved. I returned their greeting. And as always, Orvieto looked down upon us, the sun bathing its ancient walls in gold, the city seemed on fire. I vowed never to return to Rome, that city of iniquity, of torment. Here I would live a clean life, an honest life. I would strive to be kind and hardworking, like my father.

The path turned into sparse, lonely woods. Long-forgotten decayed fences were covered with vines, stones that once belonged to streams cloaked in slick lichen. The birds of the air cried their eerie song, commanding each other to return to their nests, the dangerous night approaches. There was the sound of rushing wind, or powerful wings beating through the warm air, and suddenly, a woman landed in front of me.

"You're late!" snapped Volatile.

"Would you get out of sight?" I hissed at her, instantly annoyed. "Anyone could see you!"

"Oh, stop being such a whining baby. I come past here every afternoon. Even freaks need exercise, you know."

"I've been away for an entire year, and the first thing you call me is a whining baby. Nice," I sulked.

Volatile squinted up at me. She was not petite, like a lot of the girls I had gone to class with, but tall and athletic. Still she had to crane her neck to look me in the face. "You know, I expected Rome to mature you a little. Clearly, I was wrong. Things haven't been right around here, since you've been gone. In fact –"

"What do you mean, *mature* me? You have no idea what I've been through!"

"Relax. Goodness, you're uptight. Has the eternal city made you so uppity you can't even take a little teasing? Or maybe your suitcase is too heavy for you? Want me to carry it back to the house?" She grinned up at me.

"I can manage," I replied testily.

"I expected you days ago," she said.

"Oh, because you foresaw the exact moment I would arrive? With your magical *ifrit* powers?" I was irritated, quoting what Orlando had told me in confidence all that time ago. Volatile immediately withdrew with a sharp intake of breath. "Ha!" I said, rather cruelly, but I did not know why I was delighting in being this way to Volatile.

"Shut up, Gabriel, you have no idea what you're talking about," she commanded, a little self-importantly, I thought.

"Oh, I'm sorry, I didn't mean to offend your delicacy," I offered sarcastically. "You're a great, big, mysterious anomaly. I had quite forgotten."

"Moron!" snapped Volatile, spreading her wings and flying away.

Needless to say, I felt ridiculous after that. Who did she think she was, flying around like she owned the place? Didn't she realize hunters might be on the loose? How dare she speak to me like that? Implying I was a child, that I couldn't carry my own suitcase? All I wanted was a kind welcome, was that too much to ask? I had too many things on my mind to deal with her.

My black mood lasted all night, through my Mamma's tearful embrace, and my Papa clasping me in a handshake and pumping it up and down until my arm ached. I was so incensed I almost didn't notice the way my mother coughed readily throughout dinner, crunchy, hard coughs that seemed to replace her repetitions.

"Volatile's not here," said Papa, over a steaming plate of home-made fettuccine seasoned with a thick pesto of basil, parsley, pine nuts and oil from our defunct olive grove. I had heaped fresh *parmigiano* on my plate and was on my fourth glass of wine.

"She isn't around much these days," confirmed Mamma.

"She's a good girl," reminded Papa defensively.

"But she is not like us," stated Mamma amidst coughs.

"She is a bird with human tendencies with she is with them, and a human with bird tendencies when she is with us," I said in a singsong voice, without thinking. I was probably still hungover from the night before.

"What was that, Gabriel?" said Papa.

"Nothing," I said.

"I don't know where she goes at night," continued Mamma. "She's very helpful to me here in the house. She made the pesto."

Suddenly the dish tasted strange to me, like earthworms.

"She's probably with Orlando," I offered, if not a little begrudgingly.

"Oh, no," said Mamma. "Oh, no, no, no." She began coughing again, and Papa frowned, passing her his napkin.

"I think all that business finished a while ago," said Papa softly.

"We're so worried about her future," Mamma admitted, wiping her eyes. "It was fine when she was a child and we could care for her. But it's different now. She's grown up, and you have to wonder…"

"I just don't think there's a place for her in this world," whispered Papa sadly, taking off his glasses and wiping them with his shirt.

"If only there were others of her kind she could go to," finished Mamma.

"Because what does she have here? A shutdown farm with two old people like us. She can't go out in public, can't have friends. What's a young girl to do—"

"Shutdown?" I repeated incredulously.

Papa sighed deeply. "I'm afraid it's true. The DOC has spoken. No more *Dolce Fantasia*."

"What happened? Why didn't you tell me?"

"Well, we didn't want to disturb you, we knew you were studying so hard—"

"Papa, when I think of all that money you saved for me, and it's all gone now! We could have saved the farm, we could have—" Suddenly, I wished I could hurl my incriminating leather jacket out the window. It hung tauntingly on the back of my chair, the bold testament of a selfish son.

"It's all right, Gabriel. Perhaps this farm was never meant to succeed. But you are home now. That is a blessing for us. The Laurentis family was never meant to be great or powerful. We gave our son a year of higher education and not many people like us can say that, small people surviving in this world. I'm glad you're back." Papa squeezed my hand, and I saw moisture glisten in the corner of his eyes.

That night, I tossed and turned in bed. It was hot in my bedroom, and I kept my window open, letting the strange sounds of the woods into the chamber. Was it just me, or did everything seem different? Why were the birds still chattering away like it was midday? Why could I hear distinct scurrying, the whir of insects with their blown-glass wings whizzing through the air, and roaches restlessly hurrying through the fields? Why weren't these creatures asleep, as nature demanded? Perhaps I had grown used to the sound of taxi horns and the catcalls of prostitutes.

The fact that our vineyard was shut down, that my parents were rendered destitute and defeated by the DOC, the Italian wine regulation board, kept running races around my head. Not really understanding why I did so, I leaned out of the window. "Volatile!"

I whispered. "Volatile!" I repeated, louder and more urgently. I didn't know how I knew she was there. But I just knew.

"What?" she snapped, and suddenly, she was in my room. Did she come through the window? She was so fast, like an eagle. Like a genie. Appearing when summoned.

"What were you doing, sleeping on the roof?"

"Actually, I was far away, but unlike you, I have excellent hearing. Now what do you want? I'm rather busy, you know."

"What's this about the farm being shut down?"

"Well, I wanted to tell you earlier, but you were in such a foul mood."

"I'm sorry," I said begrudgingly. "Now sit down, would you please?"

"I can't," said Volatile, her beautiful grey wings snapping closed and settling against her back until smooth, they were barely visible. I was instantly reminded that she possessed the forked swallow's tail too, and wondered what that looked like these days. With a shudder, I stopped that thought in its tracks. What was wrong with me? Had Rome turned me into a complete and utter pervert? "I have things to do."

"But I have questions," I said, shaking my head clear.

"You can ask them along the way."

"Along what way?"

"Now get your shoes on, we're going investigating."

"Aren't I slowing you down?" I complained as we hastened through the forest. The moon was high and full, and its reflection through the trees made tribal tattoos all over Volatile's bare arms. The dried leaves and twigs crunched beneath my feet, and I gazed at Volatile in wonder. She was bounding lazily along, her feet barely touching the ground. Her wings, half expanded, would lift her off the forest floor in a slow waltz, and there she would land again, on the tips of her toes. She was like a ballet dancer in the starlight, with her ivory dress pouring around her and her hair like streamers…

"What are you staring at?" she demanded, a little smile playing on her lips.

"Nothing," I muttered, and quickly averted my gaze.

"You shouldn't do that, you know," she commented drily.

"Do what exactly?"

"Extricate yourself like that. Like you don't matter. Just say what you think. It's always as if you don't think you are good enough to have an opinion, to make a statement."

"I have no idea what you are talking about," I said moodily.

"Well then, perhaps you were staring because you've never really seen a girl before."

"I've seen plenty of girls, believe me," I huffed.

"So I've heard around town," mumbled Volatile, rolling her eyes.

"News travels fast."

"A little too rapidly for my taste," conceded Volatile, somewhat sarcastically. "I thought Mariko Marino was the only one for you."

I was hastily growing irritable. She was always baiting me, always wanting to pick a fight. Why had I agreed to come with her? "She is. Was. She was."

"So much for true love," laughed Volatile.

"What would you know about it?"

"You tell me."

"You know nothing, I'll wager."

But my companion would not take the bait. She shrugged off my veiled insult like it was an ugly shawl and she was no longer cold, and continued bounding along like a midnight creature. We continued like this in silence. I did not have to ask where we were going. I knew these woods well.

"It was Alfio Gallo," stated Volatile darkly. "We all know it was. That spiteful fool."

"What do you mean?"

"I heard your parents talking one night in the spring, after *Carnevale*. I heard your Mamma crying that night, and your Papa's hands would not stop shaking." Volatile narrowed her eyes and instinctively budged closer to me as we moved along the trail. She smelled like something familiar, but I couldn't quite place it. "Your father went to the farmer's market months ago for grain, as usual. He hurt his ankle on one of his walks and he was limping a little, but I knew he was in much more pain than he let on. Alfio Gallo had come over during the wintertime, don't worry, I went straight out the window, I could smell him a mile away. All booze and tobacco."

Volatile screwed up her nose in distaste, and I suddenly recalled I had forgotten to brush my teeth before bed.

"He began pressuring your father to sell the farm. He seemed really desperate; he kept raising the price, little by little. But your father wouldn't budge. Gallo started yelling and your mamma came out of her room, she's had that terrible cough since winter you know, and Gallo started acting strange, sidling up to her and stroking her hair, and making her feel very uncomfortable. Your mamma kept coughing and saying things over and over, and Gallo was laughing at her, and your Papa got so angry, well, he punched him!"

"Bravo!" I shouted.

"Shhh!" said Volatile. "That was a big mistake. Because that day, at the farmer's market, Gallo was there too. According to your papa, Gallo followed him around the market, imitating the limp he had, just hobbling around after him. But your father didn't tell your mamma that Gallo had also imitated her too, repeating silly statements at the top of his voice, lurching around after your father, belittling him in front of all those people! Everyone laughed at him and your father couldn't hold his head up high. I only know that part because I heard your papa talking to himself in the barn."

Anger began to rise in me, a black hatred that had lain dormant for far too many years now.

"Now be silent," she commanded. "We're here."

Indeed we were. The imposing fir trees that surrounded the Gallo property had grown so tall, they seemed to extend all the way to the moon. The stone gates circled the estate, their guardian gargoyles glaring down at us. The electric lanterns were glowing all around us.

Volatile flitted up and peered over the wall. "There's no one in the garden," she called down softly. "The coast is clear."

"How am I supposed to get inside?" I whispered back. I almost shouted aloud when Volatile materialized beside me once more.

"You are going to squeeze under the gate," she directed.

With distaste, I looked over to the wrought iron gate, with barely enough room underneath for a grown man to slip through. The ground beneath was lined with powdery gravel. I glared at Volatile.

"Or you can stay out here," she said with a shrug.

I narrowed my eyes and shrugged off my leather jacket, which I now thoroughly regretted wearing. I placed my palms on the dirt and lowered myself under the iron and wood gate. It was a tight squeeze.

"Leave the jacket," Volatile hissed, as I reached my arm through the collect it.

Obediently, I abandoned it and got to my feet, the gravel making telltale squeaking noises under my shoes. I followed her into the bushes. The only sound to be heard was the soothing rush of water from the ostentatious fountain. Volatile remained in the shadows, one arm outstretched, holding me back as her eyes focused on every window in the house. Most had the curtains drawn and lay in darkness.

She crept forward, bit by bit. As we reached the back courtyard, Volatile screwed up her nose in distaste. "What is that monstrosity?" she whispered, indicating to where the second

Gallo fountain lay, its stone sea-lovers spouting dark water. "These people have no taste." I could not agree more.

A little square of light suspended in the air caught her attention. "Bingo," she whispered, pointing to the tiny glass-topped chamber in the center of the huge, church-like dome that topped the mansion. "Stay here," she commanded.

"But what am I supposed to do?"

"Keep watch." And her wings split open, and silently, they bore her into the sky. I watched in fascination. How like a real bird she appeared, especially from this distance. I sucked in my breath as she landed on the top of the dome, her wings completely outstretched, like a beautiful avenging angel. Had she always been this beautiful? She had not changed, not noticeably. How had I not realized before? And why was it so difficult for me to admit how beautiful she really was?

Gracefully, she jumped down to a ledge six feet beneath her. I held my breath and moved closer, careful to stay out of the light. She moved her head to the side, as close to the window as she could get. Her wings splayed out against the dome. She remained like this, completely frozen, for a long moment. I could not keep my eyes off her.

And suddenly, she inexplicably mewled a deliberate cry at the top of her lungs, a cry that sounded like a hunting falcon, directed right to the window. With that, she soared from the dome, coming straight at me at an astronomical speed. "Run, you idiot!" she hissed when she was within earshot. I ducked and covered my face instinctively, but Volatile flew right over me and disappeared over the estate walls.

Lights were beginning to turn on inside the house. Filled with panic, I bolted past the courtyard and the south wing of the house, my heart hammering in my ears. I could hear shouts. Sprinting up the driveway, I prayed that the main lights would delay being turned on, and I skidded on the gravel, threw myself under the gate bruising my chin along the way, snatched up the leather jacket and headed for the woods as fast as my feet could carry me.

"This way," cried Volatile, dropping to the ground beside me. "We've got a five-minute head start before he comes stomping through here with those boots and that gun!"

"Why did you do that?" I yelled.

"Oh, I love doing that to him," she screamed back. "Making him think the falcon he's always hunted is right within his reach is the second-best feeling in the world! I've been doing it for years!"

"Do you know how dangerous that is?" I thundered. "Don't wait for me, just fly!"

"And give him a perfect view and shot of me? No, thank you, I'll take my chances on the ground!" And she laughed manically.

"So this is what you do in your spare time," I roared, pumping my legs and arms at a frenetic rate to keep pace with her. "If this is the second-best, what's the best feeling in the world?"

"Sex!" she screeched gleefully.

Back at the farm, Volatile collapsed in the vineyards, in a flying roll. She was laughing and winded. She lay on her back, her wings spread out underneath her. "That was fun," she said when I caught up to her, and stood doubled over, barely catching my breath.

"You have a strange definition of fun. You gave me a heart attack!"

"Do you want to hear what I've learned or not?"

"Go right ahead."

The wildness in her eyes thrilled me more than I cared to admit. "Gallo and his wife were discussing it up there, in that room. I've been going to the estate every night just to hear what happened. Tonight was the jackpot! I knew you'd be my lucky charm."

"Come on, spit it out!" I demanded impatiently.

"Gallo paid some men to pour banned insecticides all over the vineyard, and then called the DOC with a false report. The officials came from Rome and inspected the land, and promptly shut it down."

"That bastard," I growled.

"Indeed," confirmed Volatile. "But we will not be beaten."

"What do you mean?"

"I have a plan. We are going to get the farm back."

And I believed the little renegade lying in the grass with all my heart. "And if you think we're going to stop there, you're a fool," declared Volatile.

"What do you mean?"

"We are going to *destroy* the Gallos."

QUATTORDICI

Volatile did not return that week, or the next. The farm was quiet and desolate, at least during the day.

At night, I would reach over and take the brown jar from the nightstand, swallowing down a dreamless pill with a swig of tap water. And then it would begin: birds that would not nest disturbing the leaves of trees, swooping through the air and crying their calls which were meaningless to me. I could hear mice and frogs in a rhythmic cacophony, as if they were speaking to one another. There were sounds of creatures scuttling in and out of leaf piles, slithering from under stones, emerging noisily and abruptly from the secret places of the earth. It was almost as if nature had forgotten its own nature.

In fact, as I was reading one evening, a large spider casually strolled through the window, down the wall, onto my bed and up my leg. It stopped at my thigh, and regarded me with its numerous eyes, rather deliberately, I thought. Then, as if he had sized me up, turned his back and disappeared the way he came.

Mamma and Papa had not noticed the frenetic energy surrounding our vineyard. Papa would go to the barn and count the remaining bottles of *Dolce Fantasia* each morning; as if they were free to walk out on their own once he closed his eyes. Mamma would rustle through our pantry, searching for ingredients to magically appear. After a few hours, they would both end up sitting at opposite ends of the kitchen table – Papa reading a book and Mamma mending an item of clothing I had outgrown years ago. I took long walks around our vineyard, red grapes bursting with flavor begging to be harvested, to be skinned and frozen. It would have been a productive harvest.

"Why don't you go into town to visit Orlando?" Mamma would ask over luncheon, a bread roll with a slab of cheese and raw onion. She would look me in the eye with fierce concentration, daring her body to behave, but would soon break down in a barrage of coughs.

"Not today," I'd typically reply. I had little desire to see my old friend, who had stopped writing in Rome after a few letters gone without reply. In every epistle, he asked after Mariko, and I could no longer bear to open his letters and read about his great love for Volatile while I drank myself into a stupor. The wound Mariko had left still ached terribly, and I hated reminders of it.

One morning, the sound of car doors slamming jarred the melodious melancholy the Laurentis family had cloaked themselves in since my return. It was as if we were all balancing on a tightrope, too scared to breathe loudly or speak out of turn, in case it should encourage our fall into oblivion. I knew what was on my parents' minds – when and how they should accept Gallo's offer.

Mamma appeared at her bedroom door, wiry grey hair standing on end, a dressing gown thrown haphazardly over her shoulders. Papa had already placed his reading glasses inside his pocket, and was making his way toward the door. I hung back a little, waiting to be accosted by the looming, mountainous presence of Alfio Gallo.

Instead of a shiny black Chrysler, a green van had parked on the dirt outside our front porch. Three men, all in business suits, had emerged, and I immediately knew they were city people on account of their sunglasses. It was strange, you know. That was the very last clear memory of their visit; the suggestiveness of sunglasses.

I believe they explained they were somehow affiliated with the DOC, the wine regulation board the *Dolce Fantasia* and most of the Gallo estate's labels were under. They said something about checking the PH levels, whatever that meant, and specified that they did not wish to be accompanied and could find their way around. The tallest one refused the offer of coffee and *crostini* with a simple wave of his hand. I asked Mamma if she had seen these people before but she shook her dazed head, and went inside to lie down. Papa appeared unconcerned, and took his place once more at the kitchen table, picking up his newspaper. I watched the men from my bedroom window.

I can't recall exactly what it is they did. They had no briefcases, no tools in which to measure the soil, and did not seem inclined to do so. They stood at the far end of the vineyard, frozen like statues, for an immeasurable amount of time.

They returned to the house, rapped on the door, and handed Papa an official-looking envelope. A few arbitrary statements were made, but I couldn't quite make them out, it was as if they were speaking a language that was half my own, and half someone else's. We must have understood it, at the time, because we smiled at the men and I walked them to their van. Papa reached out to shake the hand of the tallest, but the man elegantly withdrew his hand before contact could be made. After the men had left, we all retreated to our beds and slept a drugged, hazy sleep well into the next morning.

Sweet Vittoria had curled herself atop the table, half-covering the letter the men had left. Yawning deeply after emerging from my room, I extracted it, sending her yowling out the kitchen window. The letter was from the DOC, officially declaring the Laurentis vineyard reopen for business.

It was then that the very last thing I recalled of yesterday came to mind. I don't know what I was saying in farewell, but as I held the car door open for the tallest man out of a long-ingrained sense of courtesy, he lowered his sunglasses and looked at me.

His eyes were simply extraordinary, crucifixes where pupils should have been.

It was precisely one month later that Orvieto was inflamed with news of a colossal, sensational nature, news so inconceivable that many ventured to the scene just to confirm its truth. The Laurentis family was no exception. After receiving the gossip from a neighboring farmhand, my father hitched the wagon to old Tomasso's back, who grumpily conceded to the interruption of his long retirement, earned by his stiff joints and completely blind left eye. But Tomasso's comfort be damned, this we had to see with our own eyes.

And praise Zeus, it was true.

All around the road where we stopped the cart, over the hills and valleys, the green vineyards of the Gallo estate lay brown and decayed, once-luscious trees now skeletons of sticks, the vines crisp and dry, like loose hair lying scattered on the ground. Not one blade of grass had escaped; all was shriveled brown and roasted by the sun. The Gallo estate's vineyards were a wasteland.

Perhaps the most remarkable occurrence was that not a single leaf of the neighboring vineyards had been touched, they remained lush and ready for the continuing harvest. Something mysterious was afoot, whispered the Orvietani, but as police, horticultural experts, poison control and members of the DOC flooded the estate, they confirmed the original statement: the ruination of the Gallo vineyards was an act of God. No human interference was detected nor suspected. The decay had been achieved completely by nature.

My Papa had whooped in joy when he saw the ruin, but clapped his hand over his mouth and said, quite seriously, "Remember to always respect your elders, Gabriel."

That night, after habitually swallowing my medicine, was the happiest I had felt in a long time. I resolved that upon waking the next morning, I would sit with my father and plan the next year of the Laurentis dessert wine, to listen to his thoughts, which I had always tuned out before. But that night, I reflected upon the miracle that had happened, what Volatile had done. And suddenly I wanted her near, I wanted her to parade cockily up and down the vineyard, I wanted her to pick a fight with me. And this time, I'd fight back. I wouldn't, what had she said? Extricate myself. Dismiss myself.

I suddenly noticed that, outside of my window, nature seemed to have returned to normal, only the chirping of crickets breaking the deep silence.

A loud banging at the door startled my reverie, insistent and authoritative. There was still only one man I knew with the gall to knock like that, and at this hour. I flung my sheets back, slammed my bedroom door behind me, and crossed the kitchen, my one aim to get rid of the caller without involving my parents.

Alfio Gallo looked taken aback when I hurled the door open violently. "Oh, you're back, are you? Didn't have the gumption for another year of university, did you? Step aside and let me in."

"If you wish to come inside," I began steadily, "you will have to ask politely."

"What did you just say to me?" growled Gallo, and leaned forward to siphon his stale wine breath over me, but stepped back in surprise when he realized I was now taller than him, and he had to look up to me. His eyes were unfocussed and he was swaying a little.

"On second thought, you won't be coming inside. You're drunk, you stink, and you're waking the entire valley."

"Get your smart-mouthed, piss-ant *culo* out of my way," he demanded, shuffling forward. "I'm here to see the head of this pitiful winery, not some deluded little farm boy."

"The Laurentis farm is mine," I declared, without really knowing what I was saying. "*Orvieto Dolce Fantasia* belongs to me now, and in light of your recent losses, I'm the one who should be offering pittances to buy your worthless land. But I won't throw one lira your way. Now get the hell off my property."

But Gallo began to laugh, a deep, shaking braying, like a demented donkey. "Not like your father, are you, my boy? He's always been green about the gills, a coward hiding behind his books. But I like your spirit. You and I, we could be partners."

"I'd rather dine on *merda*."

"That's your retarded mother talking."

Without a second's pause, my fist found his jaw and there was Gallo, sprawled out on the ground. He straightened up, his head hanging crookedly from his neck. "Is that all you've got?" he sneered.

So I kicked him in the stomach, followed by the chest. And as the enemy of my family struggled to get to his feet, I kicked him in the face, and felt his teeth loosen as I withdrew. I readied myself for another attack when I felt a hand on my shoulder.

"That's enough, Gabriel," said my Papa.

"Listen to the old man," mocked Gallo, as he wiped a slick of blood from his mouth. He stumbled to his feet and I clenched my fists, waiting for him. He looked down at his hand, only to realize for the first time that he was bleeding.

"Look what you've done, you stupid fool!" he snapped. "You are going to pay for this!"

"Like how you paid for trying to close down my farm?"

Gallo's eyes widened, sheer hatred pouring from his stare as he hobbled forward, pointing a shaking finger at me. "I knew it was your doing," he whispered, "I knew it."

"Prove it," I sneered, and turned to go inside.

"I know all about you, Gabriel Laurentis," he hissed. "You and that *bird* of yours."

I whirled around. "What did you say?"

He grinned evilly. There was blood in his mouth. "I've seen her, the falcon. I've been tracking her for years. I know you've been keeping her here."

"You're out of your mind."

Gallo's face was mere inches from mine now. I was shaking all over, desperately trying to hide it. "Prove it," he sneered. And he spat on me.

As Papa brought me inside, I realized I was still shaking. Mamma was in the kitchen, her fists clenched around her dressing gown, eyes wide with fear. "It's over, Blanca," said my father. "It's all over now."

But Mamma just stood there, staring at the both of us, her head beginning to bob on her neck. "I'll make you some tea, and you can drink it in bed," soothed Papa, steering her back into the bedroom.

"I don't condone violence," he said as he watched me wash my face in the kitchen sink, "but I'm proud of you tonight, son. It's always been my desire for you to have the farm after I was gone. I feared you did not want it until tonight."

"So did I," I concurred with some amazement.

"It's yours."

"Papa—"

"It's yours from today on, with one condition."

"What condition?"

"Volatile must not return here again. Her life has never been more endangered. I know this is her home, but you must convince her to leave this place, this region, and never come back. I've known Gallo since the days he used to taunt me at elementary school, and he's not a man who easily discards his own threats. Talk to her. She's always listened to you."

But something sunk inside of me at his words. Something I could not name died a little, and its carcass swung inside my soul, already gathering flies.

"Do you promise me?" pressed my father gently.

"Yes, Papa," I said. "I promise."

QUINDICI

At first, I refused to recognize her.

Since the demise of Gallo and the restoration of our winery, I had been impatiently waiting for Volatile to reappear. I assumed she would return to us rapidly, strutting about congratulating herself on a job well done, and gleefully lapping up our thanks and praise. The night Alfio Gallo stormed upon our house, I sat awake at the window and waited for her. I called out to her, but she did not come. Every night thereafter, I would grossly delay my hour of sleep, and still Volatile did not return. Perhaps she had heard the promise I made to my father. Perhaps she was already acting upon it. My heart sank.

My mother's health grew worse. Speaking would often encourage a bout of violent coughing, so she refrained from most conversation. The doctor had been and gone, leaving a cabinet full of tonics and syrups behind, which Mamma took religiously. I suspected they were useless, except to lubricate her dry throat and reduce her to a numb, sluggish state. Papa tended to her as always, but this time with more care and consideration than I had witnessed before. Or so I thought. Perhaps I really was growing up.

She called me over to her side at times, to sit with her in bed. "Not now," I would say, not wanting to hear the infinite circles of her speech, not wanting to see the blood on her handkerchief. "Tomorrow, okay?" She would sigh and settle deeply into the blankets with resignation. We both knew the answer would not change then, or the next day.

Autumn was upon us now. I spent my days learning the business of the trade, and began drafting letters to wine and liquor emporiums in Rome and Milan, asking them to stock *Laurentis Dolce Fantasia*, which I kept a secret from my father for fear of raising his hopes. But I lived in a constant state of agitation without Volatile.

There was no moon that night she came. My room was flooded with a thick blackness, darkness so dense I could put it in my mouth and swallow it. I drifted in and out of sleep, caused by a fluttering anticipation I could not quell. I sensed a movement in the corner of my room; I could almost see it, like a pot of boiling castor oil being stirred.

"It's me," she said.

"Volatile?" I asked, and made to turn on the lamp.

"Don't!" came her voice, and I noticed there was no bravado there, no cocky sense of self-assuredness that I had come to associate with her, and always will.

"What is it?"

"Don't look at me," she whispered. "Keep the light off."

"What do you mean? What has happened to you?"

"Don't look at me."

I snapped on the light and there she was, standing over my bed, her arms held high, shielding her face, repelled by the radiance. "I couldn't come back looking this way," she whispered.

"Show me," I said, but she would not budge.

"Please show me, Volatile. I am not going to hurt you."

"I don't want you to see me like this," she said.

"Just show me."

Slowly, she lowered her arms away from her face, and her wings unfurled from her back.

I recoiled in horror. Her wings were nothing but a frame of stark bones, grey and splotched, so worn in the joints that I could see softening red marrow peering through. With a shudder I realized how much they resembled two enormous, broken ribcages ascending from her back. Her eyes were desperately searching mine for acceptance, and I noticed the pallor of her skin, white and chalky like aspirin. Her neck seemed too long and bony for her body.

"I tried to come when you called, but I couldn't fly."

"What happened to you?"

"It was the price," she said, "that I had to pay."

"The price of what?"

"The price of meddling with nature."

And she began to describe what she had done to save my family. How she convinced her flock to side with us, and they in turn visited the leaders of other species of birds to beg them to join the cause. How an alliance was proposed between the swallows and the insects, that the insects would not be harmed within the strict property lines of Gallo's acres, how they would be protected and encouraged to glut themselves to their heart's content. The insects took a great deal of convincing, as a deep distrust of the swallows had been long ingrained in them. They were rightly suspicious that the birds were offering them free reign of all the crops they could stomach, but had strictly forbidden them to eat or harm the nematodes, small worms and parasites that nibbled on grapevine roots, that they found so delicious. Begrudgingly, the insects agreed to the swallows' terms, provided they assured protection from not only birds, but frogs and spiders as well.

The frog king was a dull sort; often blindly following whatever trend nature wished to turn to, and agreed heartily when he realized his people would not be harmed by the larger aviary species during this time. The spiders, however, were so skeptical of the swallow's proposal that they narrowed their numerous eyes and rubbed their hairy legs together in contemplation. Tired of the birds' begging and pleading, the spiders sent an envoy to the Laurentis farm to see what all the fuss was about. The envoy had returned, unharmed, and reported that the Laurentis heir was not such a bad fellow, as the bravest of the party had dared march right up his leg, and he had neither been squashed nor brushed away. The Laurentis heir, they divulged, had hair like fine arachnid silk, and the spiders, not being half as intelligent as they think they are, agreed that anything that resembled their silk must surely be a worthwhile cause after all.

"So that's what took so long," I said after hearing this wild tale, "persuading all those creatures."

"Actually," murmured Volatile, "it was the swallows that took the most convincing." She looked down at her bare dirty feet that seemed more like claws than ever. "Because if they couldn't eat the insects, the frogs, or the spiders, what could they feed on?"

Waves of horror enveloped me and I began to shudder. My mouth filled with a sickeningly sweet taste – bile mixed with wine from my empty stomach.

"I had to protect my people," she whispered. "I had to repay them, I could not let them starve."

"So you fed them."

"I let them take what they wanted from my body."

"Volatile!"

"They didn't take much, they ate so sparingly from me, not wanting to hurt me, to disfigure me."

"You're a skeleton," I realized, as my eyes grazed over her body, which I had not noticed, stupefied by her spectral wings. The bones of her knees threatened to burst from the thin skin surrounding it. Her arms were like the limbs of long-dead winter trees. And her face was all cheekbones and sunken eyes. With a fresh wave of terror, I realized that her eyes were no longer green. The swallows had sucked the color out of them. They were now opaque and milky.

"And your wings?" I was afraid to ask.

"The larger birds took them. They stripped them and consumed them. The falcons, the hawks, all they value is power. So they took what was most powerful away from me."

"Are you dying?" I demanded, almost abruptly.

But Volatile smiled at me, and I knew then that no force of nature could take away that sweetness. "Something like this can't kill me. I will recover and replenish myself again, but I don't know how long it will take."

"Where have you been? Where do you sleep? Mamma told me you hardly stayed here while I was away."

"It had become too…distracting."

"Have you been staying under Orvieto? With the others?"

"How did you know there were others?" she demanded. "Never mind. I cannot go back there," she finished eerily.

"The dark one?" I dared to ask.

Volatile looked up at me quizzically. "Is that what you call him? How very strange. If anything he is -- but you know I cannot speak of that, Gabriel."

"Then where have you been staying?"

"With Orlando Khan, of course."

"I thought all that was over," I said bitterly.

"He is my truest friend," said Volatile, "and without him, your farm could not have been saved."

"Then I owe him my thanks."

"You owe him much, much more. He has saved your dignity and your hide since you were a little boy."

"And that's why you sent a group of swallows to him."

Volatile nodded solemnly. "To protect him as long as he lives. I sent him that gift only because you could not."

"What are you?" I breathed, and suddenly I understood what I had been living with all of these years. A phenomenon. She was not of this world. She was not like us. And I was overcome with the amazement I should have experienced a lifetime ago, when I was so full of my own self to have room for anything else. I was so overwhelmed by my own sense of self-pity and fixation upon Mariko Marino that I was numb to the miracle of Volatile. And that wasn't all. I took my only friend for granted, ignoring his letters and entertaining unkind thoughts about him. I neglected my father and took him for a fool. And I never realized, until this moment, that my mother was dying.

"You know what I am," she said, and I felt a looming recognition about to dawn on me -- bird's nests, the insides of old eggs, Lulu, *One Thousand and One Nights*, a mask --but it escaped again in the rush of my tangled thoughts.

"Volatile," I began, and hesitated, not wanting to broach the subject.

"What is it?"

"I have to tell you, to ask you, something."

"Just say it."

"You…you must not come back here again."

Her grey face seemed to collapse in front of my eyes. "But this is my home," she said.

"I know," I said, "and you have fought so hard to save it."

"But not for myself," confirmed Volatile, "it was for you."

It was then that I, Gabriel Laurentis, who had eighty-seven Roman women desiring to sleep with me, the owner of an expensive leather jacket and now a whole vineyard, realized I had tears in my eyes.

"I can't do it," Volatile finally said, "won't you say goodbye for me? I wish I could give them a gift, in thanks."

"I think you've given my parents enough."

"Won't you turn the light off?" Volatile asked gently. "I am going to leave through the window, and I don't want you to see me go. I can't fly the way I used to, you see."

"Let me go with you," I said, "I want to help you."

"There is nothing you can do for me, Gabriel, except turn off the light."

"Then of course I will," I said, and I switched off the lamp. I settled back on the pillows and in the darkness, I could barely discern the outline of the open window, and the olive branches that lay beyond it. Everything seemed shades of black and midnight blue.

I felt her slight weight on the bed beside me and her hand, so sub-temperature it was alarming, on my temple. It was shaking. There was an overwhelming fatigue descending on me, like a grim reaper claiming me for eternal sleep. And what I said next changed my whole life.

These days, I often wonder what would have happened had I not said those words. I speculate over the minor details that modulated the movement of the world. I meditate on the major outcomes that transformed the lives of so many of us in Orvieto.

"Don't be ashamed, Volatile," I said sleepily. "You're still beautiful to me."

Abruptly, she leaned down and kissed me. And she tasted so bitter, like heartbreak. She was not a skeleton of a creature to me. She was beautiful. And the seeds that dropped within me when I was a little boy, that had begun to flourish and grow during my teenage years, I now realized had become as large as an oak, smashing through my subconscious and denial.

As she broke away, I sensed the air around us unsettling as her wings of bone unfurled. A familiar scent filled the air and I suddenly recalled the night of *Donne Notte*, the dark hair, the green eyes, the spray-painted silver wings that did not come off with her clothes. "It was you," I breathed, sitting up abruptly. And I understood without a doubt that all this time, I had known it.

"Yes," she said.

"Why did you come?" I asked forcefully.

"You told me to."

"I never did."

"In your letter. You said you wished I was there."

"You came just because of that?"

"I came because I love you."

"You...what?"

"I love you, Gabriel," she said, "I've loved you my whole life."

I don't know why I said this, but I began to choke a little, and a foolish smile spread across my face. "Thank God," I said. "Thank God."

"I thought you didn't believe in God," she exclaimed, and I realized she was laughing a little.

I felt drugged, dizzy, deliriously happy. "I don't know what I believe in anymore, but thank God that it's me."

"It's all right," she said, "go to sleep."

"But will I see you again? We need to talk about—"

"You know where to find me whenever you need me."

"But I—"

"Go to sleep," she breathed. And she smiled her incredulous, iridescent smile. The smile of an angel, of a patron saint.

And because my ensnarled, uncoiled thoughts were growing dull and numb and useless in the darkness, and because her words blanketed me in a peace I had felt not once prior to this moment, I obeyed. I sunk into an unilluminated, instantaneous state of unconsciousness.

It could not have been long before a voice inside my head bleated *Wake up!* in a horrifying, throaty croak. I dashed to my feet, covered in a cold sweat. There was an unmistakable noise out there, in the woods.

And there it was again.

Gunshots.

A piercing shriek.

I screamed and hurled myself out of the bed. I grabbed a torch from the kitchen and thundered out the front door, ignoring the disturbed movements and exclamations from my parents' room. I hurtled through the woods behind the vineyard, shining the torch from the trees to the ground and up again. "Volatile!" I shouted. "Answer me!" My feet were cut and bleeding from trampling on broken trees and sharp rocks, but I could not feel anything for the pain threatening to explode in my chest.

As I continued shouting and hurling myself through those moonless woods, I heard the rustle of wings in the air, and somehow realized that in the branches above me, flocks upon flocks of ghostly swallows had gathered. They seemed to stare down at me silently for a long moment, as if they wanted to tell me something. Finally, they began to croon with uncanny, otherworld voices I had not realized swallows possessed, and I knew then they were singing a phantasmal funeral march.

I felt arms around me and heard my father sobbing in my ear, "Come home now, my son. She's gone. Won't you come on home?" He supported my weight on his shoulder and with his bad leg, he slowly led me through the woods and into the house.

"But her body," I was stammering, "I have to find her body."

"She's gone," wept my father, "he has taken her."

My Papa, as frail as he was, laid me out in my bed and poured me a glass of whiskey. I swallowed it down and he poured another one.

It was all a dream, it had to be. Tragedy like this could not happen to me. I was bone-tired, it was my imagination.

But I kept hearing the gunfire from the Winchester shotgun, and the macabre, spine-chilling song of the birds.

I needed to forget, for just a few precious hours.

I needed the memory cells to deplete, to die while I slept away the horrors of this night.

It was then that I rummaged through my possessions stacked on the bedside table for the brown jar of pills.

There was not one left.

NOTTE
UNO

Behind my closed eyelids, betwixt the right temple and the left, lies a great open plain, an entire empty world in a skull-sized radium.

The plain is white, like thick, fibrous paper from an artist's sketchpad.

It is an unvarying, unwavering whiteness. It does not move.

But even though I am asleep, I detect a slight change.

It is silent. But as I concentrate deeply, I can hear something.

Humming.

A low drone and it is vibrating. Like what most people hear after their ears pop.

On the great, white plain a grey mark appears.

Just a spec, or just like the smallest of pebbles being dropped into a still lake of milk.

It causes ripples all over the bleached world.

And then the spec begins to grow, slowly. It is humming as it elongates into a thin line. Like a line drawn in pencil on a piece of parchment.

Other lines germinate then, short lines perpendicular to the original. They are touching each other. Strange teardrops begin to fall down like rain. They attach themselves to the grey lines. The teardrops continue to mushroom all over the canvas, all over the great white world.

Finally, I can see what has been drawn in front of my eyes. I recognize the branches of the olive tree that grows outside my window, a grey, two-dimensional, child's drawing of reality.

I desire to see more, but I am being shaken, is there an earthquake in the white plain?

There are hot, salty splashings all over my face, is there an ocean in the white plain?

My name is being called, over and over, is there a friend in the white plain?

And then I am awake, and the white world disintegrates.

"Gabriel, it's your mother. She's dead."

NOTTE
DUO

Another grey, needle-thin line begins to emerge from the corner of the white world. It sails past the olive tree branch, but it is in a hurry.

It ducks and swerves. It climbs and soars, it swoops and descends. The lines fill the entire parchment with their frenetic energy.

Suddenly, the humming stops.

It takes a moment to register what lies before me.

Volcanic tuff. Hidden labyrinths of caves and caverns. Windows in the wall and lichen covered turrets. Secret chambers. A frozen well at the bottom of a double-helix staircase. Balconies that meet with a kiss, like good friends. Old, whispering piazzas with somber, metal-colored flags. Networks of spider-thin alleys and roads that rise up to a steel sun.

Orvieto in greyscale.

NOTTE
TRES

I walk through the new Orvieto. It is silent, and all I can hear are my own footsteps. They sound hollow in these barren streets. They echo so loudly, like thunder.

There is not a soul in this ghost town. But I can hear the hum of voices just behind the walls of the white world. I can hear them whispering. They are spirits, I decide. They are what endures of once-living memories. They are the remainders of dead hopes, of slain ambition.

I reach out my hand to touch something. A wall? A tree? It is hard to tell, with this lack of color. I expect my hand to fall through it, as if this new Orvieto was made of nothing but smoke and shadow. But it is solid. It feels like nothing my cells can recall. It feels alien.

I do not realize I am in a dream. Something at the farthest edge of my mind nudges me, willing me to remember, to realize. I wave it away like a persistent mosquito.

As I roam these streets, they slowly become more familiar. I recognize landmarks. I can find my way. And soon I reach the destination I never knew I had: St Patrizio's well that stands on the helm of the mountain city.

I look up at the sky. Silver stars that contain no light. And I understand the expanding feeling in the pit of my stomach. I am lonely.

I duck my head. It falls so low. It rests on my chest.

And suddenly, I am doubled over, and a pain that had always lived, dormant, inside my body breaks through, and I fall to the ground like a felled tree. I writhe. What is this agony? Why am I thrashing about?

And I let out a huge breath, as if all this time I had been underwater.

"Come back to me," I cry. "Come back to me."

And outside a bedroom window, on a vineyard that only sells sweet dessert wine, upon the branch of an olive tree, a little bird lands. She has eyes the color of frogs in the summer time. When she opens her beak, I hear her voice in my head even though I am still asleep; a voice I love like it is my own.

"I thought you'd never ask."

HALF LIFE

PART III

SEDICI

Mamma's funeral was a quiet, ill-attended affair. It took place on Saturday morning, in a small, newish cemetery in Orvieto town. It lay on a backstreet, and boasted a view of a barren kindergarten playground, as it was primarily known for its last-minute affordability and not its prestige or grandeur like the other graveyards in town.

Papa held his handkerchief to his face and unashamedly wept throughout the bare, no-frills ceremony the local parish priest, who had never met Mamma, conducted. When it was time for Papa to make the speech he had meticulously written over three sleepless nights in the barn, he broke down, gasping for breath, and Orlando Khan had to help him to his feet. He could not make that speech. The bit of paper he had scrawled it on was bunched up in his fist and sprayed with tears. I could see the ink marks all over his hands. He did, however, manage to hobble over to the little portable cassette player he had borrowed from a neighbor for this occasion.

I was overwhelmed with sorrow as the tinny tune of Mamma's favorite aria from the opera *La Tosca* poured over the tiny burial ground. I gazed down at the casket in the red earth, its cheap, unpolished pine and lack of fancy fittings. A simple box that contained the corpse of my own Mamma. I tore my eyes away from it and scanned the scene around me. My Papa had been helped into a plastic chair the priest had procured for him. There was a gravedigger standing a respectful distance away, his cap in one hand, his shovel in the other. His head was bowed as he waited for his cue, but he was fidgeting, and I could tell he was thinking about his wife and his dinner. At the entrance of the cemetery hovered a woman in a black veil that covered everything but her face. She nodded solemnly at me, and looked as if she wanted to step forward, but was afraid to enter. She held a bouquet of flowers. Ayisha Khan.

And as I wrestled with the fact that my mother lay dead, I tried to forget that I had lost Volatile, my friend so brutally slaughtered. But I shook the thought out of my head. I could not think of her now. As a fresh wave of grief threatened to envelope me, I couldn't help but take two steps back. And even though I was a grown man, I leaned my head against Orlando Khan's shoulder. I could barely stand.

Orlando Khan had arrived the morning after Volatile and my mother had died. Strange, how life worked. I wonder what I would have thought, those years ago when Volatile lived with us like a second child, picking all the meat out of her pasta. I wonder what I would have said, as I looked over at Mamma sipping red wine next to Volatile, if I had known they would die, from different causes, on the same night.

He had arrived searching for her, as she did not return to his attic room at the Emporium that night. No one answered the door, so he let himself in. There was one open bedroom door and one closed. Gingerly approaching my parents' room, he gasped as he saw my Mamma sprawled out on the bed like a starfish, and my father leaning over her with a comb, brushing out her wiry curls as they fanned over the pillow. He looked up at Orlando, dazed, his eyes bloodshot. "They aren't awake," mumbled my father. "No one in this house is awake but me."

After he had learned the truth, Orlando did not rush out of the house to avenge Volatile, as I had expected. He knocked and knocked at my door but I would not answer. I just lay there, staring at the ceiling. I was senseless, without feeling. I felt there was an iron wall separating me from reality. I had begun to dream again.

Orlando did not force his way in, that was not his way. According to my father, who told me later, Orlando lowered himself to the ground, and curled his legs beneath him, beginning a long vigil, waiting for me. He only left once, and when he returned, so did Ayisha Khan with baskets of exotic food, grilled meats and spiced curries and yoghurts infused with herbs. This type of fare continued to arrive at the house, three times a day. Mine was arranged on a tray and left on the floor inside of my door. But whoever delivered it did not enter further and did not speak.

I believe I slept most of those days. I recall that morning that Orlando arrived, screwing my eyes shut and willing myself back to slumber. It was not to avoid my friend, or my sorrow-demented father, but an anticipation to see what would happen next in my dreams. I hardly ate or drank, and when I needed to urinate, I did it out the window. I stayed in the room for three days.

On the morning of the funeral, Orlando cracked my door open to find me on my knees, staring pointedly at the olive branch outside of my window. He forced a steaming cup of coffee into my hands, and it was not my Mamma's china, but the delicate Moroccan pink and gold glass set I had sipped from so many times at the Emporium. He peered at me grimly as I swallowed it down, and I noticed there were grey pouches under his eyes, and a black shadow of a beard had spread across his jaw. His hair was unwashed and longer than I'd ever seen it, charcoal-colored ringlets tied with a leather strap at the base of his neck.

He helped me out of bed and suddenly, my Papa's arms were around me. "Are you all right?" whispered my father. "She's in a better place now. Your mother…she loved you so much. Her lungs, her heart, she just couldn't take the news about…about…" And his eyes slid over to Orlando and he hung his head. He was wearing his best suit. He smelled of mothballs.

Orlando pushed me into the bathroom and turned on the shower and left, forcefully closing the door behind him. He had not said a word. I stared at myself in the mirror. My face seemed thinner and my eyes hollow. My mother was dead. My mother was dead.

A cold slab of unleavened bread in my stomach, my wet hair combed and clothes changed, and we were in the wagon, Tomasso wheezing his way up the mountain. There was something different about the world now. Something was missing. And then I realized: I could not see or hear the swallows. Not the flock that followed Orlando everywhere he went. Not the troupes that swooped among the hills and valleys of Orvieto. They were all gone.

The priest was waiting for us and a bouquet of white flowers was pressed into my hand, which I cast down into the grave at the conclusion of the funeral, as if they had wronged me.

I waited there, at the plot, as Orlando steered my father out of the cemetery, the priest following at a tasteful distance, bearing the cassette player. Papa found himself in Ayisha Khan's arms, who would not enter the burial ground. "Shall I fill it up now?" queried the gravedigger behind me.

I did not turn to look at him. "Yes. Fill it up." My voice sounded vacant, and I turned to leave.

"You'd better take these, then," said the gravedigger, pointing to two flower arrangements I had neglected to notice, resting at the base of the grave and not the headstone. I knelt down to inspect them.

One was a perfectly adequate bouquet of ivory lilies. I tore open the envelope.

I didn't know how Everard Fane had found out my mother had died, but I did not care enough to dwell on it. At least he had sent flowers, that was kind of him.

The other arrangement was much larger and a little ostentatious, presented with splashes of exotic greenery and tropical, expensive-looking rare blooms. A creamy, gold-edged card accompanied them, set snugly against the luxurious fronds.

Dear Gabriel

I am terribly sorry for your loss.

With kind regards and sympathies,

An old friend

As I turned over the card, I saw the florist's address printed in embossed gold. Florence.

"I don't want them," I stated to the gravedigger, and turned on my heel. "Give them to your wife."

That night, not long after Orlando and his mother had left, and I could hear my Papa restacking the stores in the barn, I held the little brown jar in my hands and examined it. For so long now I had relied on the chemicals contained in the tiny blue pills to keep me from dreaming, maintaining my singular and uncomplicated life. As long as I could remember, my dreams were always far superior to real life, and I recalled the duality I felt as a child, not knowing which was the reality. I knew no one else dreamed the way I did, or even if they could, did not retain it, savor it, did not feel it so distinctly it could be mistaken for reality. Why? I thought. Why me?

I was glad to be out of pills, for now. The pharmacist, on a return visit, had warned me that this bottle was the last I'd ever buy, as the government decided to cancel the drug trail in Italy. I minded then, but I wasn't foresighted enough to care about my future psyche, so distracted by women and alcohol. And now, I was thrilled they were unavailable, if it meant I got to see Volatile again.

I was filled with dread as I thrashed in my bed, sleep mercilessly eluding me. What if she did not return? What if it wasn't Volatile, but a trick my mind was playing on me?

Before I knew it, I was wandering through dreamscape Orvieto, and she was there, falling silently into step with me, and we passed through the empty streets calmly, like it was an everyday occurrence. Unlike the rest of the white world, Volatile was three-dimensional, full of color, exactly as she always was. Gone were the wings of human bone, her body a skeleton held taut by worn, stretched hide. She looked just the way she did before the collapse of the Gallo estate. "You're late, as usual."

"Where is everyone?" I asked.

She was so unchanged, down to her expression. "Look," she said, and indicated to a set of large stone columns where a sleek cat arched its back and mewled.

"Sweet Vittoria?" Recognizing her name, she ambled over to me and I bent down and stroked her. She looked as if she was assembled from black paint and air and when I touched her, I could not feel fur but a texture I'd never encountered before.

"Why does she look like this?" I asked, and lifted my eyes to where the stonewalls, turrets and secret skyward gardens of Orvieto peered down at me, all shades of grey. It was almost as if, if I cared to walk beyond them, it would not be possible to distinguish them from cardboard cutouts. "Why does everything look this way?

"It only appears that way to you," explained Volatile gently. "The medication you took affected the part of your mind that translates dreams into images."

"But you look exactly the same."

"Your brain does not have the power to contain me," smirked Volatile proudly.

"But if you are here, then what about Mamma?"

"Shh!" said Volatile, "listen."

And as I fell silent, just like a cool breeze did the pure notes of the opera *La Tosca* drift over us, and with it, I could smell my mother's tomato puree. A sense of peace and pure joy drifted over me.

"Let's go home," I said to her, and she placed her hand in mind. And I recognized her touch, the smoothness of her skin, the smell of her hair just under my chin.

"If only," I sighed, "if only this were real life."

Volatile smiled a secret smile and leaned over to whisper in my ear. What she said next covered my skin with tiny goose bumps, and I shivered.

"It could be."

DICIASSETTE

My father, unsurprisingly, was already awake as I reluctantly dragged myself out of bed, remnants of sleep still clinging to me like a persistent lover. He nursed a cup of coffee in his hands and he seemed to be studying the pattern of the tablecloth with an absent intent.

"Good morning, Papa."

"Ah, Gabriel," he murmured, springing to life and pouring me espresso. As I sat down, through my bleary eyes I noticed he had already set out a plate and utensils for me, along with a basket of bread with an assortment of Signora Khan's condiments laid out upon the table. He had assumed my mother's job. I felt awash with guilt. Shouldn't I be serving him?

"It's not so bad, you know," he said, pointing to a tub of hummus, "once you get used to it."

"I know," I agreed, and my stomach began to churn and I realized how hungry I was. Enthusiastically, I snatched up a roll of bread. My father took this as a sign.

"I want to know when you're ready to start work on the vineyard. I know your mother just…just passed, but I find being occupied helps keep the mind off unpleasant topics. For the most part."

When he didn't receive a response, he continued. "I thought I could start by showing you the books. I could teach you how to manage the accounts and—"

"I have to go into town today, Papa."

His face fell and I felt a stab of remorse for disappointing him.

"What for, son?" he asked softly.

"I want to see Orlando."

Papa was quiet for a moment, scrutinizing me in that gentle way he had about him, like he could divine my thoughts like they were his own. "If you two are thinking up some vigilante justice against Alfio Gallo…"

"I am going to get her body back, Father," I growled.

He was taken aback by the formal use of his title. "I think you had better leave well enough alone."

"How could you say that? He killed her! He *murdered* her in cold blood!"

"He believed he was hunting an animal."

"How could you defend him? After all he has done to us?"

"I think Alfio Gallo has suffered enough."

"You think the loss of his wealth is equal to a human life?"

"She was not human, Gabriel."

I stood up, aggressively pushing the table away from me. "You cannot know what you're saying," I snapped, snatching up my jacket. "I'll leave you now."

Papa shook his head sadly. "Where has this violence in you come from? Laurentis men are men of peace. I did not teach you revenge or brutality."

"All you taught me was—"

"Enough!" my father commanded, in a stern tone that I had not heard before, freezing me in my tracks. "I will not have you spitting words that will not only wound me, but yourself, only far more deeply, and much later, after you realize what it is you have done. You cannot unsay what has already been said." He moved toward me and laid a careworn hand on my shoulder. I noticed new liver spots sprouting like mold. "Do what you must, but hurt no one."

I nodded solemnly, swallowing down the casual words I would have flung at him like a whip, words that were already dissolved and half-forgotten. I ducked my head in apology and headed for the Khan Emporium.

Declining Ayisha Khan's offer of tea, I took the familiar spiral staircase to Orlando's attic room, two steps at a time. As I sprinted hastily past the second landing, the door to the room of Imelda Khan, still a celebrated beauty yet unmarried, instinctively slammed shut. I had yet to lay eyes on her, and if not for the unmistakable girlish indications of a young woman present in the house, I would have dismissed her as entirely mythical.

Orlando was dressed and waiting for me. We had briefly discussed a plan yesterday, which could hardly be called a plan at all, it was so simple: go to the Gallo estate, get the body back, use force if necessary. I took a moment to subtly peer past my friend and into his cavernous room, once a haven of the exotic and the enigmatic to me. Two or three *huqqua* pipes sat on a floor strewn with lush rugs, silks and strips of unsold Persian carpets. The chartreuse paint that was once so bright lay flat and peeling from his walls, and tobacco smoke covered the beams. But as I peered closer, amidst the childish pictures Orlando used to draw all over the walls – peacocks and roses and mosques with domes rising like meringues, I could detect lines and lines of strange, coiled foreign writing, charts, and outlines of anatomies I never knew existed.

Orlando sensed my curiosity and budged me out of the way, closing the door firmly behind me. To my surprise, he drew a key on a long copper chain from his pocket, bolting the door behind him. Without offering any explanation, he waved me down the stairs. I could not erase it from my mind: the puddle of black satin in the corner of the room, with the hollow of a woman's body still imprinted within in. I wondered how close he would sleep beside her.

We took a shortcut through town, and began our swift decent from Orvieto, through woods and wasteland of vineyards, and on towards *La Casa di Gallo*. Swift, chilly winds soared through the valley, stinging our bare faces with icy fingers.

"What happened between you and her, anyway?" I asked, deciding I had a perfect right to do so. We had yet to discuss any aspects of Volatile since her death, excepting today's excavation plan.

"We wore away," he responded grimly. He trudged along before me, without looking back. After a long moment he continued, "Make no mistake, I knew it was you all along. When you left for Rome, she changed. When you didn't come home for Christmas, that's when I realized that she stayed for you, and not me. We were never the same after that. She could not give me what I wanted."

"I'm sorry," was all I could muster in return.

"Don't be. I was there when she needed me. I would not, *could not* abandon her. The many nights she needed comfort, someone to hold her. So many nights she could not bear to be in the same house as you. And there were the times she couldn't go back, no matter how much she wanted to."

I knew he was referring to her final days, barely being able to fly with the pain of the decaying bones on her back. Suddenly, my old friend whipped around and stared at me with a haunting expression. "I want you to know how much you did not deserve her. I don't know what it was she saw in you. Your pretty eyes, your pretty hair and face are not enough to earn the love of that creature. A part of me hates you, because you are, unquestionably, an ingrate. You never saw her for what she was. And you still don't know who she is."

I could not argue with him, even if I wanted to, because we had arrived at the heavy gates of the Gallo estate. But most of all, because I knew he was right.

A servant opened the door with a rag in one hand and bucket of water in the other. "*Si?*" she drawled lazily, frowning a little at Orlando's unsightly ensemble consisting of black jeans, sneakers, an embroidered silk shirt, and a purple fez complete with yellow tassel.

"Signore Gallo, *per favore*," I demanded.

"My husband is not at home," said a regal voice. We peered past the servant and saw a white-haired, straight-backed woman descending the grand staircase in the foyer. "How can I help you?" She gave the servant a sidelong glance, who immediately scurried away. As I looked down on this woman with her pursed lips and hard lines etched around her eyes, I recalled the last time I had seen her, noting her resemblance to her daughter. But after all these years, in my mind's eye, I could not picture Darlo Gallo anymore.

I stepped forward, about to speak, but suddenly halted. How on earth was I to identify Volatile? As a half-woman, half-bird? She would think me mad.

"Your husband shot a…a creature on my property," I begun, in my sternest voice.

"You must be that Laurentis boy," she said, but there was no flicker of recognition in her eyes.

"I am."

"Then you must mean the falcon," she stated flatly.

"Uh, yes. The, uh, falcon." I glanced over at Orlando, whose eyes were wide and upon me too, as if wondering where this was going.

"And you are?" She was addressing Orlando.

"Signora, my name is—"

"Never mind," she interrupted imperiously, "just don't touch anything. This way." She beckoned for us to follow.

Orlando and I exchanged a heavy glance as we alighted the red velvet staircase to the first landing, an enormous circular hallway of doors leading to large, opulent chambers. Original paintings in heavy gold frames lined each wall with an eerie symmetry. Signora Gallo led us through the hall, to the very last door, which opened without a creak, as if the hinges were frequently in use.

The room was wallpapered in a dark green design, heavy black curtains drawn across long latticed French windows. Silently, Signore Gallo strode across the room and unfurled the drapery. I gasped aloud.

Screwed onto four walls of the room were the stuffed heads of multiple animals, their eyes glassy, mouths wired open. There were hundreds of them, mounted on heavy rosewood slabs, brass plaques underneath stating their species and date of kill. There was no furniture in the room excepting a revolving chair in the very center, suggesting the precise purpose of the room: the hunter's viewing pleasure.

"Is this what you mean?" came the soft voice of Gallo's wife.

There, in the exact nucleus of the south wall, was an enormous head mounted on a slab of wood plated in pure gold. Orlando and

I crossed over and examined it. It appeared to be the cranium of an aviary species, certainly a falcon or possibly even a hawk.

"But it's just a bird," I breathed.

"What else did you think it was?" said Signora Gallo, a hard edge to her voice.

"No, Laurentis," whispered Orlando. "Look harder."

And as I peered closer, I noticed the features of the bird were inexplicably blurred, blurred into the contours of Volatile's face. And the eyes, burned with acid and crystalized by formaldehyde, were unmistakably hers. There was a sharp intake of breath from Orlando, and he seemed to melt to the floor in disbelief, one hand covering his mouth. I was filled with rage and horror. "How could you?" I cried at Gallo's wife.

It was my statement, not really intended for her, that made her instantly come alive. "*You want it?*" she screeched, hurling herself toward the wall. She unhooked the slab, struggling with its weight, thrusting it toward me. "Then take it. Take it away from here!"

"Are you mad?" I shouted, shielding the head away from me, not wanting to touch the thing that was not quite Volatile. I couldn't bear to look at it one more time.

But Signora Gallo, her eyes wide and crazed, pushed her face close to mine. "Do you know what my husband says?" she hissed. "He says it *speaks* to him."

All the hair at the back of my neck stood on end. Tears were streaming down Signora Gallo's face. Unable to support it any longer with unstable hands, she dropped the slab onto the ground, but it did not crack or splinter. "He said it was a sickly thing," she whispered, "not like a real bird at all. Like predators had got to it first, sucking its flesh away." She looked down to where Orlando remained stricken on his knees. "He had a hard time convincing me to keep this in the house," she murmured absently. "He said it was the head of a falcon. *How could you say that, Alfio? You've committed a murder!* I screamed that night. But he wouldn't listen, he called me a madwoman, said he'd lock me away. Because I told him what I saw, and it's no falcon. I see the face of a woman."

I stared at Signora Gallo, then back at Volatile's lifeless head, lying on the ground.

"Ever since he shot that thing it's caused nothing but trouble. Take it with you! Isn't that what you came here for?"

In horror, I backed out of the room before hurtling down the stairs and out of that property as fast as I could. But not before I saw Orlando rise to his feet, taking one last look at Volatile's features, concealed within a bird. He took Signora Gallo's hands between his, looked into her eyes, and whispered, "May she haunt you until the day you die, *Insha'Allah*."

Ever my opposite, Orlando calmly strode out of that place, head held high. We walked silently through the vineyards and the woods, until the path forked: one toward Orvieto, and one east, to my farm.

"The journey ends here," stated Orlando solemnly.

"If you want to come to the house later, I can—"

"You misunderstand me, Laurentis. Our friendship has come to an end."

"What?"

"As all things run their course, so have we."

"Is this about her?"

But Orlando was unwavering. "I have done all I can do for you. There is no road left for us to travel together. We must go on, separately, for our paths lead to very different places."

"Are you leaving Orvieto?" I asked, not quite understanding.

But olive-skinned Orlando laid a hand on my shoulder.

Orlando Khan closed his eyes as a hush descended over the whole world.

Orlando Khan opened his mouth, but all I could hear were the voices, the whispers that lay behind the white world.

Orlando Khan spoke.

"Be well, Gabriel Laurentis. This is the will of God."

"Well, I can't say that I am happy about this," I began, then stopped suddenly.

I comprehended for the first time how wrong he seemed without the flock of birds accompanying him, like he was missing a vital limb, like he was naked. And then I understood. "You're going after the swallows, aren't you?"

A strange smile spread over his face. "I suppose you could call it that."

"I want to thank you for all you have done for me."

"It was done gladly, in the service of a friend." He raised a hand in farewell and ventured down the dirt trail, the path that took him away from me, permanently.

But he turned back in afterthought. "I have one more piece of advice for you. Heed it well, for it may save you someday. *When we die, we do not live on.* Do you understand?"

"Not exactly," I admitted helplessly.

"But you will. Goodbye, my friend."

"Goodbye, Orlando Khan."

DICIOTTO

"I don't understand," I would say so often to her as we lay, her head at my feet, on the white cotton sheets in my dreamscape bedchamber. My manor in the thriving vineyard, the smell of young grapes in the air. It was magic, even though it was two-dimensional. This house, this vineyard so exact as it had always been in my dreams, only in greyscale. "Volatile, you're dead."

"Do I look dead to you?" she replied, and would laugh.

"I saw your remains," I stated. "That head." I shivered at the recollection of that ghastly thing mounted on a slab.

"Think of it as a layer," she instructed, "and of me like a snake who sheds its skin."

"But Volatile," I began, "the head – it looked like a bird, but it also looked like you. It had your eyes. And all Gallo could see was a falcon, but his wife saw a woman, she saw you."

And then she said something that terrified me, "How do you know I really look like a woman?"

She must have noticed my discomfort, the horror I tried to conceal, because she laughed, restoring my confidence. "Gabriel, I control how human beings perceive me. I wanted Gallo to see a falcon. Just as I wanted his wife to see me."

"Still messing with the Gallos' from the grave, huh?" I said grimly.

"Not from the grave."

"Volatile, you're dead." I was growing exasperated. I could sense the truth dangling right before my eyes, but try as I might, it remained just out of reach, just beyond comprehension.

"But is not death merely a migration?" she responded, and she looked at me with those eyes of hers, and I would become putty in her hands. She could tell me anything, and I would believe it.

In those moments of peace, I would cross my arms at the back of my head, and look up at the high beams that supported the soaring roof. Just outside of my room, I could hear the animated chatter of my mother, who was cooking an incredible feast and singing her favorite songs. Outside of my window lay a vast vineyard, larger than the Gallos' could ever hope or dream, and my workmen filled the symmetrical rows bursting with fertility. Nestled amongst the beams and rafters over my head were bulbous, cone-shaped nests, constructed of sticks and mud, containing hundreds of fork-tailed swallows, their round entryways blinking at me like the eyes of night-dwellers.

They were everywhere, her swallows. In the kitchen, in the hall, in the ballroom with its dome-shaped ceiling, in the woods, in Orvieto town. I often complained about them. "They go where I go," explained Volatile.

"Couldn't you have left some back at the real farm?"

"No," she responded drily.

"You even took Orlando's swallows away," I would press.

"Orlando no longer needed them."

"He no longer required protection?"

"Orlando has gone to a place where what he requires is beyond human understanding," Volatile responded mysteriously. "And don't look at me like that, Gabriel Laurentis, for I won't tell you another word!"

"You never want to talk about Orlando with me," I sulked.

"It is not your business," she replied.

"I would think it was!" I exclaimed.

"And why is that, Gabriel?" There was a twinkle in her eye; she wanted me to admit something.

"Did you love him very much?" I asked in a small voice, trying to seem nonchalant.

"I…still love him very much."

It hurt a little, to hear that. Even in a perfect dream world. "Still?"

"I will always love Orlando Khan," she stated as matter-of-factly as she would trees being green and the sky being blue, although they really weren't, not in the white world.

"The same as me?" I asked tentatively.

She closed her eyes, and inhaled deeply, as if searching for an answer inside herself. Her lips began to move, and although I couldn't hear what she was saying, it was almost as if she were consulting with something…someone.

"It is a very different kind of love. Let's compare it to fire," she began in a voice that was hers, yet not quite hers. "I love Orlando like the flames in an oven. Contained, temperate, with a purpose, and end in mind, a finished result. I am able to dictate the heat I desire, low to high, off and on. The fire does not exist outside of the oven, and the oven is useless if not for the fire."

"And me?"

She sat up in the bed, her wings unfurling around her like a fine silk parachute caught in mid-air, gently drifting down to earth. She was a vision. "Like wildfire. Fire sparked by an infidel in a patch of nature, an act of mischief. But this fire burns to bone and destroys all things." She smiled at me then, an all-knowing expression on her face. "I watched you grow up, you know," she whispered. "My flock and I would nest in the trees around this place. There were so many locations my people wanted to return to after the winter. Some wanted to see France. Others Wales, the wild Nordic lands. But every year, I would lead them back here, after migration. The first time I saw you, you were in your mother's arms. You couldn't have been more than a few month's old."

I learned forward in eagerness as Volatile continued. "She didn't stutter much in your early years, so consumed with caring for you. She would pick wildflowers and herbs in the garden, with you strapped to her breast in an old shawl. I had never seen hair that shade, like white gold. You would point at us and smile, and you sparked my interest, because I had the ability to see your spirit, your nature. And I could not forget you as we journeyed from land to land, chasing the sun. So we returned, and I watched you grow, and your simple, trusting nature brought out the protector in me," she paused then, and colored a little. I nodded at her to continue. "I had a plan, that one day I would come to you, to be the friend and playmate child you so desperately needed. I didn't know exactly the day we would meet, and although I realized Gallo was stalking me, I always counted on his shots missing. It's strange you know," she concluded, staring out of the window and into the horizon, "the first time he discovered me was not on your property, but his own. I was at *Il Casa di Gallo*, watching you through the window as that hateful little girl slapped your face with her dolly."

I must have looked as alarmed as I felt, for Volatile wiped away the eerie atmosphere with a sweep of her hand, and everything returned to a calm state. "But that doesn't matter now," she said breezily.

She gazed at me expectantly, as if she wanted me to kiss her. But I did not want to, not at that moment. She was dead. She was nothing but a dream.

"Who are your people, exactly?" I changed the subject. "The birds? Or the others?"

"What others?" she responded lightly. "There are no others."

"I saw him, Volatile. And Orlando said there were others like you that lived within the ruins of ancient cities—"

"What is it your father once said? I am merely a girl with swallow's wings—"

"Don't expect me to believe this *merda*, Volatile."

"Why must you press this?" moaned Volatile, reaching over to stoke my face. "It is not for you to know."

"But Orlando has access to this privileged information?"

"Why do you concern yourself with Orlando? You two have parted ways now. He has left your life."

And hearing this filled me with the kind of deep sadness that permeated both dream life and the real.

"You know," said Volatile, sensing my disappointment, "what went on between Orlando and I. It's not…it's not what you think."

"But I *saw* you, Volatile. I saw you in the woods. Kissing and touching each other all over…"

"There is such a thing," she explained, "called *perspective*."

"You can't tell me that what I saw wasn't real."

"Enough of these questions," murmured Volatile, sitting up on her knees and edging over to me on the soft, feathered mattress. "I have something important to ask you."

"What is it?"

Her face began to radiate, and her green eyes shone. "How would you like to live with me here?"

I began to laugh. "That's insane, Volatile. This is just a dream!"

"But it isn't."

"I'm asleep right now, in Orvieto. My mother is dead and my father works hard to forget it. My best friend broke with me, and we have a farm that desperately needs care and attention. And there's this girl, you see. She lived with us, on and off. She was murdered. *That's* where I live. *That* is real life."

"It doesn't have to be," Volatile whispered. "*This* can be real life."

"Impossible!" I scoffed.

"No, Gabriel, listen to me. How do you know your version of real life, the one you just described, isn't the dream?"

"I just know."

"But did you not frequently question that, as a child?"

"I..."

An enigmatic smile spread over her face. "That's just it, don't you see? You need to un-know it, it's so simple. It's like changing loyalties, alternating realities. You simply tell yourself that *this* is real life, and we can be together, and have all this, everything you ever wanted! All that stuff you just mentioned, *that* is the dream."

"That sounds crazy. People can't trade dreams for reality. It's impossible."

"But people don't have dreams like you do, Gabriel."

"Why am I the only one?"

Volatile's eyes were on me, focused and intent. "Concentrate," she commanded. "What do you smell?"

I closed my lids. My mother's cooking. Chicken. White wine and garlic sauce. Something roasting. The smooth, suede scent of thyme. But no, there was something beyond that, as if the scent of food were merely a mask, a veil. A familiar fragrance that had always permeated this white world, something I recalled from my childhood. And then it hit me: moss. Dried leaves. The insides of eggs, unfertilized yolks dripping over straw. Mold. The innards of insects and the slime of earthworms. The acrid, subtle trace of poultry's naked skin.

And then I realized where I was, not in my room, not in my house, not in Orvieto, not even in a dream, but the inside of an enormous nest, a nest she had constructed for me.

I tried to recall the first time I began having these dreams, but couldn't fix upon a season. It was suddenly cold in the white world and I shivered despite myself. I wanted to leave. *Wake up*, I screamed at myself, concentrating fiercely. *Wake up!*

As if she could read my thoughts, she placed a hand on my knee to calm me. "It's all right," she soothed. "And it is the truth. I created this place for you in your mind. You were so troubled as a child, filled with so much pain and self-loathing. All you had was your cat and your prayers to Zeus. So I designed a haven of refuge for you, an Orvieto where all your wishes would come true."

"Like a genie," I breathed, suddenly remembering Orlando's hypothesis of yesteryear. How long ago that all seemed now.

If she heard me, she didn't react. "I worked so hard on this place," she continued, "it nearly took everything I had."

"But those pills," I stammered, "I ruined it, didn't I?"

"You didn't ruin it," she soothed. "Look around you, the frames and the foundations are still intact. And that's all you really need. So what will you do? Will you live with me here?"

"But it's only in my head."

"Your subconscious is a place too, as real as any other."

"Volatile," I began unsteadily, "I really don't know if I can…"

"But don't you miss me?" she said, and I saw pain in those eyes.

"Of course I do."

"And isn't this place better than the other?"

"There's no comparison."

"And you can touch, feel and taste here, just like the other?"

"Much better, much more distinct."

"Then stay here with me."

"I just…I don't know if I can—"

"But Gabriel," she said, and her voice was like heartbreak. "Don't you love me?"

And I looked at her, my Volatile, my swallow-girl, my savior, my friend. I felt hope rise within me, and I opened my mouth to say what she, undoubtedly, had always wanted to hear. But I halted and the words would not come. She was dead. Volatile was dead.

"Never mind," she said, "take your time."

"Volatile…" I began, and her name was like an unsweetened lemon drop on my tongue.

But her eyes were fixed on the roof beams, as if she could detect a change of weather. "It's time," she whispered. "*Wake up!*"

And I found myself, bathed in sweat, in my rickety little bed on the farm, a new morning.

I began to sleep later and later each morning, neglecting my father who would wait for me, keeping the coffee warm over the stove, rereading articles in that day's paper just to entertain himself. He would remark on the many times he tried to wake me, shaking me and calling my name, both gently and with some force, and I would not awake. Sometimes, he said, my body was like a stone, barely even breathing. Sometimes, my eyes were wide open, fixed on the ceiling. He would become flustered and worry about losing me so soon after my mother, but I would laugh him off. As I slept later and later, he would abandon the paper and the coffee, not able to neglect the winery a moment longer. I would wander out to him then, head fuzzy and with bleary eyes, and my father would shake his head sadly and point to the barn, where new bottles of *Dolce Fantasia* were waiting to be labeled. I was entrusted with nothing new. I merely resumed the tasks I did as a child, feeling under the hens' warm bellies for new eggs.

I began to long for sleep, for the world where my father was not so old and sad, where I could rest in the arms of my mother like a baby, where the food and the music was better, and there lived a woman who loved me. I discovered I preferred the lack of townspeople in the new Orvieto, no reminders of the real world. I would too often catch idle gossip on my sunset strolls into town, which infuriated me. On the pretense of visiting Orlando, I would simply go into the nearest store and purchase bottles of whiskey, small enough to conceal inside my jacket. I needed them to aid me in falling asleep sooner, maximizing on my time in the other world.

Life seemed to go on in the real world, dull and as dreary as anything without Orlando, and a father that barely spoke to me. I began to see that Volatile was right, and I found myself unknowingly slipping more and more into her world. No one came to visit us on the farm, and when Tomasso died, my father buried it on our property and made it a little wooden headstone, as if it were a member of the family. He asked me to accompany him to the grave, to say a few words over a cup of grappa. But I laughed and waved him away, for how ridiculous it was to give a donkey a eulogy.

Time passed, and only two pieces of gossip succeeded to substantially rock me on my trips into town. It seemed that Mariko Marino was returning to Orvieto with the intent of introducing her father to a new suitor. The Orvietani were all atwitter at the news, for it seemed this beau was in a prominent position of power, as the nephew of the English ambassador. Apparently Signorina Marino, who nobody thought would amount to much being a mixed-race child, had met the esteemed man, who was by all accounts the son of his Excellency's most favorite brother, in a lowly beer shop in one of Rome's trashiest areas. And of all nights to meet, the night of that scandalous Roman tradition, *Donne Notte*.

"You crafty son of a bitch," I drawled to no one in particular after hearing this news. I took an extra large swallow of whiskey and held it up to the window, as if saluting my old friend. I might have even smiled a little. It didn't hurt anymore.

The second piece of news hit me much harder. It seemed that Signora Gallo, irritated that her husband had not come to bed the night before, had marched all the way to the other wing of their enormous manor, and into his trophy room to tell him off. She found him there, slunk down in a revolving chair, a hole in his head and his brains splattered all over the opposite wall. A Winchester shotgun lay cold on the ground, and his dead eyes were fixed upon a gold-plated plaque bearing the stuffed head of an enormous bird.

A week after Gallo's death, I was awakened by a ramming at the front door. I lay there, expecting my father to open it. When the hammering had gone on, at first hesitant and then abrasive and demanding, I pulled myself out of bed. Not bothering with a shirt and clad in dirty grey pajama pants, my long hair plastered to my face with sweat and a five-o'clock shadow spread over my jaw, I staggered to the front door. I was not pleased at being disturbed, as I had just been making love to Volatile, an occurrence in the white world that had become a religion to me. I adjusted what little clothing I was wearing out of a long-lived sense of modesty and almost swooned. I was incredibly hung over.

"What?" I demanded, throwing the door open, my eyes squinting in the sudden light.

"My, my," said a slick, caramel voice. There was something familiar about it, something in the high tones it carried, like top notes of a famous perfume. "Aren't you going to invite me in?" said the voice, and it swept past me and into the house.

I gaped at the stranger in the middle of the kitchen. She wore a tight black linen suit, with a pillbox hat adorned with ostrich feathers, a lace veil dipping artfully over one eye. Her bright hair was cut into a fashionable bob that ended just below her sweeping cheekbones, flushed to an apricot hue. "Don't tell me you don't recognize me," she stated, hands on her hips. A Chanel purse with a gold chain-link strap swayed from her wrist.

I peered at her deftly, like she was script on a page too far away to read. And then it hit me. I threw back my head and began to laugh, not a happy laugh nor a sad laugh, but a laugh of pure irony.

She stared at me until I was done, until the last sound left my lips and I straightened to stand facing her, level to level. "Darlo Gallo," I announced. "Get out of my house and go to hell."

DICIANNOVE

"What colorful language!" chided Darlo Gallo with faux-horror. "Did you get my flowers?"

"Out," I growled.

"Such hostility," remarked Darlo cheerfully.

"What can you expect," I muttered, putting my hands roughly on her shoulders and steering her out the door as one would an overflowing garbage pail, "after the way you treated me?"

Darlo stood on the doorstep, hands on her hips, eyeing me quizzically. "What on earth are you talking about?"

"Oh, I don't know," I snapped. "How about 'lady boy' and 'freak'? Tripping me in the halls and slapping me around? I recall on one such occasion, you even bit me."

Darlo's face quickly turned bright red, and I was satisfied to see her blush. But after a few moments, I realized it was not a chastised blush at all, and when her face grew scarlet from holding her composure, she burst out laughing. "Oh *that*!" she cried, "oh, Gabriel, you're not still holding a grudge about silly childhood stuff, are you?" And with that, she patted me on the forearm, sailed past me, and made her way back inside the house.

"I certainly am!" I scolded. "You made my very existence a misery!"

"Children can be so cruel," agreed Darlo amiably.

"You and your band of boys used to single me out every day."

"What a long memory you have! Delightful!"

"Because of you, I had no friends!"

Darlo's smile faded and she peered at me under elegantly tapered brows, quite seriously. "I do apologize for that," she said, and with a start I realized she was sincere. "When we started school, I remember telling everyone to ignore you. That they would feel my wrath if they befriended you. I guess they took me seriously."

"What kind of psychopath does something like that?" I demanded.

"You idiot!" exclaimed Darlo and began to laugh, revealing a dazzling row of blindingly white teeth. "I was in love with you!"

I was horrified. "*What?*"

"Yes, that's right. I wanted you all to myself! I *simply* couldn't abide anyone else messing about with Gabriel Laurentis!" She giggled at the memory, pulling one manicured hand up to her lips. "Oh, the tactics of the young! Amusing, isn't it?"

"*What?*" is all I could repeat. I could hardly believe my ears.

"But I'm sure you're far too much of a man now to let silly childhood games get in the way of common courtesy."

"Is that why you're here?" I demanded irritably, "What's the idea, are you trying to sweep me off my feet or something?"

But Darlo Gallo threw her head back and roared with laughter, a very unladylike gesture, I thought. "Oh, darling, you're priceless!" she said, holding up her left hand, where a set of wedding rings, including a diamond the size of a skimming stone, winked at me. "And despite my marital state," she continued, perusing me from head to foot, "what a God-awful mess you turned out to be!"

"I'll have you know," I bawled, "that in Rome I had eighty-seven—"

"Yes, yes!" dismissed Darlo, waving her hand in front of my face. And then the idiot started blathering on about how thrilled she was that I recognized her immediately, the trouble the Orvietani had with that these days. How much she had changed, and how they remembered her as the face of a prominent Parisian milliner in stucco-pink print advertisements, rather than her father's daughter. I gagged at the thought. I grimaced and wondered how far the company sales had plummeted since hiring that *thing*.

"Would you stop?" I moaned, "you are giving me a headache. I don't know how to get this through your thick skull, but I am not interested in your—"

"Gabriel Laurentis!" came my father's shocked voice from the back door. "Is that how you were taught to address young ladies? Your mother would be ashamed!" He walked past me glaring, taking in my lack of shirt and dirty pants, my general disheveled appearance, shaking his head with disbelief.

He peeled his cap of his head and bowed his head in apology. "Forgive my son, Signorina, he hasn't been the same since…well, I never!" he exclaimed, peering at the intruder with great interest. "Is that you, Signorina Gallo?"

"Why, yes it is, Signore Laurentis. You haven't changed a bit, not a day older, I do declare!"

"Let me look at you!" cried my father as I stared at him, my jaw hanging to the ground as Darlo took an animated twirl. "You're a vision!" he stated. "I recognized you immediately from all those hat advertisements, Signorina Gallo!"

"It's Signora Guiliani now," chided Darlo gently.

"Oh dear, I had quite forgotten," said my father. "You married that famous actor! A Florentine, no less!"

"Radio personality turned politician, but who's really paying attention to all that dreary business?" laughed Darlo.

"Well, congratulations! And I was so sorry to hear about your father," said Papa.

"Oh no, you weren't," laughed Darlo, slapping my father lightly on the shoulder, "nobody but me misses that old bully."

"We have such few visitors these days, especially ones so young and beautiful," stated my father. "Sit, sit, let me make you some coffee."

"How delightful!" exclaimed Darlo.

"Gabriel, sit down with the young lady! And be polite."

But I glared at him and in response, stomped out the front door, slamming it behind me.

"Oh, dear!" I heard Darlo chiming merrily through the open kitchen window, "we have upset him, haven't we, Signore Laurentis?"

And they both laughed.

She found me late that afternoon, roaming moodily in the woods, head down and hands thrust deeply in my pockets. Her presence in Orvieto shook me inexplicably, and I desperately wanted not to care, the way I no longer cared about Mariko or Everard Fane, or anyone else I used to know. Volatile, my dream life, had taken over my consciousness and I lived for the night.

The first time Volatile and I made love in the white world was an experience unlike anything I had before. All of that hazed, messy fooling about, the simple mathematics of it all, how many times does X enter Y to achieve the desired result? did not exist with her. It was a science. A combustion of chemistry, of experimentation, of trial and error and gradual success. The anatomy of her body was a perplexing field of study, the way her spine curled upwards in the lower back, tapering from the tailbone into a majestic feathered fork that she could wrap around her hips like a belt. Her wings, built from the misshapen arcs of shoulder blades, soared in long, elegant lengths of human bone similar to the tibia and the femur. But despite these differences, she seemed so normal, so homosapien that I would involuntarily shudder when I recalled the words: *how do you know what I really look like?*

She looks like this, I found myself whispering to myself in these moments, she looks exactly like this.

I was beginning to feel the reigns of reality and therefore sanity drift away from me peacefully, like a friend so dear a goodbye isn't always necessary. I lost appetite for most foods, and hence was obliged to buckle my belt two notches backward. My father was beginning to hint at taking me to a doctor, and on top of his workload, he often cooked a sort of meaty stew he knew I once liked to tempt me to eat, a poor attempt of burned onions and an unbalanced medley of herbs. He always forgot the garlic. He always overused the salt.

He grew especially alarmed when I began confusing the two worlds. Upon chiding me for my late mornings and lack of help in the vineyard, I would gaze at him indolently and snap, "Why are you bothering me with this? Get the workmen to do it!"

"What workmen?" he would ask.

"You know, Costar, Bianchi, Lombardi, those guys. And keep an eye on that Polish fellow, Gustav is it? I have a feeling he is filching from our stores."

"Polish fellow?" whispered my father. "Our stores?"

And then it would dawn on me, and I would literally shake the thoughts out of me, nodding my head from side to side severely. "Never mind," I would say and grimace at him. "I must have been dreaming."

And Papa would stare at me for a long time, like I was the ghost of my mother, head bobbing about uncontrollably on still shoulders.

"Your father told me you'd be here," she said, "I parked the car just down the trail," she explained, no doubt referring to the ivory convertible I saw earlier outside our house. "He knows you so well. I would have been completely lost."

"I certainly doubt you had much reason to play in the woods as a child," I said grumpily.

"You're absolutely right," she trilled, smiling at me. "I have no idea where I am! It's wonderful, isn't it, discovering things that were in front of your nose the whole time?"

"Why are you here, Darlo?"

"For my father's funeral, silly."

"I mean, what do you want with me?"

"I want to help you."

"I don't need help, and even if I did, you would be the last person I would call on."

"Because of how I was as a child?"

"Perhaps."

She sighed and threw her hands up in the air. "People change, you know."

"So you're about to try and convince me that you're no longer the spoiled, selfish brat that gets everything she wants?"

And Darlo Gallo laughed. "Absolutely not!" she exclaimed. "I am completely spoiled, and still get everything I want. Although these days, I make sure those who give me what I want are most satisfactorily rewarded."

I was beginning to grow impatient with her presence, the merry lilt of her voice disrupting my dark and somber thoughts.

"You ought to be kinder to your father, you know," she said softly.

"Oh, you've had a nice long talk, I see."

"I don't think your father's had anyone to talk to for a long time, the poor dear. We did have a rather fun time of it. We even drank some of that whiskey you hide under the bed! And he took me out to see the grave of…Tomasso was it? He said so many lovely things about Tomasso."

"Tomasso was our donkey," I stated drily, hoping to shock her with our bad taste and poverty.

"I always wanted a donkey," she replied, not missing a beat. "He must have been wonderful."

"I suppose," I conceded grudgingly, and I felt a sudden sadness creep up on me, and realized for the first time that Tomasso was gone. My mother was gone. "And now your father's gone too."

"Yes," said Darlo, her eyes on the ground. "I know what you are thinking. He was cruel to your family, but I doubt there was a family in town he was kind to. He even forbade my mother from speaking to her brother because he married a Chinese woman…"

"Japanese," I corrected, out of instinct.

"I beg your pardon, Japanese, of course. But he was still my father, so generous to me, and I will miss him in some ways. He left me the estate, did you know that?" she said quietly. "I don't know what to do with it. A winery in ruins."

"I don't want to talk about Alfio Gallo," I said roughly.

Darlo gave me a long look as I hunched down in a squatting position, poking at the ground with a stick. "I suppose you have your reasons," she said evenly.

"I do," I replied darkly.

"It's her, isn't it? That girl."

I looked up sharply. "What do you know?" I snapped. She had my undivided attention now.

"He killed her. That girl. The one with the swallow's wings."

When Darlo registered the expression on my face, her eyes widened and she continued. "I knew it! I knew she was real. I met her once, didn't I, Gabriel? At the children's parade during *Carnevale*."

"You are going to tell me everything you know," I commanded, getting to my feet.

"Oh, how I hated her, as a child. It's strange, you know. I met you both, for the first time, on that same day. We had not been introduced, and I remember seeing you for the first time, playing with my wooden blocks and other toys in the house. I just stared at you for a while, I had never seen hair that shade. You were just like the cherubs Signorelli painted in his frescoes. But soon, I began to feel like I was not alone, and all the hairs at the back of my neck stood on end. And through the window, I saw *her*. A girl on the sill, with spectacular wings and a forked swallow's tail, watching you so intently. And I was so jealous of her that I marched over to you and—"

"And hit me in the face with a doll," I finished bitterly.

"Yes," she whispered. "I did do that, didn't I? I suppose I wanted to see if she really was your guardian angel, if she would fly down and smite me. And I might have forgotten her, but every day outside our classroom was that infernal troupe of swallows that perched in the Jerusalem trees, from first bell to last, therefore she was always in the back of my mind. I dreamed about her from time to time. I pictured her, wings splayed against the back of our domed ceiling, spying on me. Our eyes would meet and I would be overwhelmed by the color of hers: a strange green, I could never quite place it. I saw a chaise lounge in Toulouse that very color, and what do you think? I purchased it immediately. Even the manufacturer did not have a name for that shade. But I am getting sidetracked. In my dreams, she would gaze at me and say, "He's mine, little girl," and I would wake up in tears. And when I saw her at *Carnevale* that day, I recognized her immediately. I'm sorry to say that I was very much aware that I tried to tear her wings. I felt them breaking, you know, the snapping of ligaments in my hands…" Her voice trailed away and she shuddered.

"You were a beast," I said coldly, "a brutal animal."

"I suppose jealousy makes beasts of us all," Darlo conceded, and had the decency to blush. "Before my father shot himself, my mother telegrammed me a few times. 'Papa sick. Stop. Hearing voices. Stop. Am afraid', one said. Another: 'He has killed her. Stop. He can't see her. Stop.' I supposed it was just my mother having her histrionics, as usual. But when she took me to the trophy room, showed me the blood she hadn't yet allowed the servants to clean, and I saw that head, I knew. It was her. He had killed the swallow-girl. And the swallow-girl drove him mad, in revenge."

I was staring at Darlo darkly, my arms crossed in front of my chest. She took a deep gulp and continued. "So I stole the head. I took the plaque right off the wall and I buried it in the woods. I came here today to show you where the grave is, because she at least deserves a resting place, don't you think?"

I was surprised. Did this fashionable thing that modeled hats for a living, in high heels and a fox fur stole, really lug that gold-plated slab out into the middle of the woods and bury it with her own two hands?

"It was with a shovel," said Darlo, as if reading my thoughts, "and my nails will never be the same." I noticed, as she held her hands up to my face, the dark edges of deeply embedded dirt and the torn edges of each manicured nail.

"This is what you are going to do," I said, after a moment's pause. "You are going to tell me exactly where you buried her."

"But if I lead you there—"

"You are going to *tell* me. And then you are going to get in your car and drive away. You will not step foot on my property again. You will go back to Florence, to your husband. And each time you return to Orvieto, you will forget my name, and you will forget hers."

"But I never knew her name," began Darlo.

"It was Volatile, *the fleeting bird*. That is who your father killed."

After she had left and I was assured she was really gone, I ventured deep into the woods, following the directions that Darlo had left for me. Soon enough, I found myself in a picturesque clearing where a mound of recently unearthed dirt lay in the center, a strangely lovely circle of polished river stones surrounding it. I was surprised by what the scene said about my arch-nemesis. Had she really searched these woods, the weight of the stuffed head bearing her down, for the most beautiful place to bury Volatile? Had she brought the memorial stones along with her for this very purpose? It was a belated atonement, somehow. A haunted atonement. Not merely for her father's sin, for her own past violence that she, too, had never forgotten.

Night was falling and I took a step out of the woods and into the clearing. In my hand was a fistful of hastily plucked wildflowers I had gathered along the way, a thoughtless ritual. Abruptly, the sound of rushing wind filled my ears, and I deftly moved back, returning to the dark cover of the forest. A monstrous shadow appeared at the grave, leaning over it and froze, like it was waiting for something. A powerful white arm, lined with blue veins like a slab of church marble, extended slowly from the silhouette, a mass of feathers, grotesque black wings.

I gasped aloud. The dark one's head whipped around in my direction and I saw a glint in his unearthly eyes.

I ran.

VENTI

Darlo Gallo, or should I say Signora Guiliani, came right back to the house two days later, bearing gifts of smoked ham, tinned peeled tomatoes and syrupy peaches, boxed *pannetone*, jars of maraschino cherries and dense Christmas cakes spiced with raisins and cinnamon. "It's going to be a long winter," she said to my father, "and I thought I'd bring you a few treats."

"You darling girl," exclaimed my father, and I heard the sound of his kisses on both cheeks, smacks of sheer gratefulness. "You didn't have to."

"You sweet old thing," said Darlo. "I can't imagine going back to Florence knowing the two of you are all alone without a woman to care for you."

"It's too kind," said Papa.

"Now then, Signore Laurentis, wait 'til you hear this! I have a boy we no longer need, after what happened to the estate. He's well trained and a hard worker, and I couldn't bear to put him out of a job."

"But Miss," protested my father, "I could not afford to—"

"He works for me, Signore," pressed Darlo firmly, "and he will begin Monday morning at six a.m."

"I simply could not accept such a generous gift," stated Papa.

"What rot!" exclaimed Darlo. "What stuff and nonsense!"

"But I—"

"I'm afraid it's already been settled, Signore Laurentis, and I am sure you would not want to deny this poor boy an honest job. No, I am afraid it is a done deal. And look what else I've brought," she whispered, drawing two bottles of *limoncello* out of her shoulder bag.

My father did not speak, so overwhelmed with emotion.

"Merry Christmas, Signore Laurentis," said Darlo.

"Merry Christmas, darling," said Papa, and his voice was muffled, as if he was choking up.

"Say goodbye to Gabriel for me," said Darlo in a loud and pointed voice directed right at my bedroom door, as if she knew that I were eavesdropping just beyond it, "and remind him that I am not far away, if he should need me."

"Has she gone now?" asked Volatile that night.

"Yes," I replied, her shins tangled around my own. I lay in perfect peace, my belly full of the rich delights that Mamma had prepared. I had just woken in the white world, and I was telling Volatile a dream I had, a dream where I lived on a tiny farm, and Darlo Gallo was there offering canned goods and cakes and labor while I hid behind my bedroom door. My Papa looked so old in the dream, so different from how he looked here.

But I shook my head and remembered. It wasn't a dream. *This* was the dream and I was getting confused again. The confusion was normal, occurring more often than not.

"Have you decided," pressed Volatile, "if you are here to stay?" She seemed unaware of my confusion.

"Must I right now?"

"You must make up your mind. If you don't want to live here with me, then I must leave."

"But why?"

"Because I cannot be in two places at once," she said huffily, as if it were the most natural thing on earth. But there was something more pressing on my mind.

"Why am I unchanged?" I asked her, switching subjects.

"Unchanged?"

"Everyone else is changing. Orlando Khan has become so mysterious and wise, so driven. He left me because he outgrew me, didn't he?"

I didn't say it aloud, but I couldn't stop thinking how even Darlo Gallo evolved from a horrid little witch to a considerate, self-possessed woman that my Papa had fallen head over heels for. Everyone I knew was transforming before my eyes. But I remained the same. I began to suspect that despite my adult appearance, I was merely a frightened little boy, holding onto the fears and grudges of the past like they were underpants with a rocket ship print. A child who longed for the night, to live in a dreamland.

"I'm just the same," I muttered.

"Let me protect you," soothed Volatile, "in this unchanging world. Isn't it beautiful, Gabriel? Isn't it everything you ever wanted? You don't need to adapt here, because everything remains the same."

I believed her. I wanted to give up. And I would have retreated completely into Volatile's world, if it were not for a irritating little thought at the back of my mind: I would not break in front of Darlo Gallo. I would show her.

I closed my eyes and breathed the aviary scent of this world Volatile had created for me. Settling into her lap, my eyelids felt like dried old leaves as they fluttered open. "I'm so tired, Volatile," I said. "I can't go on any longer."

The winter passed. Papa seemed more rested and nourished than usual, with the help of the boy that Signora Guiliani had procured for us. He spent his evenings writing long letters that he later mailed to Florence, walking all the way into town to post them, as we had yet to find the money to replace Tomasso. I knew he was corresponding with Darlo, and when he was out in the fields, I would fish about in his nightstand drawer for her replies. But once

GABRIEL AND THE SWALLOWS

I held the creamy stationery in my hands, I would lose interest and replace them in their neat, date-ordered bundle.

We would sometimes eat at the table together, Papa, the teenage boy and myself. I would watch in a mildly horrified stasis as the boy heaped helping after helping on his plate, examine the food slipping down his wet, pink throat while I toyed with my pig's knuckle and boiled peas. He would steal glances at me beneath his black eyelashes and I would stick my tongue out at him or silently heckle him on occasion. Then I would hug myself from the cold that pierced me deeper than ever before, and feel the ribs that jutted out of my skin. I knew I had to eat but had no appetite for this flavorless fare, a poor man's dinner. There was always a feast waiting in the white world. All I had taste for was liquor, and lots of it.

A man in a grey suit and a monocle appeared at the house one day and made me sit with him in the kitchen. He had a lined notepad and a silver fountain pen, and asked me a series of questions while holding up white cards splayed with strange, black, moving inkblots. He left soon after, and I watched him talk with my father, yet did not strain my ears to eavesdrop, because I simply didn't care. My father covered his face with both hands as the man drove away.

My hair grew to my shoulders and my beard with it, and I spent the days holding my mother's dressing robe around my naked limbs, perched up near the window, watching the grey snow drift down to earth, the faint outlines of Papa and the boy moving in a rigid dance.

Darlo Giuliani reappeared with the spring, racing down the road in her convertible, auburn hair flying from a headscarf, and a brilliant smile on her lips.

"It's a gorgeous day," she said after greeting my father with a flurry of packages and embraces, "won't you come with me for some gelato?"

I stared at her in horror when I realized she was addressing me, and not my father.

"Shan't," I said rudely, and turned my back on her.

"Gabriel Laurentis," commanded my father sternly, "you are going to get dressed and accompany this young lady into town for gelato."

"But I don't like gelato," I moaned childishly.

"Yes, you do," he said firmly. "He does," he confirmed to Darlo.

And so, dressed in pants that swam on me and a shirt that the boy had washed, and badly too since he had taken over the laundry chores, I sat in the front seat of the convertible, pressed up against the door to get as far away from Darlo as possible. I felt assaulted by the fresh air as she sped the vehicle through the narrow streets and under the old stone canopies, their protective gargoyles shaking their heads at me as we passed. She whizzed through Orvieto town, without a care for potholes or the state of her poor tires, honking her horn at the tourists that gathered to photograph Il Duomo, sending them scattering and cursing in English. I had whiplash as she suddenly braked, stopping the car in front of an unimposing, candy-colored ice cream store on Corso Cavour.

"Out!" she said, slamming the car door behind her. I had no choice but to follow her. I moved slower than I supposed, and everything about Orvieto hurt my eyes. People moved so fast, like lightening. They spoke with an animation I hadn't seen in months. The sound of their laughter was like warm, salted bathwater over old scabs that the owner can't stop picking. They did not seem to notice me as they clung to each other's arms, striding with purpose, praises on their lips, curses too. What did they live for? Why were they here? It felt like my first time in Orvieto. Had I ever really been here before? I glanced down the road. There was Montanucci's, my favorite bakery with its sticky *torrone* I loved as a child, the venue where I first laid eyes on Mariko Marino. Mariko. What did her face look like again?

A little bell chimed as I pushed open the door of the *gelateria*. Darlo was standing at the glass counter where a rainbow of flavors met my eyes, jabbering away with a serving woman in a comical pink hat. I sat down weakly and a paper cup overflowing with green, pink and white spheres was pushed in front of my nose. "Eat," she said, and dove into her chocolate cone, keeping her narrowed eyes on me.

I was so unnerved I did as she commanded. An explosion of taste made my eyes water. "That lemon is quite sour, isn't it?" sympathized Darlo.

"I thought," I said, once I came to myself, "that I told you never to return to my house again."

"And I thought," replied Darlo smoothly, "that you knew I wasn't the type to take orders from a man."

When I didn't reply, she directed my gaze outside of the window. "I like to come here to watch the tourists," she said, referring to a loud group rollicking up the cobbled street. "The Americans always wear the strangest clothes. Things that don't really fit them, and the most obnoxious colors. The British, they are on either end of the spectrum. Too formal, or too sloppy, but almost always inappropriate."

"Do you come here a lot, then?" I muttered.

"When I am in town," she responded.

"What does your husband think," I began, "of you coming back here? Doesn't he want you in Florence?"

But Darlo began studying the grains in the wooden table intently, a jaded expression passing her face. "My husband certainly wants a woman by his side, several, if he can manage it," she replied softly, "and does not permit me to comment or complain." She looked up at me, her eyes bright with tears. The first sign of weakness I had ever seen in Darlo Gallo inexplicably moved me. The child in me wanted to throw my ice cream in the air and dance a victorious jig around the table, laughing at her misfortune. But I couldn't move. I could not even find the tiniest sliver of joy in this revelation. Instead I felt sad, sorry that this Florentine did not want Darlo anymore.

"Oh, just look at me," she said, producing a linen handkerchief and dabbing her eyes daintily, "you'd think the world was coming to an end." She sniffed loudly and smiled brightly at me. "What my husband just realized is that I am, unapologetically, a one-man woman. And I expect equal treatment. We're getting divorced," she announced.

"What will you do now?"

The whiteness of her teeth were blinding, and suddenly, I could see that face encouraging women to buy the hats all around Europe. I had finally seen the print advertisements, clipped from the newspapers and placed proudly next to her letters in Papa's beside table. "I think I will restore my father's estate," she said softly.

"You're going to stay in Orvieto?"

"Does that meet with your approval?" she asked mockingly.

"I don't care." I shrugged and was shocked to see the empty paper cup on the table, milky pink pools staining the bottom.

"Do you hear that?" she asked suddenly, and her shoulders began moving up and down. I stared at her, bewildered.

"Just listen!" she said. And a joyous, melodious clash of high voices met my ears. I had never heard anything like it. "They're called ABBA!" she said, singing a few bars of an upbeat tune.

If I had to do the same again, I would my friend, Fernando.

"I saw them in concert in Madrid last year," she shared.

They were shining there for you and me, for liberty, Fernando.

We sat there, listening to the entire song blasting out of the radio, both enraptured. I watched as Darlo closed her eyes and mouthed the words, as if she had forgotten her husband, her divorce and all her troubles. As if, in the entire world, she only cared about Fernando.

"Why have I never heard of them before?" I wondered.

"Because you never leave that dreary room," she said and winked. "Stick with me, kid, and I'll show you a thing or two."

"Darlo," I said urgently, as the radio announcers squabbled. She sat up straighter at the use of her name, spine like a new knife. "I'm hungry," I realized with some astonishment.

And an enormous smile spread across her face, and that was the moment it occurred to me: that someone who wasn't Volatile, wasn't a heavenly creature of spirit and fire, could be so enchanting. How someone I hated for so long could reverse everything. That despite myself, a stubborn affection for Darlo Gallo was growing within me. Life; the ultimate backstabber, the scheming court jester.

"Then," stated Darlo, "we are going out for spaghetti with clams, and wild boar steaks with mounds of potatoes!" And she seized my arm, throwing a bundle of lire on the table.

Later that night, stuffed to the brim with fine Umbrian fare and chilled golden chardonnay, Darlo and I strolled down Corso Cavour. All of the street lanterns had been turned on, their flame dimmed by glass casing covering the streets, oily and slick from a light downpour, in soft honeyed light. Orvietani children, called by their mothers on balconies overflowing with bougainvillea and piano music, hurried up the stone steps to bed. Gentrified couples made their way to the Teatro for the night's performance, tourists adjusted the lenses on their cameras to adapt to the dark, and young people snuck away to the tiny bars of the alleyways, to smoke and drink in secret. It struck me that I was one of those young people. I had, for so long, felt ancient, as ancient as the bones of this town. "Come on," I said to Darlo, "let's go and smoke cigarettes."

She laughed and we soon found ourselves parked on a ridge near St Patrizio's well, smoking Camel cigarettes and drinking Irish cream out of a brown paper bag. She turned the car radio on, and we listened to ABBA, Aerosmith and a scandalous new band called The Rolling Stones.

"What are you humming?" asked Volatile.

"A song," I replied, "called *Fernando*."

"Stop," she said, "I don't like it."

"But Volatile," I said, "don't you like ABBA?"

"What?"

"ABBA."

"No, I don't like it. Please stop."

I steadily regained weight, and when I began waking at a decent hour to help my father prepare for harvest, he gave me a hint of a smile but said nothing. I was more alert than the previous year, and began to find a strange satisfaction at the end of a day's work, as simple and meager as it was. And every Thursday evening, Darlo appeared in her convertible to take me out for dinner. She always invited Papa, who politely declined on every occasion. "All that rich food," he would complain. "I'm happy with my bread and onion, and a little peace and quiet."

At Darlo's insistence, and also because I would never get used to the stares, I consented when she pushed me into a barbershop, who promptly shaved my beard and cut all my hair off.

"Much better," said Darlo when I emerged from the shop, nodding with approval.

We ate pizza topped with zucchini and generous, thick shavings of wild truffle. At nine o'clock, the lights went down in the pizzeria and a disco ball descended, patrons rushing to sign up for the night's karaoke list. "Dance with me," yelled Darlo amidst the chaos, and we joined a group of clumsy, careening Orvietani on a floor peppered with shivering lights, shouting lyrics to the popular songs at the top of their lungs. A group of tourists danced among us, distinguishable by their hemp belts, sideburns, and trousers with hems so wide they reminded me of a bride's train. They shouted lots of foreign words aloud, especially "Groovy". Darlo laughed and tested this word with her own tongue. "What did I tell you?" she shouted in my ear. "They have horrible taste in clothes!" I surprised myself with how many songs I recognized, how many words I knew. I forgot my awkwardness and my sorrow. I forgot my past and my dreams too.

I was pleasantly inebriated when Darlo dropped me back at home, and I leaned against the door of her convertible, laughing at something only the drunk could understand.

"What is it?" she demanded playfully.

"You're so stylish," I muttered, twirling a finger in the air. "Darlo's so fashionable."

"So?" she laughed, smoothing down a yellow silk skirt.

"You're a fashion model," I said, "you're too pretty to be seen with the likes of me."

"But I want to be with you," she said, "and I am only a hat model. They only photograph my face."

"It's your best feature, I think."

"Gabriel?"

"Yes, Volatile?"

"Aren't you hungry?"

"No, I'm stuffed."

"You were late again tonight, Gabriel."

"I'm sorry. I was out."

"With her?"

"Yes, Volatile, with her."

"Do you want to stay with her?"

"No, Volatile, I want to stay with you."

"Are you in love with her?"

"Of course not!"

"Promise me you won't fall in love with her."

"I promise."

Little by little, the pull of the white world weakened. I drank less and hardly ever alone, often pouring a night cap for my father and I after a hard day's work. We began to talk of many things, the future of the vineyard, the progress of the farmhand, memories of Mamma, Darlo Guiliani. Some nights, the helper, whose name was Alfredo but who Papa nicknamed Freddy, joined us. When it became clear to Papa that Freddy was an orphan who lived in town with an aunt that did not want him and sorely neglected him, Papa cleared out Volatile's old closet-room and Freddy became a part of the Laurentis household. I did not mind. Two wine emporiums in Rome and one in Milan had responded to my letters last summer, requesting bottles of *Orvieto Dolce Fantasia* to be sent to them for sampling. Such written requests also arrived from Florence, a city I had not inquired with in the first place.

"I think it's about time," said Darlo one night at a caffe, moving a glass of red wine out of her eye-line, "that you tell me everything." Summer had come and gone, and still the swallows had not returned.

I readjusted my chair and leaned forward, and for the first time in my life, told a human being the inmost secrets of my soul.

To her credit, Darlo did not ask questions or comment on my tale. It was only weeks later, as winter once more approached, that I asked her for her opinion.

"I think," she began after hesitating a moment, "that you know what you must do."

"And what is that?"

"She's dead, Gabriel. And she won't come back, no matter how much you love her."

"You think I love her?"

"Oh," she said, "very much so. But you won't admit it to a soul, not even yourself. It's your deepest, longest secret, and you will carry it to your grave."

"Why can't I live in both worlds?"

"I doubt any man can bear that burden. One reality here, one over there! I mean, just look at you, darling. You were absolutely bonkers last spring, and such a fright! Trust me, I'm quite an expert, you know. I would entertain stark raving mad politicians in Florence every weekend, one foot in this policy, one in the other! They would attend my dinner parties and eat all my imported goose liver, acting quite deranged, I simply couldn't make heads or tails of what they were saying at all! No, I'm afraid you must choose one or the other."

"But I will lose her. This is the last link I have to her."

"Nothing lasts forever. At one point in life, we will always have to say goodbye to everyone we have ever known."

"But how will I stop her from coming into my dreams?"

"You must take control over your own consciousness. You must be strong, and no matter how much you miss her, you can't return to that world where she is waiting for you. It's your mind, Gabriel. Only you can control it, no matter how magical she may be."

"Sounds like Alcoholic's Anonymous."

"You're a dream-aholic," she said with a laugh.

"I'll think about it," I said. "But Darlo," I said in afterthought, "will she let me go?"

"If she loves you like you say she does, she will."

"And do you think I have the strength to go through with this?" I questioned.

"I've always perceived you, Gabriel Laurentis, as someone who has the ability to do precisely as he wants."

I knew she was right. I had to choose. But a choice between a life full of disappointment or a life I loved, based on a simple perception of reality, did not seem like a fair choice at all. But I knew the truth: as real as the white world seemed, it was manufactured. And if other human beings did not have a supernatural creature protecting them, building them sanctuaries and their own private caves, yet still managed happiness, then why couldn't I? *When we die, we do not live on*, Orlando had said. What was his meaning, that Volatile was dead? It had to be. Even if her spirit and the memory of the Orvieto she had created remained, she was slain, extinct. Had I not seen her grave, the earth that cradled her remains?

I let the weeks go by, like a coward, after the decision had been made. I held Volatile in my arms and made love to her. I ate my mother's food and praised it. I played chess with Papa, who hadn't a single grey hair. She and I walked arm in arm, lost in the maze of the enormous Laurentis vineyard. It was always summer, and the swallows stared down upon us watchfully like guardian angels, humming a strange vibration. They seemed to sense what I was about to do. They appeared poised and ready for flight, to migrate to warmer climates.

I drudged through that final day. I drank espresso after espresso, willing myself not to fall asleep. "Are you feeling unwell, Gabriel?" asked my father as I sat, head resting on the kitchen table, unblinking eyes staring at my shoes. He ruffled my hair affectionately as he passed by, with a book and a nightcap. "It will be all right, son," he murmured, and shut his door. Freddy, taking his cue, leapt up from the table and sealed himself inside his room.

It was very, very late when I entered the white world, and I found Volatile asleep, curled in my sheets. I approached her timidly, making my footfall as light as possible. Softly, I sat down next to her as a weak red sun rested upon her face. She was curled up; knees tucked under her chin, just like a child. I stroked the lengths of her hair, so long it reached her waist. It curled on the ends. I hadn't noticed that before. Emotions never before experienced welled up within me, like an ocean's savage waves.

Something salty trickled down the left side of my face, but I brushed it away violently and steered myself. "Volatile," I whispered urgently, although it broke my heart to watch her eyelids flutter, to see her stir and sit up straight.

She said my name groggily.

"I have to go, Volatile," I said, forcing my voice to sound as steady as possible.

"Where are you going?" she asked, but she already knew.

I reached for her hand and I held it for a long time. The red sun rose and fell again into the horizon. The swallows were eerily silent.

"Thank you for everything you have done for me," I whispered when it was time, raising her fist to my mouth. It seemed like our hands were fused together. I felt an age of clamminess between our palms and I did not want to disengage. "Without you, we would be ruined. Without your sacrifice, I would be nothing. Without you, I would have been friendless, alone, all of my life. You saved me, Volatile. Every good thing I have in my life came from you. You were the first person, I believe, who truly loved me."

"I was," she said slowly. "But you don't love me, do you, Gabriel? Not really. That is why you're leaving me." She looked down at our entwined hands. "I suppose they were right," she muttered in disbelief. "They were right all along."

"Volatile…"

"It's going to be dawn soon, and you will have to wake up."

"I will never forget you," I said, and a very peculiar thing happened. The humming began again, and grew loud and uncanny, raucous and bizarre. My ears seemed like they would soon split open from the murderous noise, and I covered them with my hands. I watched, dumbfounded, as Volatile walked to the center of the room, the nucleus of the white world, her wings suddenly unfurling and stretching to their full, monstrous capacity. She stared at the sky and held her arms straight out over her head, two undeviating lines. Suddenly, the dreamland began to break apart. The grey walls started to crack and splinter into a hundred pieces, hunks of the roof shattered and rained down in thick, vicious shards. I made to shield my head, but realized I didn't need to. The debris avoided me completely. Through the open space where a wall once was, I watched Il Duomo split apart, brick by brick. The labyrinths of Orvieto unraveled and slithered like snakes, before disintegrating into useless grey fragments. My Mamma and Papa, our workmen too, all glided past me, their faces frozen and their eyes lusterless, like marbles. They bent and swayed with the current, like paper dolls. Sweet Vittoria naked, separated from her fur.

And Volatile, her arms and wings stretched out like an angel of death, was like a violent vortex, and all the matter and molecules of the white world whirled around her amidst that deafening shriek, until she swallowed all of Orvieto whole.

All that remained, in my dream, was she and I facing each other, suspended in nothingness.

"Don't go," she said, and her expression was that of a child whose trust had been broken for the very first time, hands held palm-upward toward me, an act of humility.

And then I woke up.

VENTUNO

Carlo Gallo had that enviable talent of making friends effortlessly with a wide range of personalities. I would watch her at parties, clinking glasses with old Orvietani patriarchs, gossiping merrily with other young women, laughingly waving away scores of well-dressed men with romance on their minds. Her divorce had finally come through and she now wore her wedding rings on a long gold chain dangling around her neck. "Because a diamond this size deserves to be shown off on a daily basis," she would explain, and drop a fresh strawberry into her champagne. No matter who would engage her in conversation during a gathering, she would refuse to neglect me, returning to me often and linking her arm through my own, leading me around and introducing me to people like a long-lost brother.

She developed her own reputation amongst the Orvietani, away from the shadowy public opinion of her father. She was a style icon, they decided, with immeasurably good taste, despite a French education. She was trustworthy, they said, not flighty like other girls her age. And even though she was once married to that scandalously sleazy politician -- an alcoholic and a womanizer, if the tabloids were to be believed -- she was the height of worthy opinion when it came to food and entertainment, a cuisine and wine connoisseur.

At the mayor's dinner, an affair highest on the scale of importance on the Orvietani social calendar, Darlo Gallo had praised her way through twelve courses, to the delight of the infamously particular chef. However, after the gateaux and cheese platters had been served, and the guests were presented with a Tuscan dessert wine the color of cherries, all eyes were on the illustrious Ms. Gallo as she took one sip and declared, "Take this away at once. I only drink *Laurentis Dolce Fantasia* after a perfect meal."

After this famous event, every restaurant, bar, caffé and *trattoria* in Orvieto and the entire Umbrian region stocked our wine, and the people, inspired by Darlo Gallo's declaration, followed suit, ordering *Dolce Fantasia* after every dining experience. Within the year, our entire cellar stock, going back some sixty years, was sold. I was soon obliged to develop a waitlist for emporiums and cellars throughout Italy and France, and Papa had no choice but to hire extra hands to speed up production. What was it that the school children used to say about Darlo Gallo? That she owned Orvieto? Those who don't heed the words of children are fools indeed.

When it became clear that we needed more land, Darlo shrugged and offered her own. And so a partnership was formed, and Laurentis wine took over the Gallo estate. On the day that the contract was signed, as an omen of good faith, Darlo appeared at the farmhouse with a bottle of *Gallo Premium Trebbiano* in one hand and a young donkey on a lead in the other. "His name is Tomasso *Duo*," she stated heartily, "and he's all yours, Celso!" She was now on a first-name basis with my father.

People began to question my relationship with Darlo. Whenever Papa saw us together, his eyes would alight with pleasure. Young, rich Orvietani men would clap my back with envy, and our names became entwined on their tongues: Gabriel-and-Darlo. Darlo-and-Gabriel. It was assumed that we were an item, we were so frequently together. Those that knew us intimately, and I did develop a little clique of my own, knew we were nothing more than business partners, although they could not help but speculate.

Sometimes, when I watched her work a room, I could not help but admire her for her intelligence and excellent conversation, covering a wide range of secular and highbrow topics. A shrewd businesswoman, she had retired from the modeling industry, and was often away for lengthy periods promoting *Dolce Fantasia* and a new range of dry white wines we were developing on the Gallo land. I would worry about her when she was gone, and would not go out socializing much in her absence. I grew to fear the inevitable; that someday she would meet a man, marry him, and bring him into this tightly knit partnership we had, ruining everything.

I began to love the outdoors, the smell of manure and ripening grapes, and the cries of birds that would flood the woods at nightfall. I watched them always, an unfurling of wings, a twitch of the tail, and they could all be *her*. I began to sense her presence out there in nature, and saw her shadow accompany every living creature. Yet there had been no swallow sightings in the region, and all the farmers complained of it, perplexed.

Sometimes I would whisper her name to the air, hoping it would carry over deserts, oceans, and oriental lands filled with spices and opulent carpets. When I closed my eyes, I could feel her breath on my face and her hair wrapped around my wrist. But then, I would command myself: enough. If I indulged myself this way, I lectured myself, I would certainly go mad this time. Really insane. Institution-worthy.

It was hardest just before bedtime. I would hold my pillow to my chest and stand at the foot of the bed, staring at the sheets. It was in this bed, in reality and in the white world, that I grew to know her so well, her body, her mind. I remembered when I was a child; she would sit there with me and listen to my woes. And I would glance at this swallow-girl and not realize how limited our time was, the effort I would go to these days to change this. My fists would whiten around the pillow and I would remind myself to breathe. It became my constant companion, the living sadness.

It was difficult at first, learning to shut my mind. To retain my will and consciousness during sleep, and not slip away with abandon. I learned not to dream, and during sleep, I was suspended in nothingness, quite alone. I often sensed the shadow of a door, calling out for me to turn its handle, and I would struggle violently, wanting to push it open and see her one last time. But I was forgetting that she had gone. She would not be waiting for me, that world had been destroyed. How many times can you say goodbye to a person? I kept wanting to do that, to say goodbye. A complete sucker for punishment.

Time passed. Darlo and I began to hold tasting parties for our new wines, resurrecting and recalibrating the old classic reds that her family had successfully produced for generations. We started sponsoring events in Rome, and held an annual ball every spring at *Il Casa di Gallo* around the time of *Carnevale*, reminding our customers of the wealth, glamour and prestige of the ever-expanding Laurentis winery. Old Signora Gallo presented no objection, as she had long ago moved to Naples to be with her sister.

As I wandered through the halls of this mansion, a glass of the ruby elixir I had created in my hand, I was surprised at the effort Darlo had put into remodeling the old place. She had taken down the gilt-framed masterpieces and replaced them with minimalistic modern art, all bare lines and block colors that I couldn't pretend to understand. All the heavy velvet curtains, old world sculpture and ostentatious chandeliers had been donated to charity, to be replaced with practical, slatted bamboo drapes, African death masks and fat, laughing jade Buddhas. She had burned every one of her father's stuffed heads, painted the room pink, and used it as a shoe closet. During such a party, I snuck into the master bedroom and examined the four-poster bed with its elegant scattering of oriental silk cushions. I felt a sharp, unexpected pang of jealousy as I noted the imprint of two bodies on the cotton sheets. Well, why shouldn't she have a lover? I thought as I slammed the door shut behind me, no longer caring if I was discovered, she's a grown woman.

And I made my way to the back courtyard, looking up at the fountain that Darlo decided should stay right where it was. I smiled to myself as I remembered the words of a little renegade I once knew: "These people have no taste". I laughed to myself loudly, startling two elderly people mingling nearby.

It was after one such party, when Darlo was overseeing the cleaning contingent well into the early hours, that I approached her, tuxedo jacket in one hand, keys to my car, a sensible Peugeot, in the other. "Let me walk you out," she said, looping her arm through my own. I remember what she was wearing that night, pearls around her wrists and a short cream dress with a beaded hem that soared up her thighs, a lack of pantyhose revealing the freckles on her knees.

In the driveway, as I sat in my car with the window down, she leaned against the doorframe and said, "Don't you think, darling, that it's time we got married?"

"Married?" I guffawed, waving her suggestion away.

"I do believe I am ready to marry again," she continued, "and you and I, well, we're the greatest of friends. We get along so well together. And we do throw a mean party."

"Well, how about your countless other suitors?" I laughed, "good men, most of them. Rich too, and distinguished. How about that mustachioed fellow that followed you about all evening with his tongue hanging out? You're ruining your chances with a dreary old bachelor like me."

"Why, Gabriel Laurentis," she chided, "you're not yet thirty years old! Dreary old bachelor, indeed."

"Goodnight, sweetheart," I said in response, and plucked at the tip of her nose, a habit I had developed in recent years.

"Do think about it, won't you darling?" she drawled, turning to go back inside. "I'd love to have dear old Celso as a father-in-law."

"And I'm sure that was your prime motivation for asking me, you sly thing, and my own father too! Why don't you marry him instead, he'd have you in a heartbeat!"

Darlo giggled. "I'd rather have the younger model," she said.

"Very well, I will consider your proposal of marriage," I said, mock-formally. She laughed and swatted at me before sashaying away in that mini-dress and high heels, tousling her chin-length hair.

I tossed and turned in bed that night. Marry Darlo Gallo? Could I? I had never considered marriage, never assumed it was for me. I had devoted myself entirely to the business, deviating only to build a small extension to the house, a proper room for Freddy who was now in his early twenties and a damn fine overseer, and a large new shed and cellar. I knew Darlo Gallo was serious, she never joked about this kind of thing. I imagined a life with her: breezy, elegant, and easy. Business trips and luxurious vacations to exotic lands tempted me, as well as the thought of having her in bed again, which was something I fondly fantasized about from time to time.

We had slept together once, two years ago, after signing a contract with one of the biggest hotel chains in Europe. We had gotten wildly drunk, and had run naked through the vineyards on the Gallo estate. She ended up sliding on moss and bruising her knees, and I ended up taking a bath in the courtyard fountain. In the morning, we woke up and I opened my mouth to say something romantic, but she laughed at the moles on my buttocks and went inside to prepare strong coffee, never mentioning the incident again.

This is my wife, I imagined my future self saying. May I present Darlo Laurentis? And she would step forward, the women would gasp at her stylish attire, the men at her beauty. But I did not know, you see. I did not know if I could go through with it, now or ever.

There was something I had to do first.

VENTIDUE

Is this the one? I thought to myself as I knelt at the rock wall. There was trash at my feet, a cola can and a couple of empty crisps packets, numerous stubs of cigarettes. Teenagers, I thought with disgust, lowering my head just under the ridge, a boy-sized hole.

A heavy wave of stench socked me in the face like a well-aimed fist. Stale air, dank green mold, the rotted yolks of a thousand cracked eggs and the unmistakable smell of damp poultry. Easing my right arm through and then my leg, I almost lost my balance as I realized a cobbled stone staircase waited for me, so narrow gnomes might have constructed it, so steep I could surely fall and break my neck. My hand grasped at the stonewall, but it was so chalky with age it slipped. I squeezed my other leg through the hole, and then my hips, thanking God they were so slender. Bending over backwards like a novice contortionist, my head was last to be stuffed into that tiny cavern, and I straightened out as best I could, shuffling timidly down the stairs, hands on each opposing wall for balance.

Yes, I mumbled to myself upon my ginger descent, this was most definitely the place. I was finally able to unlock my spine at the chamber with the water troughs, its high ceiling and the hollow resting places for yesterday's carrier pigeons carved into the opposing wall. I looked down into the trough where I had rediscovered Volatile all those years ago, a naked child. I had run down here to hide from someone who was molesting me in the bathroom – what was his name? Michael. No, Christopher Esposito, that's the one. I hadn't thought of him in an age. But then again, the image of the dark one had scared the living daylights out of me then, no wonder I didn't remember a pimple-faced child-pervert. I steeled myself and gritted my teeth. I was a grown man now. I would not be frightened away.

There were more steps leading away from the cavern. These twisted in a spiral formation, only about a meter wide. The powder on the stonewalls, a mixture of dry mold and bird's dander, brushed against my jeans and collared shirt and flew up my nose. The light from the window in the pigeon's chamber was draining away, and I pulled a battery-operated torch from my pocket. It was growing cold and I wondered where exactly I was, and how far down in the earth. I moved cautiously onwards, flicking my torch from ceiling to floor, the stairwell becoming narrower and its height shortening until I was crouching as I walked. Markings lined the walls of the staircase that reminded me of the caveman era. But I did not have time to examine them.

A rush of air, as hot as a furnace, assailed me and I froze, directing the light to my feet. And just in time too, as I found myself wavering over an enormous opening in the volcanic tuff, and I staggered two steps backwards, landing on my behind.

Instinctively, I switched off the torch. I was breathing heavily, the shock of almost plunging to my death overwhelming. I sat there for some minutes, collecting my wits. And then, attentively budging forward on my knees, I gripped the rim of the opening with both fists. It was solid rock. And with a deep breath, I ducked my head under it and opened my eyes. Nothing. Pitch black.

And then, an orange light. Two orange lights. I blinked, and squinted my eyes. Was I dreaming, or were there now a hundred tiny lights blinking in the darkness? And as my eyes adjusted, I realized the lights were the lanterns of thousand rooms, of a thousand houses carved from the depths of Orvieto, an entire underground city before my eyes. The words of Orlando Khan drifted back to me: *they have their own society, kings and queens and families and clans that live underground with them...*

This was it. This was their spirit world.

I was beginning to think that the use of my torch would aid in illuminating the city better when I was knocked violently off my knees, the torch rolling away from my grasp, disappearing into the opening. I was sprawled on my back, my neck cradled dangerously by the last step of the staircase, my feet dangling perilously over the edge. I felt hot breath on my cheek and heard the bristling of a thousand feathers, sharp as daggers, standing on end.

And through the darkness, my eyes focused upon him. I could see his crucifix-shaped pupils glaring down at me, inches away from my face. And his mouth opened slowly, forming a horrifying red 'O'. Monstrous words began to pour from his mouth, although his lips did not move.

I am the guardian of the gate, he said, and his voice sounded like the creak of a door when you are assured you are all alone. *You shall not enter.*

"I'm sorry," I stammered, inching away from the terror of his unmoving mouth, the scent of old blood and children's tears on his breath.

I let you live once, said the voice. *You have trespassed for the last time.*

"I offer you this in payment," I said, speedily thrusting a hand in my pocket and withdrawing the single black feather I had collected on that day, many years ago.

I care not for your trifles, whispered the creaking old voice, *you shall die.*

"That's not true," I stammered bravely. "I know what this is." I held the feather up to his terrible stare. "This is power. I hold some of your power in my hands."

Give it to me.

"Let me go free."

There are few human beings that can enter the city of spirits and leave unscathed. You are not among them.

"How do you know?"

Foolish human, said the dark one. And with one silver fingernail, more like a deathly talon than any human appendage, he drew a circle over his heart. As his leather clothing fell apart, I could barely make out lines and lines of eerily familiar coiled writing protruding from his bare skin, and with a jerk, I realized they were not quite script, but shapes made from his indigo veins. *I am the guardian of the gate*, he repeated. *And I determine who lives and dies.*

"But if you kill me, she will never forgive you!" I declared. "I saw you with those men, claiming you were from the DOC. I know you were involved in her plans. She did all that for me, for *this* human being. And if you helped her, that means she has power over you. So you will not dare touch me, in fear of her wrath."

She's dead, laughed the voice. *The accord is broken.* But his eye blinked a little too rapidly, and I heard a quavering in his speech.

"Liar!" I stated, and I began to smile from deep within. "She's alive, isn't she? You beings, whatever you are, you can't really die, can you?"

If you do not leave this moment, replied the dark one, *your blood will be my people's wine this night. Fresh warm wine sucked from your every artery, your body deflating like an old wineskin as we pass you from one to another. And we will eat bread made from the marrow of your bones.*

"I am not afraid of you," I lied.

Give me back my power.

"No. I'm going to save it. Maybe it will buy me free entry one day."

But the dark one's head lowered until his face nearly touched mine, and all the light left his eyes. I sensed his enormous presence growing smaller, softer, more compact. Silken hair fell onto my face and shoulders and engulfed me in its familiar scent. His voice changed and when he spoke again, the voice was that of a woman's. It was hers.

"You must never come back here, Gabriel, do you hear me? You must promise me never to come back to this city of death."

And the dark one's face transformed into hers. I blinked twice.

"This is not your path. Your path lies in Orvieto, not under it. You must forget all you have seen here today. Do you promise me?"

And the dark one leaned forward and kissed me on the mouth, a deep kiss full of longing. I didn't care that it was him, because in my mind there was only her, and I wanted that kiss to last forever. So I sunk into it, into her, into him.

"Swear a blood oath," said her voice, "because blood oaths last forever."

And even though I did not know how it was done, I swore it in my soul.

Her eyes looked down at me and with a mighty sound of rushing wings, she was gone. All the lights in the underground city went out.

As I staggered to my feet, I slipped on my own blood, seeping from a wound in my right hand. It looked as if a sharp beak had gored through it, but I had already forgotten how that had occurred.

The feather was gone.

And so was any inclination that I could ever marry Darlo Gallo.

GABRIEL AND THE SWALLOWS

I found Orlando Khan in the public house on Via Sant Angelo that I recalled one of his thirteen uncles owned. He was sitting at the bar, his back bent, his curved nose and olive skin almost exactly as I remembered. He was wearing a light-colored tunic belted at the waist, which was still trim, over tight blue jeans. His hair was short, curls cropped close to his skull, evening shadow on his jaw.

He did not look up as I sat down next to him, and at this short distance, I noticed subtle changes: the grey bags under his eyes, the ash in his complexion, descending lines around the mouth that signified too much recent disappointment. I had seen him, upon occasion, as I careened down the boulevards with Darlo Gallo and friends. He never returned my waves or shouted greetings. He looked right through me, as if I were invisible. I would shrug and say something to my companions about the oddity of foreigners, and they would all laugh. And then terrible guilt would descend upon me, and I remembered all he had done, and how I had loved him once. And Darlo would sense my awkwardness and cover it up by exclaiming, "I don't know, darling. He's still awfully handsome." And much worse, I would imagine Volatile overhearing my pompous, petty comments, her disappointment in me.

"Ah, Laurentis," murmured Orlando, eyes on his glass, "I've been expecting you."

"Have you?" I said, motioning to the bartender.

"I expected you to come sooner with your questions, your incessant questions and unwavering lack of understanding. But then again, you are a big man about town these days." This he said without a trace of mockery or rudeness, as if stating simple fact.

"I didn't think Muslims were allowed to drink," was all I could come up with in response.

"This is *raki*," said Orlando, holding up a glass full of what looked like water. "The men in my family have been drinking it for generations. It was one of the Turkish customs my father couldn't leave behind. Whenever I saw my father drinking this," he continued, taking a small sip, "he would say: *God will forgive me, on this one occasion.* And so now, I say the same to you."

"If you say so," I replied.

"But what God really wants to know," began Orlando, turning to face me, "is why you have tied your fate to a woman you hated for years on end."

"She's different, Orlando. She's changed."

"Tigers cannot change their stripes," he stated drily, drinking from another glass that had appeared before him.

And I laughed then, remembering my dreams before they became the white world. How Orlando was always depicted in them – an alien young boy with tiger's claws for hands. "Are you sure about that?" I chuckled.

"What is it you want from me?" he asked directly.

"I want to know if she is really dead," I responded.

"What do you think?"

"Don't play games with me, Orlando."

"Just answer the question: do you believe she's dead?"

"I thought I did. I mean, you told me she was."

"I never said such a thing."

"*When we die, we do not live on*," I quoted. "Wasn't that your last piece of advice to me?"

"It was," he concurred, "but you mistook my meaning. No, that advice was about you, not about her. I know what your life has been like after she was shot. I heard the rumors, saw the evidence."

"What evidence?"

"You were wasting away in a half-life, unsurprising to all who really knew you, because your character has never been strong. You will always need a protector. First it was me, and then it was her, and now it is this woman you claim has changed. They will always shield you from the real world, from making your own decisions. Don't you ever wonder what your life would have been like if the ifrit had never chosen you?"

"I've never thought about it," I responded truthfully.

"You being involved in *all this*," he held his hands up and stretched them wide, "it's all kinds of wrong. It's like you've always been the anti-hero in a story that was never about you to begin with. Oh, you have the looks of a hero -- the height, the build, the face. Some might even say you have the *air* of a storybook hero, if they didn't know you at all."

"And who's the real hero then, you?" I scoffed, inhaling the strong scent of the whiskey the bartender had set before me.

Orlando didn't respond. He didn't have to.

"I knew that she would come for you in the night, she loved you to the point of obsession," he continued after some moments. "I knew she was capable of it the minute she announced she was going to Rome, how she spied and stole and plotted to bed you that night. I knew she would manipulate your mind, because that is what they do. They are master tricksters, don't you remember me warning you? They assume the shape and nature of animals within our world, a single disguise of their choice that lasts their entire existence. Do you think anything *good* could ever rise from the blood of a murder victim? And instead of becoming your own man through the pain and the sorrow of loss, there you were, escaping back into your own mind, returning to your protector. *When we die, we do not live on.* We. Not they. There is no life after death for us, do you hear me, Laurentis? We have just one life so painfully short, granted to us by Allah, and we must live it no matter the cost, what it takes away from us. I think it is time, my friend, for you to protect someone else now, in repayment for all that has been done for you, and all the world's wrongs you have been sheltered from. Now what are your other questions?"

"I think," I said slowly, taking a sip of the whiskey placed before me, "that I have no further questions."

"No more?"

"Well, maybe just one. You outgrew me, didn't you? That is why you left me."

And this was the gentle response of my first friend: "Of course I outgrew you. You are a simple man, Laurentis, made for a simple life. You were never meant to contemplate other worlds or see the things you have seen. Do not complicate it any further. Your path is straight ahead of you. Go and walk upon it, and may Allah bless you and your children."

"Children?" I started, surprised. "You think I will have children?"

"Oh yes," answered Orlando, smiling a little. "You will have many."

"Will I ever forget her?" I asked then, filled with sadness.

"No," he responded. "But you will live like you have forgotten. And you will never forget the honor she bestowed upon you. For a creature like that to love you so completely, it is unheard of in this world and in theirs."

"Was there a price," I hesitated, "for loving me?"

"Trust me on this, Laurentis. You do not want to know." Orlando leaned over the pressed his forehead to mine, and I did not understand then why he did so. "God be with you, my old friend," he breathed.

It was not long after that I heard the news: Orlando Khan had disappeared from Orvieto, leaving not a trace. His sister Imelda Khan, the famed beauty, had vanished alongside him. After an extensive search conducted by his family, they were presumed dead. Their bodies were never recovered.

It was late that night as I sped the Peugeot up the driveway of *Il Casa di Gallo*. I left the keys in the ignition and didn't bother closing the door behind me.

Enough, I told myself as I hurried past the fountain and its water dark and peppery, like stardust. Enough of being the secondary character in someone else's story. It's time for change.

The front doors were unlocked and I pushed them open, feeling the heavy oak swaying under my strength.

She looked up in surprise from where she knelt in front of a suitcase in the bedroom, burrowing through color-coded piles of neatly folded clothing. "What are you doing here, darling?" she asked, getting to her feet and smoothing out her satin kimono.

"Where are you going?" I demanded.

"I told you already, you silly man. I'm off to Rome in the morning."

"Do you love me, Darlo?" I stammered abruptly.

Her mouth hung open with surprise. "Well, of course I love you, you dear fool. Why ever else would I hang about, unmarried, all this time?"

And I got down on one knee, like all the leading men in Americano movies with their side-parts and square jaws, and reached for her hand. "Darlo Gallo," I said. "I haven't an ounce of jewelry on me at present, but I promise you a diamond double the size of your fist if you just say yes. Will you marry me?"

She had tears in her eyes, quickly brushing them away with her newly polished nails, a lacquered apricot. "Oh, darling," she cried, "does it even matter that I asked you first?" She reached for me and held me close, and I felt her heart beating near my own, and it was no dream. But what was that long-forgotten feeling rising within me?

Happiness.

It was happiness.

FINE

On the morning of my wedding, I awoke alone in my bed on the farm. We had agreed to sleep separately the week before the ceremony, and I missed Darlo terribly at nights. I threw on my dressing robe and hurried to the kitchen, where my father's newspaper had already been leafed through and discarded on the bench. No doubt he had been in the vineyard since early light.

I made myself an espresso using the remains of the coffee grounds in my mother's favorite canister. I sighed when I thought of her. How she would have loved to see this day. Her favorite aria from the opera *La Tosca* would be performed later that day in her honor, Darlo had arranged it.

Instead of having the coffee in the kitchen as was customary, I took my cup and the rolled up newspaper to my bedroom. I opened the curtains and slid up the glass plating, feeling the summer warmth on my skin. I settled again on the bed and thought about my auburn-haired bride, our honeymoon on the white beaches of Thailand. "You're going to love it, darling," she shouted, waving travel brochures in the air like banners, "the feel of the ocean on your skin." She had bought us matching pairs of sunglasses, despite my protests, for the occasion.

I slipped a vinyl record on the player I had procured on a business trip, a beloved old record that I had once listened to over and over.

Can you hear the drums, Fernando?

When it was almost time to leave for the church, and I could smell from the hallway my Papa's rarely used aftershave, contained in a glass bottle so yellow with age it must have been at least fifty years old, I opened the box Darlo had left for me.

True to her impeccable taste, there lay encased in tissue a beautiful black suit made from the finest material I had ever touched. It ran through my fingers like a river. I dressed slowly in front of my little mirror, and slicked back my short blonde hair with water from the nightstand. It was still so light colored that it was difficult to notice the strands of white that had begun to creep in. I had shaved the night before, and my face was still smooth and pristine, without a hint of a shadow. I slipped into worn yet comfortable leather shoes that Freddy had kindly polished, placing them outside my door.

When I was done, I sat back down on the bed. It was silent in the room, and I couldn't hear my father hobbling through his preparations anymore. I looked around my chamber for the last time. I felt between my fingers the bed sheets I would never lie in again to dream the dreams I don't dream anymore.

GABRIEL AND THE SWALLOWS

I turned to face the window and saw the farm beyond it, the vineyard that my forefathers had toiled upon stubbornly, refusing to give it up to strangers or bullies. It was in its age of glory now, and I could only be happy my father had lived to see this day.

And then I heard something. It sounded just like the call of the swallows from so long ago, but I had to be mistaken.

Suddenly, a breeze disturbed the branches of the olive tree outside the window, and I crossed over to inspect it. My mouth fell open as I looked up: there in the sky flew a familiar flock of swallows, a gust of wind bearing bodies of silver and sapphire and ivory. I watched in awe as they descended into all their old haunts as if they had never left – the vineyard, the awnings of our roof, the barn. Some perched in the olive tree and I leaned out the window to study them with wonder. I'm not sure what made me say it – nostalgia? But I said it anyway. "Where is Volatile?" I asked them.

Nothing. Just the breeze, the trees, their chatter.

Then: *She's here*, they sang.

And my eyes alighted on something. A swallow. As I peered at the bird, its curving speckled wings, I realized with a jolt that its eyes were not the customary black. They were green, like the bellies of pond-frogs in summer. The swallow's head bobbed about in a funny little nod and it had no shadow.

I began to speak, but my voice sounded strange and frothy, and I knew that I was crying.

And then the swallow turned and she spoke to me, not in a voice I heard with my ears, but in that lovely, familiar speech she had, and I heard it with my heart.

"I've brought my flock back to Orvieto," she said.

I was speechless, as I always am when dumbfounded, when I am full of wonder.

"I've come to tell you that though the swallows stay, I am migrating," she continued.

"But it's only summer," I reasoned.

"You are my winter," she said, and I understood.

"Will you come back after I am gone?"

"Yes," she replied, and the happiness I felt at knowing she would return home, to this farm where she belonged after I had passed on, was the kind of happiness I could never again hope to achieve in this lifetime.

"Goodbye, my love," she said, and after a moment of gazing right inside of me, she spread her wings.

I gripped the windowsill and watched as she flew away, as she left me for the final time, left me safely in the grip of an ancient city atop a volcano, Orvieto bathed in light.

And I whispered then to an easterly wind, the kind created just to carry messages.

I whispered the words she'd always wanted to hear.

COMING IN 2017

Orlando and the Spirits

THE VOLATILE DUOLOGY BOOK 2

Things are not going well for Orlando Khan. After being discovered in an illicit tryst, he's been banished to Istanbul, his clan's hometown. Watched over by his rigid Uncle Ahmed who seems determined to set his nephew back on the righteous path, Orlando's life is soon whittled down to prayers at the mosque and meals in his room, with no one but his sister Imelda – both blessed and cursed with ethereal beauty – for companionship.

When Imelda disappears without a trace, it's up to Orlando to recover her and save the family honour. Already walking a tightrope between reality and the spirit world, Orlando calls upon the ifrit, legendary spirits of fire that he previously encountered as a boy in Italy. But this time, the ifrit demand payment for their services, and Orlando may not be able to afford the price: to abandon all he knows to descend into the world of the spirits.

From the sweat-stained, pulsing clubs of underground Istanbul to the eerie catacombs of Paris, Orlando must risk all he has in this vibrant, cross-cultural reimagining of *Aladdin*. As Orlando discovers the terrible truths buried in the Khan clan's past, he is forced to choose between his honour, his family, and the love of his life.

ACKNOWLEDGEMENTS

Gabriel and the Swallows has been, like Volatile herself, a creature of many faces. After going through numerous title changes, plot redirections, characters being killed off and then resurrected with a sex change, and even the setting transported firmly from a small town in France to an even smaller town in Italy, it was not without a trove of wonderful people that *Gabriel* exists, in this form, today.

I would firstly like to thank my team of editors and beta-readers: you know who you are. To Katie and Conor, whose advice made me cringe at best and wish for death at worst. Thanks for making me creep up on my darlings in the middle of the night and murder them with a pick axe. You've made *Gabriel* so much cleaner and tighter. For Giselle, emergency copyeditor – thank you for picking up on those issues these eyes could no longer see, so used to these sentences I could recite them in my sleep .

For the team at Of Tomes Publishing – ah, where to begin? For Ben, obviously, such an enthusiastic supporter of my debut *Drown*, and an even more ravenous supporter of *Gabriel*: you are the publisher every author dreams of pairing up with. Your love for the written word, your cutting-edge industry knowledge and involvement in the project down to every layer of the cover design: it's been an honor and a dream come true. Never had I thought a relationship between a publisher and author could be boiled down to flagrant excess of emoticons and exclamation points, side-splitting FaceTime conversations and inside jokes.

For Xina, my first reader in the Of Tomes house, thanks your contagious support. Kim and Nadege, designers extraordinaire for the insides and outsides of *Gabriel*, thank you for giving a face to a pile of words, and for making the intangible tangible - because of you an idea I once had, the hours I spent at a computer, can now sit comfortably in the hands of people around the world.

To the fellow authors I've especially connected with in the brief period since my first novel's publication – especially Tegan Wren, for the encouragement and support, Carol Riggs, who lets me rant and complain about things, Anita Howard, for the sage advice, Jen Wilson, for being generally amazing in all the categories of amazingness. Michelle Madow and Danielle Page – author crushes and girl crushes all rolled into one. You inspire me and give me worthy examples to look up to.

To Mark, who gave up the honeymoon idea of a golfing trip around South East Asia, exchanging swimming trunks for thermals, in order to return to Orvieto in the greyest, bitterest winter to complete the second stage of my research. Thank you for counting the steps from Fontana De Leone to Orvieto's summit, for finishing all the dishes I wanted to write about but didn't fancy eating, for trudging through the underground tunnels, holding my purse patiently at the bottom of St Patrizio's well as I took notes. Thank you for cringing through three hours of the worst tango production on earth just so I could get a feel of the Teatro Mancinelli. You're the most supportive best friend in the world. You're the storybook hero everybody wishes for. And you gave me Florence Finch.

Heartfelt thanks to the handful of good friends in my little Berlin community for being so supportive of me as a writer. It's difficult to be far away from home, living this life flittering from country to country, forging friendships at lightning-speed and then uprooting yourself away from it all. Thanks for keeping me sane. Thanks for letting me rant and rave to you about my many, many issues. For Angus, my partner in creativity for over a decade, thank you for forgiving me for that disastrous fish and chips incident at Bronte Beach. Thank you for not outgrowing me, for always making time for me in your glamorous world. And for Jess (whom I imagine to be the epitome of the adult Darlo Gallo), your encouragement has never wavered and you celebrate my successes with utter abandonment, like they were your own. I am deeply grateful for your friendship.

To Jasmina, the wonderful translator-slash-hostess, for showing me around Orvieto, for housing me in your wonderful medieval chambers, for sending interviewees my way and sitting through conversations you've undoubtedly heard over and over, translating for me. I wish I could have used your truffle-hunting dog in this novel, but Sweet Vittoria won that competition. Maybe in the sequel.

For the esteemed Signore Montanucci, of the 100 year old institution Caffe Montanucci itself (yes, it is a real establishment and it's more delightful than I could ever describe) thank you for the hours you spent enthusiastically regaling me with the local history of Orvieto. I have been so strongly inspired by the gossip about its people, the history of even its smallest spaces and the story of your ancestors. You truly gave me inside access to Orvieto's culture and mindset. Gabriel's personality was crafted specifically from the story you shared from your boyhood – when you would creep around the alleys of Orvieto, scared out of your wits in the dark, to deliver the daily bread.

And finally, to the citizens of Orvieto: bottomless gratitude for accommodating me, permitting me to nose around in your beloved nooks and crannies and to commit your fantastical city to a work of pure fiction. Thank you for giving Gabriel and Orlando a home in the most magical place on earth.

Printed in Poland
by Amazon Fulfillment
Poland Sp. z o.o., Wrocław